TANYA CHRIS

With sincere thanks to K. Evan Coles for lending me her Boston expertise throughout the series.

Table of Contents

Prologue Arlo

Why had he ever thought being caged would be sexy? It was boring, mostly. Lonely, scary, uncomfortable. And boring.

Arlo rolled over onto his other side, presenting his back to the room. Not being able to see what might be sneaking up on him made him nervous, but the cage didn't allow for many positions. He could lie down, but not all the way flat. He could kneel, which he only did when Master was in the room. Or he could sit cross-legged. A mat on the bottom of the cage provided some cushioning, but otherwise it was all bare metal, and either the mat had worn down or his bones had grown sharper because he could feel the cage right through it. Kneeling was the worst, but none of the options were comfortable.

Uncomfortable, lonely, boring. Scary.

When Master came back, he might take Arlo out to play with him. Whenever Arlo was in the cage, he listened for the sound of the front door with sharp ears, eager for something to happen. Eager for *anything* to happen. Because anything would be better than this. But then sometimes it wasn't.

Those fantasies he'd had—of someone loving him and caring for him, of a gently controlling master who would fix all his troubles and make him delirious with pleasure—those had just been fantasies. Reality was a steel cage, a long wait, and a mind that could no longer tell the difference between anticipation and dread. He couldn't wait for Master

1

to get home. He didn't ever want to see Master again. Both true.

How long had he been living like this? Long enough that the mat had worn thin and his bones had grown sharp. Months maybe. Two months, at least. Or four. Maybe it was only one. He hadn't been counting the days at first because he hadn't realized he would need to. Later he'd tried, but he wasn't always sure. When he woke up in his cage, was it tomorrow or still today? The shades were always down, the vague glow of light behind them only enough to divide day from night, no way to tell if it was morning or afternoon, yesterday or today.

He rolled onto his back for a bit, his feet on the floor because the cage wasn't long enough for his legs, short as they were, to stretch all the way out. His eyes went to the clock on the wall to his left. It was the old-fashioned kind, with hands, and it made a ticking sound as the hands moved. Tick, tick, tick. He could only see the minute hand—just the tip of it when it was between seven and eleven and not at all otherwise—but it was the only clue he had to the passage of time.

Was every tick a second? He'd tried counting them, seeing how many ticks it took before the minute hand moved, but he always lost focus. Master said he didn't pay attention, that that was why he needed to be punished so often. Maybe if he were better at paying attention, he would've been important enough for his parents to care about. Maybe he wouldn't have jumped on the contract that'd been offered to him. But it had sounded so good. Master would feed him and house him and clothe him and dominate him and fuck him. All Arlo had to do in exchange was submit. And he *wanted* to submit. It hadn't been a hard choice to make. He was being offered everything he'd ever wanted.

But it turned out housing meant a cage with two bottles—one to drink from and one to piss in. Clothing meant jockstraps for playtime and a track suit for the rare

2

occasions he got to leave the house. Feeding meant not much. Master liked his boys boyish, which meant skinny. Master said he didn't like *children*—which was why they pretended Arlo was eighteen already—but he didn't want Arlo turning into a big, hulking man either.

Arlo had been five-five since he was fifteen, and he didn't figure he would ever be anything other than five-five for the rest of his life, no matter how much he ate. He was built small. Small hands, small feet, ribs that were visible even before Master put him on a crash diet, and collar bones like coat hangers. He'd been called a cherub, but his cheeks had been rounder then, his face more filled in.

A waif, Master called him now, meaning it as a compliment. Those were the good days—when Master would take him out and clean him up, pose him and admire him, tell him he was pretty and good. Arlo liked being pretty and good. Then Master would order him to suck his cock, and Arlo didn't mind doing that. He liked sucking cock, even when Master pushed too hard and almost choked him. Maybe *especially* when Master pushed too hard and almost choked him.

Arlo's cock would get hard too, and sometimes Master would play with it and they'd both come and Arlo would feel very at-home, with his head on Master's thigh and all the happy hormones rushing through him. Then he would remember why he'd signed the contract, why he'd wanted to be a slave, kept and coddled and made to kneel and suck.

But it didn't last. Too many days were bad days, and mostly it was this: boring, uncomfortable, scary. Lonely.

God, he missed people. His friend Tripp, especially, but people in general. Talking. Talking was a thing he hardly remembered how to do. He used to be shy about talking to people, but he would talk to anyone now. Sometimes he talked to the clock. *Hello, clock. How's the world turning? Can you see anything from there, or is this all there is?*

A television hung on the other wall, the wall he and the clock faced, but he didn't have any way to turn it on.

3

Sometimes Master turned it on in the morning while he was getting ready for work or at night before he fell asleep. Those were the best times. The TV was like a window into Arlo's old life.

But of course his old life hadn't been so great. He had to remember that. If Master got tired of him, if Arlo got too big or too old, if he disobeyed, he would be back out on the street, all alone with no one to take care of him or pet him. Then he would remember again why he'd signed the contract.

He just wished it wasn't so boring.

The raspy sound of the front door sliding across the tiled entryway had him scrambling to his knees, transitioning from bored to anxious in a heartbeat. Master was back so soon. Was it for a good reason or a bad reason? Maybe Master wanted to play. But maybe something had made him angry. If he was angry, there would be punishments, whether Arlo deserved them or not. Master said Arlo *always* deserved punishments, that it was only thanks to his kindness that Arlo didn't get punished every night. Which meant there was no way to predict punishment, no way to prevent it. But there were definitely ways to make it more likely, and despite what Arlo had once believed about punishment being caring and sexy, he knew better now. Punishment was bad.

Knees wide, back straight, head bowed. The cage wasn't tall enough for him to raise his head fully, but he dropped it all the way down so that his chin touched his chest, keeping his eyes on the floor and his hands behind his back, every muscle tense and waiting. But Master didn't come.

Maybe Master had only forgotten something. Maybe he would go straight back out without coming upstairs. Arlo maintained position anyway—wanting to submit, wanting to be good, wanting Master to be in a good mood and be pleased with him.

Finally the sound of footsteps and then... voices? A

4

man's voice—not Master's—and a woman's answering it. Then other voices. How many people were in the house? So many. Arlo could hear footsteps going this way and that, one set coming straight for the bedroom with an even, measured tread like Master's but not Master's.

The door swung open. Shoes appeared in the doorway. Men's shoes, light brown chukkas with darker laces, a strip of cream-colored socks.

"Found him," the owner of the shoes said, his voice relieved but exasperated, as though Arlo had strayed from where he was supposed to be. But he was right here where Master had left him.

"Arlo?"

Master didn't call him Arlo. Master called him boy. He hadn't been in the cage so long that he'd forgotten his name, but he wasn't sure how to respond to it. It might be a trap. Master might be behind this man, waiting for Arlo to pick up his head or speak out of turn. He kept his mouth shut and his head down, being very good.

"Arlo?" The man was directly in front of the cage now, crouching so their heads were at the same level, though Arlo still didn't peek. "You *are* Arlo, right?"

"Does it matter?" a woman asked from somewhere closer to the door. "Whoever he is, let's get him out of there. Hey," she yelled to someone farther away. "Call an ambulance. And find some bolt cutters."

THE MAN WHO'D COME FOR HIM WAS NAMED Harrison Fisher. He was a private investigator from Boston who Tripp had sent because Tripp was worried about him. The woman with Mr. Fisher was named Stephanie Ludlow and she was a police detective from Philadelphia, which was the city they were in. Arlo had been in Philadelphia for ten weeks, which was two and a half months. It was August now, which meant he was eighteen and didn't have to pretend anymore.

Mr. Fisher rode with him in the ambulance and told him all these things—about the city and the date and Tripp being worried about him. When they got to the hospital, Arlo was put in a room and given a gown to wear, which was funny because he'd been naked that whole time, but now that he had a gown on, he felt underdressed.

A doctor came and listened to his heart and said he was malnourished. Then a technician came and took his blood, which made him dizzy because Master never fed him in the morning. Master was always rushing in the morning, and Arlo was lucky if he got to use the real bathroom before he had to go in the cage.

He wanted to ask for food, but then he remembered Master would send him away if he got too big, and besides, there were so many people, all of them asking questions. If he said he was hungry, they would expect him to say other things too—to answer all those questions they had—and he didn't *know*. So he closed his eyes and let the dizziness take him away from the bright room overly full of people. He'd been wishing for company earlier, but now it was too much.

It was cold in the hospital. Master always kept the house warm. For *him*, he would say, telling Arlo how much Arlo cost him. Arlo hadn't always remembered to appreciate it, but he did now. He wrapped his arms around himself. The gown was thin and scratchy, and the bed had only been made up with a sheet. His body shook beneath it.

Another doctor came in and talked to the detectives about him like he wasn't there—saying he didn't have any drugs in his system, which he knew, and that he seemed out of it because he had an infection making him feverish. Arlo touched his thigh, the one Master had burned, where the sores had gotten so yucky. Maybe they would finally heal.

"Arlo!" The sound of a familiar voice had his head jerking up in surprise. It was Tripp, climbing right onto the bed with him and wrapping him up in a giant hug. God, it was good to see him. Arlo ducked his head onto Tripp's

6

shoulder, ignoring the people who'd come in with him. Ignoring everything.

Tripp rocked him, whispering to him and running his hands over his body like he was checking him for injuries or maybe like he wanted to have sex, but Arlo couldn't allow that. He had Master now, and Master wouldn't like him having sex with someone else. Not unless he'd said to. Arlo struggled to get away from Tripp so there wouldn't be any mistakes he would have to be punished for, and Tripp let him sit up, but he kept an arm around his neck.

"How are you, buddy?" Tripp whispered into his ear. "How are you *really*?"

"The tox screen came back negative," Mr. Fisher said. It sounded like he was answering Tripp, but actually he was talking to one of the other men. "But he reminds me of Kimi. He won't talk, for one thing. I know you don't like it when I say things like this, but there something's wrong in his head."

Arlo touched his head. It seemed fine. He was only a little dizzy. Having Tripp next to him was nice—warm and human, what he'd been missing. As long as Master didn't see it and get mad. But of course Master would be mad he was out of his cage, that he was here, in a hospital, with these people.

"Arlo?" Mr. Fisher said. "Are you hungry? You want something to eat?"

"Maybe a Philly cheesesteak?" Tripp suggested. "When in Rome, right?"

Bread. Meat. Cheese. Arlo's stomach hitched as he imagined swallowing an entire sandwich, just inhaling it in one big bite. It sounded wonderful, but not like something he could really have. Tripp had been joking. Arlo could hear it in his voice.

"Anything at all," one of men who'd come in with Tripp offered. A big guy with brown hair that fell over his forehead. Arlo was careful not to meet his eyes. He didn't know who any of these people were, and there were so many of them. "I'll go get it."

"Come on, Arlo." Tripp jostled him. "That's Cash talking to you. He's a Dom. A nice one. What do you say?"

What did you say to a Dom asking you if you wanted something you weren't allowed to have?

"No thank you, sir," he tried. He braced himself, not sure whether that'd been the right answer or not.

"You don't have to call me sir," Master Cash said, but Arlo *did* have to if Master Cash was a Dom. "I'm going to bring you some food. You can eat it if you want."

The big man went away, which was a relief because Arlo didn't know how to make him happy. Sometimes Master asked Arlo what he wanted, but it was always a trick. Later, Master would say he hadn't meant it, or that Arlo hadn't earned it, or that if Arlo were a good sub he wouldn't have desires, that his only desire would be to do what his master wanted.

More people came and went and asked him questions he didn't know the answers to. Another man had come in with Tripp and Master Cash—a handsome one with close-cropped, dark hair and blue eyes like Arlo had, only his were darker, like sapphires. They sparkled when he spoke, and his voice was a melodious rumble, as if everything he said were meant to comfort. Looking at him made Arlo happy, but he was careful to do it discreetly.

The handsome man stood up so straight, and everything about him was so neat and controlled. Arlo wondered if he might be a Dom too. If Arlo needed a new Dom, could he have this one instead of the big guy with the bangs? Master must've decided he didn't want Arlo anymore, that Arlo wasn't good enough to keep. It was a relief, in a way, but if he hadn't been good enough for Master—who had signed a contract promising to keep him and protect him—would he ever be good enough for anyone?

A little noise rose out of his chest. He tried to choke it back, but it escaped anyway. Tripp hauled him in closer and said. "I've got you."

Tripp couldn't take care of him though. Tripp was hardly any older than he was, and he lived in a dorm most of the year. His parents put up with him being gay, but they didn't like him bringing home "friends." Besides Tripp was a bottom, a sub. He couldn't own Arlo, not the way he needed to be owned.

Master Cash came back with his arms full of food. Chips and crackers and cakes—things Arlo hadn't seen in months. He must've looked as overwhelmed as he felt by the shower of snacks being dumped in his lap because Tripp made a little show out of offering them to him, describing Oreos and Cheetos to him like they were foreign delicacies.

Tripp opened up a whoopie pie and held it to Arlo's mouth, trying to get him to eat it. Arlo shook his head. Until he knew who his new Dom was, it was safest to stick to the old rules. Eventually Tripp gave up and ate the treat himself, dropping crumbs on the sheets and talking with his mouth full, telling Arlo how they'd been looking for him all this time and had come to save him.

So maybe Master hadn't rejected him?

No, Master hadn't rejected him. He'd been taken by the police because Tripp had been worried about him. He remembered now. It was just that he was very hungry and the whoopie pie looked so good, all chocolatey and oozing with frosting.

Arlo's stomach rumbled. Master hated when that happened—said it was rude—but it wasn't like he could stop it. Would he be punished now? He checked on Master Cash and found him not paying attention, but when he shifted his glance to the other one—the handsome one with the blue eyes—the two of them accidentally made eye contact. Arlo dropped his gaze quickly.

"Arlo?" The handsome man was coming over to the bed. To hit him maybe. "I'm Officer Brixby from the Boston Police Department. I want you to look at me, please." He said it gently, but also firmly enough that Arlo could be certain he meant it, that it wasn't a trick. He picked up his head and found Office Brixby sitting on the edge of the bed right in front of him, those blue eyes staring straight at him. He dropped his gaze again. Dizziness washed over him.

"Arlo," Officer Brixby repeated, and there was an insistence in his voice Arlo couldn't disobey. He made eye contact as best he could. "I'm not going to hurt you. No one is going to hurt you. I'll make sure of that." He held out a granola bar. "I want you to eat this."

Arlo hesitated, even as saliva pooled in his mouth. It was a chocolate chip granola bar, the chewy kind. It would be sweet, almost like a candy bar.

"Anything you're allergic to in there?" Officer Brixby asked when he didn't take it.

Arlo shook his head.

"Hate granola bars?"

Another shake.

"Then eat it. Now." There was no mistaking what that was. That was an order. Arlo had to obey, thank God. He took the bar, fumbling to open it with hands that shook from how hungry he was until Officer Brixby opened it for him. He held it up to Arlo's mouth, and Arlo took a bite.

"Good boy." The approval in Officer Brixby's voice was more nourishing than food. "You hold on to that." He released the bar to Arlo's hands, watching him as he worked his way through it, trying to savor it in small bites so it would last, but it was gone too soon nevertheless.

His stomach made a grumbling request for more, but Officer Brixby took the wrapper from him with slow, controlled movements and said, "That's enough for now. If you eat too fast, it'll make you sick. We'll give you some more in a bit."

Arlo nodded even though he was still hungry. He would obey this kind man with the mesmerizing eyes and good-natured smile and crisp black hair that Arlo wanted to put his fingers in. Master hadn't been a particularly attractive man, not one Arlo would've picked out on the street. Arlo had been disappointed when he first saw his new master because he'd had a childish fantasy of a handsome prince, a dark-haired, bright-eyed man with a strong jaw and wide shoulders. Exactly like this one who was watching him as if he were precious, as important as a glass slipper or the princess who fit it.

Looks didn't really matter. Arlo wasn't as superficial as all that. He'd given himself fully to his master, wanting to form a bond that would last forever, one built on his master's loving control and his own willing obedience. He didn't need a Dom who was as handsome as Officer Brixby. He just wanted one who would look at him that way—like he mattered.

He didn't mean to start crying because crying was something he got punished for—unless Master was already punishing him, and then he was supposed to cry—but tears pooled up in his eyes until they spilled over and ran down his cheeks.

"What's wrong?" Tripp asked, giving him a squeeze. "You're safe now. It's all going to be okay."

But it wasn't. It wasn't going to be okay. This had been his big chance, and he'd messed it up, not been grateful for Master when he'd had him, been bad and disrespectful and questioned him in his head. He'd spent his days bored instead of remembering that this was what he'd wanted, and now where was he? In a white room with white sheets and no master anymore.

The bed dipped from the weight of Officer Brixby's hip settling back onto it. Officer Brixby opened his arms wide. "Come here, little one. Come on. I've got you."

Arlo went. He scrambled out from under the sheet and threw himself into Officer Brixby's arms, and then there was no stopping him. His tears came hard as everything flowed out of him—the uncertainty and fear and relief.

He'd been rescued. Freed from a cage he would never have to go back into. He would have food and clothes and

11

Tripp, but no master or home or illusions about a secure and happy future.

"Shh," Officer Brixby whispered in his ear, cradling him close with strong arms. "It's going to be all right. I've got you, and it's going to be all right."

And oh, if only that were true.

Chapter 1 Brixby

HELL'S
BEDROOM

Cade Brixby, being only twenty-four and a new enough member of the Boston Police Department that he was only barely allowed to patrol on his own, had never had any reason to be in the captain's office before. His summons today might be either good or bad. On the one hand, the sting he'd participated in over the weekend had led to the rescue of a human trafficking victim. On the other hand, the sting had taken place in Philadelphia, not Boston, and wasn't something he'd been authorized to get involved in.

His official responsibility had only been the routine investigation of a possible missing person, and even there he hadn't exactly had the case assigned to him. More like he'd borrowed it from the patrolman who'd taken the initial complaint. Truthfully, he'd been working the case as a side job, providing backup to a private investigator named Harrison Fisher who was giving the case more attention than the Boston PD had been willing to. Someone was out there preying on subs—using their kinks to trap them in bogus contracts with unethical Doms—and a golden-haired angel had been caught in their web. Finding Arlo had become Brixby's priority, whether the Boston PD thought it ought to be or not.

Brixby rapped lightly on the captain's door, which stood mostly ajar.

"Brixby," Captain Murphy acknowledged from behind his desk—a huge slab of wood designed to intimidate. The entire office had been furnished in a bureaucratic version of elegance, decorated in gold and blue with lots of American flags and eagle insignia.

In the back corner, a person Brixby didn't recognize stood looking out through the window. The stranger had short, flat hair in a dark brown and was dressed in a suit—one hand casually stuffed into the pocket of their trousers, the other raised as if to intentionally shield their face. The stranger didn't turn around in acknowledgement, and Captain Murphy didn't introduce them.

The captain was a big man with a florid face who'd worked his way up the ranks over a forty-year career. Brixby knew him by sight but had never talked to him in person. He pulled himself up to attention, ready for his dressing down. He looked good in his uniform at least, far better than the captain who wore his like he'd pulled it off a rack at Target. If Brixby had needed any confirmation that the captain was straight, the way he looked in his uniform was it.

"Went a little outside the lines on this case," Captain Murphy said with a frown. "I'm hearing you spent the weekend in Philadelphia."

Actually, Brixby had spent most of the weekend in New York. He'd only detoured to Philadelphia when word came that Arlo had been found there. But if the captain didn't know that more than one jurisdictional line had been crossed, Brixby wasn't about to fill him in.

"The situation seemed to warrant it, sir."

When he thought about Arlo—about those light blue eyes dimmed with fear and the golden curls matted and limp, about his prominent ribs and frail wrists and the sores on the inside of his thigh above his contradictorily chubby knee—Brixby knew he would make all the same decisions again, even if he got fired for them.

"You're not a detective yet, Brixby."

"No, sir."

"In the future, if you come across something that

14

appears to need additional investigation, I expect you to hand it off to the detective bureau."

"Yes, sir." Every use of the word sir grated. He was expected to say it, but the term was so tinged with a sexual dynamic, courtesy of his kink, that he hated having to choke it out. Working with Harrison, this kind of subservience hadn't been necessary. Though Harrison had spent some time on the force, he'd left the formality of it behind him when he quit.

Captain Murphy contemplated him for a moment, leaving Brixby to wonder if this was the end of his career with the Boston PD, but instead of dismissing him, Captain Murphy told him to sit down. Brixby sat in one of the guest chairs without allowing his body to relax in the slightest.

"Detective Ludlow from the Philadelphia PD tells me she appreciates our cooperation and that you should be commended for the work that led to the exposure of what might be a human trafficking ring."

Brixby smiled in acknowledgement. That'd been nice of Detective Ludlow to put in a good word for him, considering he'd barely met her.

"Fisher called me too," Captain Murphy continued. His expression told Brixby how much weight Harrison's recommendation carried. "And I don't discredit his appreciation of your efforts, but aside from the inadvisability of partnering with a private investigator on official department business, which I can't emphasize enough—"

"Yes, sir," Brixby interjected, cutting Captain Murphy off before he got too deep into that particular lecture. "Understood."

Captain Murphy harrumphed. "Right. Where I was heading with that is that Fisher isn't the sort of person you want to associate with. Unless he is?" Captain Murphy didn't expound on his meaning, but Brixby got it. The captain wanted Brixby to disavow Harrison, who was known to be gay, in order to prove he wasn't gay himself.

15

"I only know him through the investigation." That was as far as Brixby was willing to go, and even that was a lie. Yes, he'd originally met Harrison because of the case, but they were friends now.

"He wasn't a bad detective," Captain Murphy said like he hated saying it. "But he's not a team player, couldn't make it on the force, and this case he got you involved in—inappropriate involvement of civilians, misuse of department resources. I could write you up a hundred ways."

Brixby didn't ask Captain Murphy to list all the ways he could be written up. He could probably name them himself. Like that time he'd used his squad car to stake out a house party while Harrison was undercover. Or the way he'd convinced the department's cyber specialist to help them bid in an online slave auction.

"Fisher led you astray," Captain Murphy said. "You're young, excited to save the world. I get it. I was the same at your age, which is why I'm not going to hold this against you. But now that the case is closed, I'd strongly suggest you keep your distance from Fisher and anyone else of his ilk."

And that was why Harrison had bailed from the force and why Brixby wasn't out himself. The homophobia in the Boston PD might not be overt, but everyone knew being gay wasn't good for your career.

"The case isn't closed though, is it, sir?"

The stranger at the window gave a light cough. Captain Murphy ignored it.

"As far as the Boston PD is concerned, the case is closed."

"What about Kimi?"

"That's the Native American woman you, ahem, purchased from Chicago using private funds?"

"She was abducted—"

"From Chicago," Captain Murphy interrupted. "The Chicago PD has been informed, which would've been the

16

appropriate action for you to take when she first came to your attention. The Chicago PD will cooperate with the FBI. Same goes for that other woman."

"Jessica Chambers," Brixby supplied.

"Who skipped bail in Rhode Island. Maybe she came to Boston, maybe she didn't, but there's never been a missing persons report filed in Massachusetts, and Rhode Island hasn't asked us to assist, which means she's not our problem."

Brixby opened his mouth to protest, but the captain cut him off with a quick chop of his hand.

"Not our problem," he repeated. "I have limited resources, limited funds. I'm glad you found what's-his-name—Arlo. Our missing person. But the ongoing investigation is being transferred to the FBI, where it should've been transferred as soon as you suspected there was trafficking across state lines involved. I'm being generous, Brixby. Don't fight me."

Brixby really wanted to fight. Someday, he told himself. Someday, he'd be the one behind the big desk giving orders. But if he ever wanted that someday to come, he had to shut up and take orders for now. He'd played sub before. It wasn't his jam, but he wouldn't be a good Dom if he didn't know how to be a good sub. So that was his role today. Good sub.

Harrison never could toe a line, which was what made him a terrible sub and probably also why Captain Murphy screwed up his mouth like he was biting into a lemon every time he said Harrison's name—not just because he was aware of Harrison's sexuality.

"What about the guy who sent Arlo to Philadelphia?" Brixby asked, daring to poke just a little because he hated the idea of the Boston PD completely washing their hands of this. "Isn't it our job to find him?"

"Got any leads on that?"

"Not yet. Arlo has had a rough couple of months. He's a little... uncommunicative."

Uncommunicative was a charitable term for it. Brixby had driven Arlo back from Philadelphia because he hadn't wanted to let the wounded angel out of his sight, but if he'd imagined being allowed to comfort the boy on the ride back, he'd aimed too high. Arlo had slid silently into the back seat and spent the long ride huddled against the window. Tripp, riding shotgun, had chatted up a storm, but Brixby's efforts to draw Arlo into the conversation had been fruitless. The best he'd been able to do was coax him into eating a little more.

"Well, if you learn anything else from him, turn it over via the appropriate channels," Captain Murphy said. "The reason I asked you here wasn't just to chew you out. It was so you could meet the agent who's heading up the case. Nothing's being dropped, all right? Only transferred. Agent Dobransky?"

The figure in the back of the room turned from the window and took a few steps toward the desk.

"Agent Mark Dobransky, FBI. He's—" Captain Murphy glanced at the stranger, as if to check something. "He's out of their San Francisco office. Comes highly recommended. Agent Dobransky, meet Cade Brixby, one of my officers."

Agent Dobransky's dark hair was cut in bangs that fell partway over his forehead. He had a small frame, hardly bigger than Arlo's, a delicate clean-shaven chin, deep brown eyes behind wire-frame glasses, and a chip on his shoulder. Or so Brixby surmised, given the scowl Dobransky greeted him with.

Brixby rose to his feet. "Would you like to sit?"

The offer earned him an even deeper scowl. Brixby lowered himself back down into his chair, and Dobransky remained on his feet next to the Captain's desk.

"Agent Dobransky will want to interview your vic," Captain Murphy said. "That girl too. Kim Whoever. I expect you to cooperate with"—Captain Murphy cleared his throat—"him. With Agent Dobransky. Him."

"Of course. Whatever you need, Agent Dobransky."

18

"Once you've debriefed him, I expect you to stay out of it. You understand me, Officer?"

"Yes, sir."

Dobransky approached with a thin piece of white pasteboard in hand. "My card."

His voice was unexpectedly high in pitch, and between that and his lack of Adam's apple, Brixby suddenly got it. Dobransky was trans. That was why Captain Murphy had been hesitating over his pronouns, to let Dobransky know he'd been "made." Brixby scrambled to think of something to say to align himself with Dobransky and disavow his boss's attitude, to assure Dobransky he had absolutely no problem with his gender identity, but he couldn't come up with anything that wouldn't make the agent self-conscious. He settled for shaking Dobransky's hand, making sure to keep his grip firm and his eyes steady.

"Let me know when you want to get together," he offered. "I'm at your convenience."

"If you'd give me a minute to finish with Captain Murphy, we could do it right now."

Brixby saluted the captain and went out to linger in the hallway, standing a few feet away so he wouldn't appear to be eavesdropping. He hadn't been fired, but he'd definitely been warned—not just about his actions with respect to the case, but about his prospects in the department if he came out as gay.

Harrison, being an unsubtle, in-your-face kind of guy in all ways, had started his career out, but Brixby had thought it would be better to ease his way into it. To make friends, get promoted once or twice, let his co-workers get to know him before he dropped the bomb, so they would understand he was just like them—a regular guy and a good cop. Now, thanks to this case, rumors would already be flying.

Maybe Harrison had made the right choice in leaving. Why work in a place where you had to either hide who you were or be unwelcome?

Dobransky joined him in the hallway. He looked the way Brixby felt—relieved to be away from Captain Murphy. Some of the stiffness in his posture had dropped, and he actually smiled as he indicated that Brixby should lead the way.

"For what it's worth," Dobransky said, "I think you did a great job. You found Arlo."

"That was luck as much as anything." What if Arlo hadn't been in one of the cities they'd had covered? What if Terzini, the douchebag who'd been keeping Arlo in a cage, hadn't brought him to the club that weekend? What if Harrison hadn't caught a glimpse of Arlo through the crowd?

"If you hadn't found him this weekend, I imagined you'd have gone back the next," Dobransky said.

"Definitely. We weren't giving up on him."

He ushered Dobransky into the brightly lit black-and-white squad room and pulled his working file out of the shared file cabinet. The squad room was mostly empty, the shift having started a half hour ago, so they were able to grab an entire table for themselves. He handed over the folder, and while Dobransky flipped through it, Brixby pumped him for an update.

"Has the Philly PD arrested Terzini?"

Dobransky responded without glancing up. "Not yet. We're letting him think Arlo's a runaway—waiting to see what he'll do with that information."

"Arlo was locked in a cage. How could he have run away?"

"One of the Philly techs had some skills. He picked the lock and left a paperclip behind to give the impression Arlo had managed to get himself out. Fisher thought it might be better not to broadcast the fact that law enforcement was involved. We don't just want Terzini. We want the whole ring."

"But if they think Arlo's an escapee, they'll be out looking for him."

"That's what we want them to do. We're monitoring Terzini. Hopefully he'll lead us to some panicked bad guys. People make mistakes when they panic."

"Yeah, but—" Brixby didn't like the idea of Arlo being bait. "What does that mean for Arlo?"

"Where do you have him stashed exactly? Captain Murphy said something about reprobates."

Reprobates. Great. Harrison and Brixby and people of their ilk. Gay, kinky reprobates.

"He's with a guy from the club where all this started."

"Hell's Bedroom."

"Right, Hell's Bedroom. Some of the members helped with the investigation."

Brixby gave Dobransky a rundown on the players involved: Cash, who'd helped Harrison get into the club undercover; Francesca, who'd pretended to be the kind of Domme willing to buy a sub; and Sebastian, the Dom who'd provided the funds to do it.

"So you've taken these trafficked persons, these... submissives, if I'm using the term correctly, and placed them with civilian dominants—Kimi with Francesca and Arlo with Sebastian."

"Kimi wanted to be with Francesca," Brixby explained. "Insisted on it, actually. It was the best place for her, given her mental state."

And as for Arlo, Brixby had hated dropping him off with Sebastian, but it wasn't like he could've kept Arlo himself. Arlo was a victim and Brixby was a police officer. Their relationship needed to remain professional, even if Brixby already had strong protective feelings toward the blond angel.

"I don't want Arlo used as bait," he insisted strongly.

"Don't worry," Dobransky said. "We'll find somewhere to stash him—a safehouse or something. We're going to take good care of your boy."

Brixby's heart seized. Dobransky had thrown the word boy out as a joke, but Brixby had held Arlo in his arms—

21

had comforted him and fed him. An emotional connection like that didn't end just because he put on a uniform the next morning. But realistically, there was no reason for him to ever see Arlo again. He'd been taken off the case. His work here was done.

Chapter 2 Brixby

Brixby was off the case. He was off the case. He told himself that repeatedly over the next twenty-four hours, but it didn't stop him from thinking about Arlo and wondering how he was doing. Was he remembering to put salve on his knee and take his antibiotics? Was he still with Sebastian, or had Dobransky picked him up? Wouldn't he be lonely and confined in a safehouse? A safehouse was like a cage, just a bigger one.

So when Harrison called and suggested they drop in on Sebastian to ask Arlo a few questions—see if they could get any more out of him than they had that first night—Brixby jumped at it. The prospect of seeing Arlo carried him through the rest of his shift and all the way home.

Sebastian's condo was on the waterfront where cheap parking was impossible, and since Brixby had been explicitly told he was off the case, he left the cruiser at home and made his way over to Sebastian's on the T. When he'd dropped Arlo off, Sebastian had come down to the lobby to pick him up. Brixby had watched the small, golden-haired figure walk away next to Sebastian's imposing, dark-haired one, resisting the urge to run after them and snatch Arlo back. Or at least give him a hug goodbye.

Today, he rode the elevator up to the twenty-third floor where it appeared, based on the number of doors, that Sebastian owned a full quarter of the floor. His place was... impressive. Brixby tried not to let his jaw drop.

"Nice view," he said, choosing the most obvious feature to comment on. Sebastian's living room overlooked Boston Harbor through a wide bank of windows. Outside, the sky was fading to purple and lights sparkled off the water.

"I like it," Sebastian said casually, one-upping Brixby's attempt at understatement. "Can I get you something to drink?"

He moved to a bar on the far side of the space, drawing Brixby's attention with him until it got diverted by the figure sitting on a black leather couch facing the windows. All Brixby could see was a profile, but he knew whose profile that was.

"Anything's fine," he told Sebastian as his feet carried him to the couch. "Hey, Arlo."

Arlo glanced up when he came around in front of him, his eyes the same light blue Brixby remembered—as clear and soft as a summer day. The shadows beneath them had lessened somewhat, and Arlo's plump lips curved in a smile that made them glisten.

"Hello, Officer Brixby." He was so small, surrounded by a veritable fortress of burgundy throw pillows and dressed in the clothes Tripp had lent him for the drive back. Brixby wanted to strip Arlo naked and dress him all over again— in something cuddly that fit him, not black nylon basketball shorts that bagged at the waist and an orange rayon athletic shirt that gaped at the neck.

"Oh, you'll talk to Brixby, will you?" Sebastian came over with two glasses. He handed one to Brixby and waved the other in front of Arlo, who only blinked at it. "First thing he's said all day. I don't think he likes it here." Sebastian took a seat on a couch to the left.

Sebastian had, for some reason, three couches, which were arranged in U around a giant coffee table as if this were a hotel lobby rather than a private residence. He brought the glass he'd tried to tempt Arlo with to his own lips.

Brixby took a seat next to Arlo instead of using the third

of the three sofas. It put him between Arlo and Sebastian, which satisfied his protective urge. He glanced down at what Sebastian had handed him—a highball glass half filled with an amber liquid. "What is it?"

"Scotch. I seem to recall you're a whiskey drinker. I thought you might enjoy some good Scotch."

Brixby took a sip and barely managed to hold back a moan of approval. God, that was good. He didn't know what it was, but it wasn't Chivas, that was for sure.

"Arlo's eighteen," he pointed out, rather than compliment Sebastian on the quality of his liquor cabinet.

"This is lemonade." Sebastian lifted the glass he was drinking from in a mocking toast. "I haven't corrupted my precious guest. Much."

"Have you been playing with him?" That would be even worse than giving him alcohol. Arlo was in no condition to be played with. And besides, Arlo didn't belong to Sebastian. He belonged to—

Well, to no one.

"Define playing," Sebastian said with a quirk of one sculpted eyebrow.

"You know what I mean."

Sebastian laughed. The intercom buzzed, and he rose to answer it rather than answer the question, though Brixby suspected he hadn't planned to answer it anyway. Brixby took advantage of the time alone with Arlo to check him over.

"Can I see?" he asked, hovering his hand over Arlo's right leg. The basketball shorts were so long they hung well past his knees. When Arlo nodded, Brixby slid the fabric higher, careful not to touch any flesh, and peeled back a corner of the bandage covering Arlo's sores. They already seemed less raw, with some healthier pink skin showing around the edges of the scabs that'd started to form.

"Does it feel better?" He stuck the bandage back down and lowered Arlo's shorts as carefully as he'd raised them, suppressing the urge to get between Arlo's knees and kiss

25

him all better. Arlo might look like a lost puppy, but Brixby had no right to pick him up and snuggle him.

Arlo nodded. His gaze was mostly through the window in front of him, but he was taking occasional quick peeks Brixby's way, flashing those pretty blue eyes. Brixby put his hands in his lap and eased himself farther away. Arlo was a mighty temptation.

"He's seriously still not talking?" Harrison asked as he plowed into the room with his usual energy.

"I talk," Arlo grumbled. "I can hear, too."

"He doesn't talk to *me*," Sebastian said. "I told you—he doesn't like it here." His tone conveyed how wrong he thought Arlo was.

"You didn't answer my question," Brixby reminded him. "Have you been playing with him?"

"I haven't applied a paddle to his ass if that's what you're asking. But remember how Kimi was when we picked her up? She wanted someone she could serve."

"Fuck that. If you've been taking advantage of him—"

"He's a sub."

"He's not *your* sub. I don't want you messing with him."

Arlo had just been through a hellish experience. If Sebastian wanted a playmate, he could find one capable of consent.

"Oh, for fuck's sake," Sebastian said. "I haven't been messing with him. I was messing with *you*. He's been watching television. Took a shower, ate half a sandwich. No one's hurting your boy."

It was the second time in two days someone had called Arlo his boy. Brixby's brain was starting to believe it. He sat back down. He hadn't intentionally stood up in the first place. He took a deep swallow from his drink and glanced at Arlo who'd scooted forward to the edge of the couch like he might need to flee.

"That was an entertaining show you two just put on." Harrison arched an eyebrow at Brixby, silently reminding him that Sebastian liked fucking with people, and yes,

Brixby had fallen for it. Risen to the bait. The thought of Arlo on his knees to someone like Sebastian made him want to hit something, and Sebastian seemed like the obvious choice for what to hit. "But Arlo won't be staying here much longer, one way or another, right? You told me the FBI's going to take charge of him."

"Where am I going?" Arlo asked.

"A safehouse, probably." Harrison shrugged. "They'll have someone watching over you, don't worry. You're their star witness."

"Witness?" Arlo shrank back into his fortress of throw pillows.

"You're going to have to testify," Sebastian warned him.

"He doesn't have to do it today," Brixby snapped.

"No, we'll need to build some kind of case first. And you know what I think about our chances in court."

Brixby did know. Sebastian was a prosecutor for the State of Massachusetts and had expressed his highly valued (by him) opinion on the subject more than once. Arlo had been underage at the time of his disappearance, but only barely. Seventeen, nearly eighteen—past the age of consent. And he'd gone willingly, as best as they understood it. Just like Kimi had.

Selling people wasn't legal, of course, but Sebastian said there was no proof people were being sold. The auction they'd bought Kimi at had been vague and discreet—a picture on a screen with the option to bid without any text explaining what the bidder was buying, and Kimi had arrived in Boston unchained and unescorted. So where was the crime?

"Since you're up to talking," Harrison said, coming over to sit on Arlo's other side, "maybe you can answer some questions for us."

Arlo shifted closer to Brixby, away from Harrison. Brixby couldn't help flashing a victorious grin. Arlo liked him.

"I thought jurisdiction had been turned over to the FBI,"

Sebastian said from the spot he'd reclaimed on the other couch.

"I'm not Boston PD," Harrison reminded him, "which means Captain Murphy's not the one who decides when my case ends. I have a client to answer to."

Harrison's client was Tripp, except that Tripp had never paid him as far as Brixby was aware. Brixby had stopped charging Harrison for his own services at some point too. This was about community, about taking care of their own.

"So, Arlo," Harrison said. "Can you tell me what happened the night you were at Hell's Bedroom?"

Arlo shrugged. "I got caught, for being underage. They took my ID and made me leave."

"Who were you playing with there?"

"No one. The guy who signed me in was a sub. Uncle Bob."

They'd interviewed Bob Jones while they'd been searching for Arlo, so they already knew he mentored new subs and occasionally signed them into the club—not to play with them but because Hell's Bedroom made it difficult for unaffiliated subs to get in. Supposedly, Jones hadn't realized Arlo was underage, though Brixby had a hard time believing it. Arlo had turned eighteen in custody, but he still didn't look any older than sixteen.

"I got caught almost right away," Arlo said, sounding put out about it. One of the curls that'd been tucked behind his ear fell across his cheek. Brixby resisted the urge to smooth it back for him. "I hardly even saw anything before one of the guards grabbed me. I had my picture taken by a big Black guy with a bald head and then a guard walked me out."

"And then what?"

"I was hanging around outside the club because I didn't have anywhere to go. I'd been staying with this guy, but he didn't like me being under his feet, so I always made sure not to turn up too early."

"Staying with in a sexual way?" Brixby asked, being

28

careful to keep his voice neutral.

Arlo didn't answer the question.

"All right," Harrison said after a moment. "We'll leave that for now. Can you tell me how you ended up in Philadelphia? Did someone approach you? Grab you?"

"A guy came up to me. He asked me if I liked that sort of thing—what they did in Hell's Bedroom."

"And what did you tell him?"

Arlo shrugged. "I like it."

"Which is fine," Brixby assured him. "What happened wasn't your fault. You didn't deserve it, regardless of your kink."

"I wanted it though. Or at least I thought I did. Look, you-all are wasting your time. No one did anything bad to me. This guy showed me a contract and said if I signed it, he'd get me a full-time master, so I signed it. Then he bought me a coffee and a bus ticket and waited with me until the bus came. That was it."

"What can you tell us about this guy?" Harrison asked.

"He said his name was Mike. He had short, brown hair and he wasn't very tall. Like you."

Harrison grimaced at that. "You were alone on the bus?"

"I was seventeen, not twelve. I didn't need an escort to ride a bus."

"See, there's the trouble," Sebastian said. "I don't even know if a charge of transporting a minor across state lines would hold up. Doesn't sound like anyone transported him."

"What about that contract?" Harrison asked. "People aren't allowed to sell themselves."

"We sign contracts in the BDSM world all the time. They have no legally enforceable consequences, which means they aren't really contracts from a legal point of view. They're just rules we're agreeing to play a game by. What did they tell you would happen if you broke your contract?" he asked Arlo.

29

Arlo blanched. "I did break it," he whispered. "I didn't have Master's permission to leave the house. Or wear these clothes." He plucked at the basketball shorts. "Or any of it."

"So the fuck what?" Harrison blustered. "Don't tell me you still care what this guy thinks."

Arlo shook his head in the smallest of movements.

"All right then," Harrison continued. "So what happens if you break your contract?"

"Then I'm a bad sub. Then Master won't want me. Then I'll get sent away. I don't *know* what will happen. What do you want me to say?"

"We were hoping you'd say someone threatened you." Sebastian tinkled the ice cubes remaining in his glass of lemonade. "There wasn't anything in your contract about hunting you down like a junkyard dog and stringing you up by your testicles if you dared to escape, huh?"

It wasn't funny. Whether Arlo's contract had included any explicit threats or not, there was a definite threat hanging over his head.

"Now do you get my point?" Sebastian asked, shifting his attention from Arlo to Harrison. "He voluntarily signed an absolutely unenforceable document, and then someone bought him a bus ticket. There's nothing to prosecute in Boston."

"So we go after Terzini," Brixby said. He hoped Sebastian wouldn't try to justify keeping a human being locked unattended in a cage day after day. Or those festering burns on Arlo's thigh either. Regardless of how Arlo had ended up in Terzini's hands, Terzini was responsible for what had happened next.

"The State of Pennsylvania will have to go after Terzini," Sebastian said. "And the parent company for Hell's Bedroom—DDD—is headquartered in San Francisco, which means any kind of racketeering charges would have to be brought there."

Which Brixby figured was why the Feds had assigned a San Francisco-based agent to the case. "Want to hear

30

something funny?" he asked. "The FBI agent told me what DDD stands for. Dom, Domme, Dominant."

Sebastian let out a surprisingly attractive laugh. "Someone's over-compensating for something."

"Maybe the fact that they can't get a sub without buying one."

Lifestyle BDSM was a choice—a choice Brixby had mixed feelings about for himself—but it didn't mean treating your submissive without regard to their welfare. Exactly the opposite. It meant being a hundred percent concerned with their welfare, with every facet of it.

If Brixby had a cutie like Arlo as his sub, there would never be a mark on him. If he had to discipline the boy, he would do it with no more than his own hand, leaving nothing worse than a temporary blush on the cheeks of his perky ass. And Arlo wouldn't ever need any more discipline than that, Brixby was sure. He would be a perfect angel. Brixby just knew it. He snuck a peek at the boy who was all the way up against his side now—small and vulnerable in the overlarge clothes.

"Are you going to be okay?" he asked, allowing himself a brief touch as he tucked back that curl that'd been tempting him.

"How long do I have to stay here?" Arlo's voice was low, riding beneath the argument Harrison and Sebastian were having over legal semantics.

"Probably not much more than a day or two. Is it so bad here?" So help him, if Sebastian was fucking with Arlo...

"I'd rather stay with you."

"You can't stay with me, Arlo."

"Why not?"

Because he was a police officer assigned to Arlo's case. Except he wasn't anymore. The case had been closed. Boston PD had washed their hands of it.

"My place is really small."

Compared to this palatial waterfront condo, his apartment would be a serious downgrade. He lived on the

31

top floor of a three-family house, in what he suspected had originally been an attic. From the outside, it looked like a fanciful pagoda perched on top of the building. From the inside, it was more prosaic—only half the size of the other two floors with ceilings that sloped down steeply on all sides, rendering much of the space unusable.

"I don't take up a lot of room," Arlo said. "And I promise I'll be good. Can I please stay with you, Officer Brixby? Please?"

Brixby might be risking his career by agreeing to take Arlo home, but if he couldn't bring Arlo's kidnapper to justice, then he could at least do this—answer the plea in Arlo's pretty eyes.

Chapter 3 Arlo

What little there was to see of Officer Brixby's apartment was visible from the door. There was his bed, unmade and half-hidden behind a screen painted with bulrushes and butterflies. And there was his kitchen, dishes stacked by the sink and crumbs scattered across the eighteen inches of free counter space. Officer Brixby didn't have a bar or a marble foyer, and the view through his windows was of a suburban neighborhood, not Boston Harbor, but Arlo finally felt safe.

"Make yourself at home," Officer Brixby said. "There's no television, but the Wi-Fi password is taped to the router."

"I don't have a phone."

"Right, sorry." Officer Brixby scooped a pair of sweatpants off the floor and tossed them into the laundry basket behind the screen. "Maybe the FBI can help with that. Here, sit."

He steered Arlo over to his two-seater couch and started stripping the sheets off his bed.

"I like your house," Arlo said.

Officer Brixby gave him a look like he didn't believe it, but it was true. He liked how he could see everything at once—how no one could sneak up on him—and he liked the soft blue couch that matched Officer Brixby's eyes and wasn't all slick and crinkly like the leather at Master Sebastian's.

"Why do I have to go a safehouse?"

"They're worried Terzini might come looking for you."

"Who's Terzini?"

"The guy whose house you were at."

"Master?"

"Don't call him that."

Arlo flinched at the rebuke. He'd always called Master Master. What else could he call him?

Officer Brixby came over and sat next to him. Now his voice was low and even. "Terzini isn't your master anymore. He wasn't really ever your master. That's not how a master behaves, not a good one. That was your first time in a serious power exchange relationship, wasn't it?"

"I've done stuff before." He'd had all kinds of sex anyway, and he'd spent years and years *imagining* having a master.

Brixby clucked his tongue. "No one should've been playing with you. You were underage."

"But now I'm eighteen, so it's okay, right?"

"I'm not sure. Is that still what you want?"

"I don't know." It hadn't turned out to be what he'd expected, but that left him without anything to hope for.

"You don't have to figure it out right now." Officer Brixby put a hand on his shoulder. Arlo leaned into it until he was all the way up against Officer Brixby's side. Officer Brixby was so warm, and he was firm but not hard, in a way Arlo could sink into. The tension he'd been carrying the last couple of days melted out of him. Officer Brixby dipped his head down to kiss the top of his head, and Arlo just wanted to stay right there and never go anywhere, especially not to a safehouse.

"I doubt Master will come looking for me. I don't think he liked me that much."

"What makes you think so?"

"He was always mad at me. I'm untrained."

"Training is a Dom's job. If a sub isn't well-trained, that reflects on the Dom, not the sub. Doms need to set clear—"

"He was pretty clear."

34

"You didn't let me finish. Clear, *achievable* expectations. Terzini was a terrible Dom and you, little angel, did nothing wrong. Nothing. Even if you were a brat sometimes or failed at a task he set you, it's the Dom's job to manage those things, to correct them."

"He corrected me. A lot." And Arlo had still never gotten it right.

"Not like that. He *scarred* you, Arlo. I hate that he scarred you. I hate that he touched you at all." Officer Brixby sounded like he wanted to fight Master over it. He rubbed his cheek against Arlo's hair. His beard had come in a little, making his handsome face even more rugged. The stubble rasped through Arlo's curls. "Are you hungry? I can find something for you to eat."

"I already ate."

"Sebastian said you only had half a sandwich though. You've got some pounds to make up."

"Master doesn't like fat boys."

"Yeah, well Master—I mean, Terzini—can go fuck himself. You can be as fat as you want. It won't make you any less beautiful."

Arlo turned his head up so they were nose to nose. "You think I'm beautiful?"

"I think you're too beautiful for words."

Arlo waited for Officer Brixby to close the gap between them, to kiss him and claim him. If Officer Brixby thought he was beautiful, maybe Officer Brixby could be his new master and it would be different this time.

"Well." Officer Brixby hopped to his feet and clapped his hands together. "Those sheets aren't going to change themselves. Why don't you help me?"

Arlo would rather kiss, but this might be a test to see if he could be a good sub, so he got to his feet and waited while Officer Brixby fetched a set of sheets from a cupboard. He unfurled the bottom sheet and handed one side to Arlo. The sheets were light blue, decorated with the repeated image of a shirtless man striking a muscle pose against a background of snowflakes.

"That's Iceman," Officer Brixby told him as they worked together. "These were the sheets I used as a teenager. I was pretty dorky. And gay."

"I can't imagine you being dorky."

"Well, you'd be able to imagine it if you'd seen me then." He shook out the top sheet, on which a giant flexing Iceman was centered. "I'm still a dork, but the uniform hides it pretty well."

"I've never seen you in uniform."

"You'll get to see me in it tomorrow morning. I have an early shift. There you go." He patted the bed where Iceman had been covered up by a navy blue fleece blanket. "Hop in."

"Where are you sleeping?"

"On the couch." He took the sheets he'd stripped from the bed and started to tuck them around the couch. Arlo sized up Officer Brixby's six-foot-two frame compared to his own five-foot-five one, then went over and plunked himself down on the couch.

"I'll sleep here."

"I'm sure you had a bed at Sebastian's."

"I slept in a *cage* at Master's. I can sleep on a couch."

"But I don't want you to." Officer Brixby sat down next to him and took his chin in his hand. "I'm not Terzini. I can't ever be comfortable knowing you're not comfortable."

"These sheets smell better than the Iceman ones though. The Iceman ones smell like laundry. These smell like you."

Officer Brixby dropped his hand down to his lap and gave his dick a squeeze. Arlo glanced away because he didn't want to be creepy. Officer Brixby probably had a nice dick. It took up a lot of space in his jeans.

Officer Brixby cleared his throat as he let it go. "We could put these sheets back on the bed if you'd rather."

"Can't we sleep together? The bed will smell even more like you if you're in it."

36

Officer Brixby glanced over at the bed as if it held an answer, but it was just a navy blue fleece blanket and a couple of pillows covered in pillowcases to match the sheets. Arlo imagined putting his head on one of those pillowcases and having Officer Brixby's on the one next to him. He would sleep so good. The bed at Master Sebastian's had been soft but big, stretching endlessly away from him in every direction so he couldn't tell if he was where he belonged or not.

"If sharing the bed with me would make you feel safer, then I guess we can do that."

"Thank you, Officer Brixby."

"Most people just call me Brixby."

Arlo shook his head. He couldn't say Brixby without a title. That would be disrespectful. "Master Brixby?" he suggested.

"No, please. Master is a monster who locked you in a cage. I'd rather not hear that word out of you at all, to be honest."

"But you're a Dom, aren't you?" He couldn't remember if anyone had told him Officer Brixby was a Dom or if he'd just known it.

"I'm not *your* Dom, Arlo, so you don't have to call me by a title. If you don't like Brixby, then how about Cade? Pretty much no one calls me that except my parents, but since you're staying here, I guess you're family in a way. Come on. Into bed with you." Officer Brixby turned down the blankets.

"You're coming, too?" He sat on the edge of the bed to kick off the sandals Mr. Fisher had loaned him, then shimmied out of Tripp's basketball shorts. The boxers beneath them were Master Sebastian's because after wearing Tripp's for two days, he'd really wanted clean ones, but he hated them.

"Let me get you something to sleep in," Officer Brixby said as Arlo pulled Tripp's t-shirt off over his head. It was dirty too and probably smelled bad. "One wrong move and those boxers will fall right off you. Here, put these on."

He held out a pair of plaid flannel boxers, and Arlo took them with a happy smile. He got out of bed to drop his drawers—well, they practically dropped themselves, just like Officer Brixby had said—and Officer Brixby averted his eyes with a choked cough.

"Are those better?"

Master Sebastian and Officer Brixby weren't so different in size, which meant the new boxers didn't fit any better than the old ones. They dipped low on Arlo's hips, low enough that if he had any pubic hair left, it would be peeking out over the top of the waistband. But they were Officer Brixby's boxers, so yes, they were better.

"Yes, thank you."

"Want a shirt?"

Arlo shook his head as crawled into bed. He'd always slept naked at Master's. Even the boxers felt like an alien extra, like something he might get in trouble for wearing. Officer Brixby stripped down to his own boxers, which were plain black cotton ones. He pulled his shirt off over his head, plugged in his phone, and turned off the lights.

"Have everything you need?" he asked as he slid into bed from the other side.

"Yes, sir," Arlo said dutifully, but all he could feel was the endless space telling him he wasn't in his cage, which meant there would be consequences.

He separated his legs, sending the one closest to Officer Brixby out across the mattress until his little toe connected with Officer Brixby's furry calf. That felt so nice that he scooched over until he could touch his whole foot to that warm, firm flesh. Then a little more until they were pressed side by side, with most of the length of their bodies touching.

He nuzzled into Officer Brixby's arm, seeking out the rich, masculine smell that had infused those used sheets and finding it. He inhaled deeply, feeling more settled now that he had a boundary, a limiting edge. Officer Brixby sighed and stretched his arm up and around so Arlo could curl under it and be right there on Officer Brixby's chest. He hooked his fingers into the waistband of Officer Brixby's boxers and fell fast asleep.

Chapter 4 Brixby

Another long day of what used to be his normal routine—patrolling in his cruiser, sweeping the streets for trouble, and responding to calls as they came in—had Brixby eager to be done with it. He missed strategizing with Harrison, missed being involved in something more important than a traffic stop, missed exercising his brain instead of his badge, missed working with people who knew who he was and didn't hate him for it. And he missed Arlo.

Poor Arlo, who spent his days locked in Brixby's apartment with strict instructions not to answer the door or leave the building unless it was on fire, which made Brixby feel like he wasn't much better than Terzini. Who was he to tell Arlo where he could go? He wasn't Arlo's keeper. He wasn't even Arlo's Dom.

He'd never had what he could call a sub of his own, unless he counted Shane, his first ever play partner—a guy who'd been as new and inexperienced as he was. Two neophytes exploring such potentially dangerous territory together wasn't ideal, but Shane not knowing any better had given Brixby enough confidence to exert authority, to pretend to be in control until he'd learned enough to really be in control.

Their time together had been play in all senses of the word—an exploration and an experiment, more like they were hiking partners jointly admiring the scenery than lovers. When they'd outgrown each other, they'd gone their separate ways without any hurt feelings or regrets. Since then, Brixby had bounced from sub to sub in public scenes, not sure what he was looking for but knowing he hadn't found it yet.

If he were going to catalogue what he wanted out of a power exchange relationship, he would start with submission—for someone to turn themselves over to his caring hands—then add punishment when it was warranted. He didn't have any appetite for sadism for the sake of sadism, and seeing a sub get humiliated only made him want to defend them from the monster making them feel bad, but a touch of subjugation and a hot wash of tears? Yes, please.

What he wanted most, though, was a partner who *wanted* his protection and correction. Not a brat who sassed him or a constant battle for control, but peaceful belonging, quiet presence, a harmonious exchange of power. And he couldn't find that at a club.

He couldn't afford it either, he reminded himself with a rueful shake of his head as he clocked out at the end of the day. A rookie's salary didn't go far in an expensive city like Boston. He needed to establish himself before he could think about taking care of someone else.

Nicholas Popinjay—the guy who'd signed Jessica Chambers into Hell's Bedroom with his multi-million dollar row house and bespoke suits—had told them he didn't want a fulltime sub like Jessica, but Popinjay could've kept Jessica if he'd wanted to. His wife might not have appreciated it, but he could've afforded it. Sebastian had a waterfront condo, and Terzini had a mini-mansion in the suburbs of Philly—both of them big enough to keep a whole harem of subs in without anyone needing to sleep on the floor. Meanwhile, Brixby lived in an attic.

Why was it always the asshole Doms who had the financial wherewithal to really spoil someone? If Brixby had a house and a six-figure income, he would set Arlo up like a prince. Like a perfect spoiled pet. And love him and love

41

him and love him. Instead, he went to work every day and left Arlo in a studio apartment with nothing more than a window air conditioner to beat back the ninety-degree heat.

Brixby was in a hurry to get home to his temporary angel—take him out for an ice cream, at least—but he had an errand to run first. He swung by the office of Gina Harlow, one of the techs assigned to his unit. Gina had attached a GPS tracking device to the back of a medallion so Harrison could it wear when he was undercover in places where he had to be weaponless, phoneless, and nearly naked. Harrison had managed to slip the medallion into the pocket of Terzini's suit jacket, and that was how they'd followed Arlo back to his cage.

Brixby would trade any number of medallions for Arlo's safety, but this particular medallion had been a present from his mother when he'd graduated from the police academy, and he would love to get it back. Thanks to the tracking app on his phone, he knew it was still in Philly. Presumably in Terzini's closet. But knowing where it was didn't tell him how to get it back.

Gina Harlow looked nothing like Jean Harlow, the forties bombshell with rolled blond hair and voluptuous curves who was her near-namesake. At first glance, she gave an impression of bulk, but that was only due to the sheer number of layers she typically wore. Beneath her homeless-person ensemble, her limbs were thin and spindly. When Brixby came in, she had her head buried in a human-sized metal cabinet bristling with wires, which he hoped wasn't a bomb she was in the process of defusing. You could never be sure with Gina.

"Got a minute?" he asked, pitching his voice low so he wouldn't startle her into detonating whatever she was trying to defuse. It didn't work. She jumped and hit her head on the top of the cabinet. A handful of screws rolled into the corners of the cluttered room.

"Well, I don't suppose I'll ever see any of those again," she said, as though the screws had grown legs and run off on their own. Brixby was just glad nothing had exploded.

"Hey, Brixby."

"Hi Gina. Sorry I startled you."

"Oh, no worries. Screws come and screws go. You can't get attached to them." She yanked open a drawer overflowing with parts and unearthed an embroidered coin purse exactly like the one Brixby's grandmother had carried. It turned out to be full of screws. Extracting a few of the smaller ones, she turned back to her cabinet.

"Could I ask you something?" he said before he lost her attention again. "You remember that medallion you modified for me? You put a GPS tracker on it."

"Uh huh." Her voice sounded eerily robotic from inside the cabinet.

"I'm wondering how long the battery will last."

"Maybe a month if it's getting a good signal. Less if it's not."

Brixby had no idea what the signal was like inside Terzini's closet, but if a month was the max, then his time was almost up. Oh, well. The medallion was a minor loss in exchange for Arlo's freedom. He logged out of the tracking app as a way of mentally letting go of the medallion and headed out to his car. He was on his way home when his phone rang. He accepted the call using the Bluetooth, and Harrison's voice greeted him through the speakers.

"We're having a conclave tomorrow," Harrison said. "At Cash's."

"A conclave?"

"A dinner. A social gathering. A get-together of friends. None of whom have any official role in a human trafficking investigation. Mere friends who happen to enjoy partaking of food and drink. You know how much Cash likes to entertain. Bring Arlo if you still have him."

"I still have him. I haven't heard anything from Dobransky about getting him into a safehouse."

"Does Dobransky know he's with you?"

"Um, it's possible he doesn't. I'll have to shoot him a

43

text." Something he should've thought to do over the last few days because there were undoubtedly more accommodating places for Arlo to be than the lonely austerity of his apartment. But he couldn't find the urgency to move Arlo to one of them, despite the torture of having Arlo's sleeping body draped over his every night.

He was so uncomfortably horny at this point that literally anything could get him up. To make matters worse, he hadn't even been jerking off in the shower because doing so would feel like an admission that he was lusting over an eighteen-year-old victim. Meanwhile, he was lusting over an eighteen-year-old victim.

The sight of Arlo naked that first night was permanently etched on his brain, despite how careful he'd been since then to look away when Arlo was changing. Arlo was completely waxed, smooth like a boy but with a man's cock, which Brixby knew because its spongy weight got jammed into his thigh each and every long night. But still, he didn't want to let Arlo go.

Having Arlo's curly head tucked under his arm gave him a thrill he couldn't label. It wasn't sexual, though there were tinges of sex to it. It wasn't domination, though there was some of that too. It wasn't brotherly, though it felt a bit like family. It was fuller, more complete, than anything he'd ever felt before, as if every positive emotion he'd ever had toward anyone were wrapped up in this single yearning for the heart beating next to his.

Physically, Arlo was healing, but his physical wounds were the least of it. Terzini had convinced Arlo he was a bad sub. *Untrained.* Which was why even though Brixby's accommodations were less than luxurious, it might be best for Arlo to stay right where he was. He needed a Dom. Not to fuck him or punish him, but to give him positive reassurance, to guide him toward understanding that what had happened with Terzini wasn't his fault. Brixby's challenge was to top Arlo just a little without giving in to his own baser impulses.

"What are you up to these days?" he asked Harrison, eager to hear about something more interesting than traffic stops and noise complaints.

"You should see this dude I've been following." Harrison whistled appreciatively.

"Gay?"

"No, he doesn't play for our team, but he's still a hot piece of shit. And also a total scumbag. I'm collecting evidence for a divorce case, and there's an abundance of it. Different woman every night. At least, I think they're different women."

"So that's what you do? Follow philandering husbands?"

"PI work isn't all human trafficking rings, Brixby. Why do you think I jumped on Arlo's case even though I didn't have a paying client? Well, that and I wanted to see the inside of a BDSM club." Harrison snorted. "But this case is a goldmine. Mr. Philanderer is going to earn me five figures."

"Ever think about taking a partner? Like a junior partner," he clarified, since he had no capital to bring to the table.

"Are you thinking about jumping ship?" Harrison didn't sound surprised.

"Not seriously. Only, you know, considering my options. Patrol work is boring."

"And you've got a lot of years left to do it before you make detective. That was what I kept hanging in there for. I thought when I made it detective, it would be different."

"But it wasn't?"

"Eh. The case work, yes. The attitude, not so much. And even the case work.... I don't know if I can explain it, but it never felt like I was deciding what to work on based on how important it was. Either I was cherry-picking the easy stuff so I could improve my close rate, or I was being told what to do by higher-ups based on what *they* thought was important. Like vandalism of corporate property beat out the murder of a prostitute."

That was exactly how Brixby was feeling. He was spending his days handing out speeding tickets when there was a kidnapper preying on vulnerable kids loose.

"Of course now I decide what to work on based on how much I can earn," Harrison said. "Maybe not so different. But at least I'm the one making the call, and I don't have to put up with any shitty attitudes other than mine." Harrison barked out a laugh. "If you ever want a job, Brixby, hit me up. Fair warning, I'm going to pay you like shit because that's what I can afford, but at least you'll be earning an honest living." He laughed again and hung up.

Nice of Harrison to offer to hire him, but that warning was really valid. If Brixby stayed the course with the Boston PD, he had a comfortable future in front of him. Working for Harrison, he'd be starting over at the bottom again, and he'd be at the bottom of a scale that might never go all that high. Harrison might even have to let him go if work got lean, whereas belonging to the police union meant his chances of being out of work were practically nil. He would have to kill an unarmed victim to get fired. Probably twice.

Better to put up with a little boredom. If he ever wanted to stop jerking off in the shower and live the real-life dream of having a sub of his own, one he could cosset and care for and spoil every bit as much as Arlo—or whoever—deserved, he needed to focus on advancing the career he had, not playing Cade Brixby, Private Eye.

Chapter 5 Arlo

Arlo stood next to the bed, naked and a little damp from the shower, trying to figure out what to put on. He loved living with Officer Brixby, who was nice to look at and kind to him besides, but the days were long and all the same—not so different from when he'd been in the cage. And he liked being allowed to put on clothes, except those were all the same too.

He had Tripp's basketball shorts and t-shirt plus three pairs of boxers—one from Tripp, one from Sebastian, which he never wore, and one from Officer Brixby—and a t-shirt Officer Brixby had given him that he said was from when he'd run track in high school. It was a little big on Arlo but not huge, so Officer Brixby must've filled out since high school, and it was the same bright blue as Officer Brixby's eyes. Arlo loved it, but after two days in it, he was really wishing for something else.

He opened a dresser drawer and found stacks and stacks of t-shirts. Would it be okay to borrow one? Officer Brixby hadn't said he could, but he had so many. He wouldn't miss just one. Arlo hesitated, torn between the audacity of taking something without permission and a strong distaste for putting on one of the two dirty shirts he'd folded and stacked on the bottom shelf of the nightstand, like the shirts were his wardrobe and the nightstand was his dresser.

The shirt on top of the pile in Officer Brixby's drawer

was deep red. Well-worn and soft to the touch. Arlo pulled it from the drawer and shook it out, finding it as broad as Officer Brixby and graced with a picture of Captain America, somewhat crackled from repeated washings. If he put it on, Officer Brixby might punish him, but maybe that wouldn't be so bad. Imagining getting turned over Officer Brixby's knee for borrowing one of his shirts without permission had Arlo chubbing up, but then the reminder of what punishment was really like intruded. Punishment wasn't the sexy, caring act of kinky love he'd imagined it being. Punishment sucked.

He was returning the shirt to the drawer, trying to fold it back the way it'd been so Officer Brixby wouldn't know he'd touched it, when the door opened. Caught.

"Hey, Arlo," Officer Brixby called. Cheery like always. Sounding so happy to see him.

Arlo crammed the shirt into the drawer and pushed it shut. He turned, knowing he couldn't hide what he'd done, not in a room this small, and found Officer Brixby standing just inside the door holding a paper bag and staring at him. Arlo dropped his eyes. Maybe if he seemed very, very sorry, punishment wouldn't be so bad.

"Why don't you have any clothes on?" Officer Brixby asked.

"I just took a shower." He ran a hand through his damp hair. His curls were drying in a mess around his face.

"Oh, that's good." Officer Brixby didn't sound like it was good. "I brought dinner."

Arlo dared to raise his eyes and saw Officer Brixby holding out the paper bag.

"Do you think you want to put on clothes for dinner?"

Was that a trap? Officer Brixby had seen he was in the drawer. Was he trying to get him to lie about it so he would deserve even more punishment? Arlo took a deep breath. He would confess and get it over with.

"I just wanted a shirt. All mine are dirty."

"Oh, shit. Of course they are." Officer Brixby dropped

the paper bag on the table and came over to him. Arlo backed up into the dresser but Officer Brixby only brushed him out of the way so he could open the drawer himself.

"Borrow whatever you need. I should've said that before. I know none of this is going to fit right, but here." He picked up the very shirt Arlo had been fondling, the one with Captain America on it, and held it out to him. "The red will look nice with your hair. Underwear is in this drawer," he said, pulling open the drawer above it. "Just take whatever seems like it'll fit best. I have no idea what to do for pants though."

"It's okay," Arlo said, happy just to have the shirt and not be in trouble.

"We need to get you some clothes of your own. I should've thought of it before, but I wasn't expecting you to stay so long."

"I don't need anything." Not if it meant he had to live somewhere else.

"You do though because we're going over to Cash's tomorrow, and I'm not bringing you there dressed in clothes you've been wearing for a week." Officer Brixby went into the kitchen and started pulling dishes out of the cupboards. "Do you remember Cash? You met him at the hospital."

Arlo nodded. "Master Cash brought the food."

"Don't call him master. And put some fucking clothes on."

"I'm sorry." Arlo scrambled into Tripp's basketball shorts without even bothering to put on underwear beneath them. He looked up to find Officer Brixby next to him.

"I didn't mean to snap at you." Officer Brixby opened his arms and Arlo dove into them, grateful he was being forgiven for having messed up again. "You can say master if it makes you more comfortable, but Cash would never ask you to. It's not a title he uses. There are going to be a few Doms at his house tomorrow, but none of them are *your* Dom, Arlo. No one has the right to tell you what to do or to hurt you."

"It's not a play party?"

"No, not a play party. Just dinner. And talking about what happened to you and the other victims."

"I'm not a victim. More like a failure."

"Stop, please." Officer Brixby hugged him harder. "I can't stand to hear you talk that way."

"You don't know how bad a sub I was."

"I know you *weren't* a bad sub. You'd be beautiful on your knees. Perfect for me. Perfect for anyone, I mean. And yes, you were a victim. You were abducted—"

"I wasn't. Mike said he could hook me up with what I was looking for, so I did it. It sounded like a sweet deal."

"What about it sounded like a sweet deal?"

"The kink part. It was what I wanted. And the part where I would have a place to live." He'd been essentially homeless—couch surfing, crashing with friends, sleeping with guys he hooked up with one or two nights at a time. He could've gone home if he'd wanted to. His parents hadn't thrown him out. They just hadn't cared when he left. Or noticed.

"How long had you been on your own?"

"Since I graduated in the spring. I was only seventeen when I graduated because when you have a summer birthday, you either start school when you're already six or else you start when you're barely five, and my parents chose five."

"Because you were a prodigy?" Officer Brixby teased.

Arlo figured he was smart enough, but Doms didn't like boastful subs, so he didn't say that. Instead he gave what was most likely his parents' reasoning.

"I think they wanted the free daycare. They don't hate me. They're just really, really involved in their own dysfunction. I thought I could do better on my own, but not so much. It was already getting old when that guy Mike hit me up. It sounded too good to be true, so I guess I should've known it was. Master was a disappointment to me, and I was a disappointment to him."

"I sincerely doubt he was disappointed in you, but if he was, that just means he has bad taste in addition to everything else that's wrong with him. You're going to find the right Dom, Arlo. One who'll treasure your submission like the gift it is. Not every man is worthy of you, and Terzini definitely wasn't." Officer Brixby tipped his chin up, forcing him to meet his eyes. "Can you try to believe that for me?"

"Yes, Officer Brixby."

"That's my angel." Officer Brixby kissed his forehead. Arlo tilted his chin higher, hoping for a real kiss, but Officer Brixby eased him away. "Let me change, and then we can eat."

"Do you have to? I really like your uniform."

"I've been in it all day," he said as he unbuttoned his shirt. He was so sharp in his uniform, so authoritative without being scary. When he dropped his shirt on the bed, Arlo snatched it up and brought it to his nose for a deep inhale. He wouldn't mind wearing dirty clothes if they were Officer Brixby's dirty clothes.

"What cologne do you wear?"

"Right Guard Sport Stick," Officer Brixby answered with a laugh as he shucked his pants, leaving him in just his undershorts.

Arlo lingered by the bed, not wanting to miss any of the show. He liked Officer Brixby in his uniform but with it off, he could see all of Officer Brixby's body—his strong, furry chest, his muscled arms and shoulders, and those thighs that felt so nice under his own when he dared to throw his leg over Officer Brixby's in bed. Arlo never got very hairy anywhere except his groin and armpits, and Master had made him wax his cock and balls, even the crack of his ass and his thighs, though he only had a little bit of peach fuzz there. Now he had stubble, and maybe Officer Brixby wouldn't like that.

"After dinner, we'll do some shopping," Officer Brixby said when he'd dressed himself in a pair of jeans and a plain green t-shirt. "Buy you some clothes that fit. But first, I want to see you eat."

Arlo took a reluctant seat at the table. He hated this part of the day because the food was so good and he was hungry. It was an ordeal trying to hold himself back from scarfing it down, but even if Officer Brixby wanted him to eat, he wouldn't like seeing him wolf down food like an animal. Subs ought to eat lightly, that was what Master said. As if they didn't have any needs except the need to submit. Unfortunately for Arlo's appetite, the spaghetti smelled as awesome as Officer Brixby.

Arlo served himself what seemed like a reasonable amount—a small pile of pasta and one meatball. No garlic bread because carbs made you chubby, but Officer Brixby put a piece of bread on his plate, then added more pasta and a second meatball.

"You must be bored eating what I've got in the house for breakfast and lunch every day," he said as he tucked into his own food, eating it with the gusto Arlo was trying to suppress. "We should do some grocery shopping while we're out, get what you like."

"It's all right. I don't need anything special."

"Arlo." Officer Brixby's tone was stern. "You *have* been eating breakfast and lunch, right?"

Arlo hated tricks like this, where there was no way to know what the right answer was. It sounded like Officer Brixby wanted him to eat breakfast and lunch, but Master had fooled Arlo before. Sometimes Arlo was pretty sure there hadn't even been a right answer, that Master had been planning to punish him either way, but Officer Brixby wasn't like that. He probably meant what it sounded like he meant.

Arlo nodded. Just a small nod, one he could take back in case it turned out to be wrong.

Officer Brixby smiled. "Good. As long as you're staying with me, just help yourself to anything you need. Anything I have. And if you need something I don't have, speak up. I feel bad about you being stuck here all day, but until they arrest Terzini, I'm not comfortable with you running around on your own." Officer Brixby's smile dimmed. "I guess you'll be in FBI custody soon, but as long as I've got you, I'm going to take good care of you."

Oh, that was lovely. Arlo smiled so big. He didn't need lunch or new clothes or anything if he could have that.

Chapter 6 Brixby

Harrison hadn't been kidding about calling a conclave. By the time Brixby arrived at Cash's garden apartment with Arlo in tow, the place was full. Sebastian was there, kicked back on a couch with a drink in his hand, talking to Harrison. Brixby gave him a brief nod as he steered Arlo past him. Sebastian was lecturing about something, and neither he nor Arlo needed to be lectured to.

In the kitchen, he found Cash—Harrison's boyfriend and Dom-in-name-only—checking on something in the oven while he chatted to Aldous Knight, Hell's Bedroom's chief of security and their mole. Knight and Cash were both big men, meaning they took up a lot of the available space in Cash's small kitchen, but Cash had a disorganized tumble of brown hair while Knight's black dome was completely shaven. It gleamed under the strong fluorescent lighting.

Brixby reintroduced Cash to Arlo, then started to introduce Knight.

"We've met," Knight reminded him.

Arlo shrank back against Brixby's chest, trying to disappear right through him. Right. The last time Arlo had seen Knight, Knight had been having him pitched out of Hell's Bedroom.

"Knight's not here to get you in trouble," Brixby assured him. "We never would've found you without his help."

But Arlo still seemed uncertain, so Brixby didn't linger in the kitchen. He escorted Arlo outside where the weather was so pleasant half the party had spilled out of Cash's cramped subterranean living space into his garden. The pale cast of Arlo's skin told Brixby that Arlo hadn't seen much of the outside since the night Mike put him on a bus to Philadelphia, and Cash's garden was like an Eden—an unstructured jumble of colorful plants interspersed with seating areas and fanciful lawn ornaments, many of which featured rainbows.

The sun was still high enough that Brixby put his sunglasses back on, and the temperature was a perfect seventy-five. Francesca sat on a wrought-iron bench with her sub, Ilona, kneeling on one side of her and Kimi, the Algonquin woman from Chicago, kneeling on the other. Francesca's shiny dark hair was coiled into a twist on top of her head, and the two subs were in matching rompers with their hair dressed in pigtails. It would appear Francesca was taking her job as Kimi's temporary Domme seriously, but from the way the two women had their bodies angled away from each other, Brixby could guess the unplanned triad wasn't harmonious.

Ilona had a right to be displeased. She and Francesca had had a long-term monogamous D/s relationship for years before the case thrust Kimi into their lives. Brixby felt bad for Kimi, who'd been misled into believing she was going to be a full-time slave to a doting Domme, but he felt nearly as bad for Ilona, who'd had to make room for her. He didn't envy Francesca either. Two subs would be too many for him.

Arlo hadn't strayed from his side. He was eyeing the two women on the ground, either envying them or confused by them, when Tripp bounced up with a giant hug for his friend. He had a rubber ball, and he pulled Arlo away to play.

Brixby took a seat on a canvas camp chair that'd been placed among the more ornamental seating and greeted

Francesca as he stretched his legs out in front of him. He left her subs unacknowledged. He only knew the Korean Domme well enough to know she was high-protocol—the sort who thought subs should be more seen than spoken to.

"How was New York?" Francesca asked. They hadn't seen each other since the weekend Arlo was found. "Was the club much like Hell's Bedroom?"

The only parts of Hell's Bedroom Brixby had ever seen were the reception lounge and the back office where Knight worked because he wasn't a member—and considering Hell's Bedroom's prices, he wasn't ever likely to be—so he didn't have much of a basis for comparison.

"Their security guards wear the same uniforms," he said, sticking to what he knew. "And they keep a close eye on you."

"You think that's how potential victims are being identified?"

"No talking business," Cash interrupted. He'd come out to the patio with a giant fork he looked about ready to stick someone with. "We're going to eat before we get to the serious stuff. Food's up in the dining room."

Francesca sent Ilona to fetch her a plate, but Brixby went inside himself since he didn't have anyone to fetch for him. He made small talk with Harrison as they filled plates next to each other, then went back out to the patio. Tripp and Knight were already out there, digging in, and Francesca was handfeeding her subs from the plate Ilona had fixed.

Brixby looked around, wondering where Arlo had got to. He found him along the back edge of the garden, tossing the ball up in the air and catching it again.

"Arlo." He waited until Arlo looked at him. "Come here."

It was an order, and Arlo obeyed like it was one, dashing over to stand between his spread legs.

"I want you to eat," Brixby told him in a clear, unmistakable tone. "Do you understand me?"

"Yes, Officer Brixby."

"Then let me see you do it."

Arlo plopped down to his knees, right there between Brixby's legs. What the fuck? Brixby had meant Arlo should make a plate, not suck his dick, although his dick had thoughts on that subject that were going to quickly become apparent. Then Arlo opened his mouth, and Brixby realized he was mimicking Kimi and Ilona. Well, if that was the way to get Arlo to eat.... He offered up a forkful of macaroni salad, and Arlo closed his mouth around it.

"How come no one's feeding me?" Tripp complained. He was on the ground too, but cross-legged rather than kneeling and doing a fine job of feeding himself.

"If I feed you, I won't make it easy," Sebastian said.

"Hit me," Tripp challenged. Sebastian plucked a cherry tomato from his plate and lobbed it in Tripp's direction. Tripp managed to catch it. He bit into it lasciviously, sending seeds bursting out of his mouth.

Brixby turned his attention back to Arlo. He broke off a piece of Cash's unbelievably delicious homemade cornbread and handed it to Arlo to eat while he stuffed a forkful of salad into his own face, getting one of those cherry tomatoes with it. They were too good to be used for target practice.

He held one up to Arlo's lips. Arlo sucked it in with a succulent pout, then his eyes went wide as he got a flavor bomb. Brixby imagined the tomato bursting in Arlo's mouth like a cock going off, spraying him with its seed. When Tripp had mimicked something similar, Brixby had only rolled his eyes, but Arlo doing it hit different. He leaned down and held Arlo's chin still while he licked across his lips to catch a trace of the tart sweetness.

Their almost-kiss was interrupted by a crashing sound. Brixby looked up to see Tripp sprawled across the pavers with an upended planter spilling dirt over his legs.

"Must you?" Francesca asked with a harsh look for Sebastian, who'd instigated the foolery.

Tripp righted the planter, and Brixby went back to what he was supposed to be doing. Which was making sure Arlo ate, not kissing him.

Tripp stopped horsing around with Sebastian and came over to sit next to them. He regaled Arlo with the entire plot to the movie he'd watched last night, mostly with his mouth full. Arlo listened more than he talked, but he obediently opened up every time Brixby held something out for him.

"Here."

Brixby glanced up to find Cash standing next to him with another plate of food. "You gave most of yours to Arlo."

It was true. He hadn't managed more than a few bites himself.

"Did you get enough to eat?" he asked Arlo.

Arlo nodded.

"I don't want you lying to me," Brixby told him sternly.

"I won't, Officer Brixby."

"All right, then. Good job. You did very well."

Arlo's lips curved into a smile. He leaned his head against Brixby's thigh, his hair brushing the skin below Brixby's shorts. It was a little tickly, but not tickly enough that Brixby would trade it for anything else in the world. He tucked into his new plate. Everything Cash made was so tasty.

"What's up with your arm?" he asked Cash, who'd finally sat down with a plate himself.

"Tattoo." Cash tapped the adhesive square plastered over his forearm.

"Harrison finally talked you into one, huh?"

"Him and his sister. Apparently I can't marry into the family unless I'm marked up."

"Are you guys getting married?" Kind of quick, but not unexpected.

"Just an expression," Cash said, but Brixby doubted it would be just an expression for long.

"So what did you get?" Sebastian had made Tripp run his empty plate into the kitchen and bring him back a beer.

Now he was sitting with his feet up on Tripp's back while Tripp pretended to be an ottoman for him.

"You'll have to wait for the grand unveiling like everyone else," Cash told him.

"It's Harrison's initials, isn't it? He totally owns you."

"Whatever. I've got a sub. Where's yours?" It was unlike Cash to be nasty, but Sebastian had that effect on people.

Sebastian pointed at his human footstool, which Cash shrugged off.

"Games. You're nothing but games." He stood up and took Brixby's plate, which Brixby had already managed to empty because it'd been that good.

"I'm serving dessert in the living room so we can talk without being overheard." Cash gestured at the three-story building looming over them. "Come in when you're ready."

"Do you want to come inside?" Francesca asked Kimi. "I'll give you permission to stay in the garden if hearing us talk about the investigation will be too triggering."

Kimi pursed her lips in Ilona's direction. "I'll come."

Francesca went inside with her subs scrambling to crawl after her. Brixby felt for their knees.

"How about you?" he asked the boy at his feet. "I'd like for you to be part of the conversation since it concerns you, but you don't have to be."

"Of course he's coming," Tripp said as he tugged Arlo up off his knees. Well, that was good. Brixby preferred not to leave Arlo out here alone, and he certainly hadn't been planning to make him crawl. Feeding someone was sweet—domestic and loving. Making them crawl, especially over a brick patio, just felt mean. To each their own, of course.

When the door slid shut behind Arlo and Tripp, Brixby realized he'd been left alone on the patio with Sebastian.

"I thought Arlo was too fragile to play with."

"I'm not playing with him."

"Only feeding him. And kissing him. And having him kneel at your feet."

"I'm trying to help him. What were you doing?"

59

"The same thing. He seemed to need something, so I tried to offer it. But perhaps he needed something... safer."

"Not every sub is looking to have his ass handed to him."

"Very true, and safe isn't my thing. Can't I be happy Arlo has found a Dom who suits him?"

"You *could* be." But he was pretty sure Sebastian wasn't, not with that sneer he was rocking.

Brixby was glad he'd gotten Arlo away from Sebastian before Sebastian's luxurious lifestyle could persuade Arlo into another bad relationship. What Arlo needed right now was a way to support himself and a place to live, friends and family—found family, since his own sucked—and the confidence to insist that his Dom treat him right. What he *didn't* need was a high-handed asshat like Sebastian using a bullwhip on him.

He probably didn't need Brixby hand-feeding him either. That'd been inappropriate. And a little out of nowhere, not something he'd ever done before. He was supposed to be acting like the big brother Arlo needed, not the Dom he didn't.

"Shouldn't you be inside?" Sebastian asked with deceptive politeness. "I thought you were a cop. One might imagine you'd be interested."

Fuck, that asshole really knew how to push a guy's buttons. Brixby brushed past him to get to the door, letting his shoulder bump against Sebastian's as he went. It was childish, and Sebastian's low laugh told him Sebastian knew it.

Chapter 7 Brixby

Brixby leaned up against a wall, automatically scanning the room with a cop's eye. Cash's apartment was an overcrowded space even when it didn't have this many people in it, full of cushioned furniture in a rainbow of colors. Every wall was covered in memorabilia or artwork, some of which Brixby suspected might be Cash's own. But what he was scanning for was Arlo. He found him on one end of the longer couch with Tripp in the middle and Knight on the other end

Arlo waved when Brixby spotted him and indicated a narrow strip of empty space between him and the arm of the couch. It was much too small for Brixby's hips, but he went over and wedged himself in anyway so that Arlo's ass ended up half across his thigh.

"There's a cat," Arlo whispered with a nod toward the window.

Cash's apartment sat mostly underground on the street side, so the window in the living room was high and long, stretching in a letterbox from one side of the space to the other. Cash had built a platform there, and his black-and-white chonk of a cat was in its usual spot, surveying the stream of feet passing endlessly by on the darkening sidewalk.

"That's Mr. Moo."

"Do you think he wants to sit with me?"

"I've never seen him sit anywhere except there, and

there's an awful lot of people here. Cats tend to be shy around strangers."

Arlo made various faces in the cat's direction—first eager, then pouting—as if the cat might be swayed by either Arlo's beauty or his desperate wish to be friends, but Mr. Moo only swished his tail and looked even more studiously out the window.

Brixby accepted a cup of coffee from Ilona who was passing them around with pretty manners, calling everyone sir—even Tripp, who goggled at the title—and curtseying as she went. He declined to take any brownies from the tray Kimi followed with. He'd already eaten well, and he'd missed his workout that morning. A warm and clingy Arlo had made it hard to get out of bed, resulting in an extended lie-about while Brixby half dozed with blond curls tickling his nose.

Arlo didn't take a brownie either, which made Brixby wish he'd taken one just so he could feed it to him, despite the resolution he'd made not five minutes ago. Arlo was looking at something on Tripp's phone now, laughing like a typical guy his age—one who'd never had anything traumatic happen to him. Brixby nodded at Knight over their heads.

"How'd your tattoo come out?"

The last time he'd seen Knight, Knight had had one of those same white pieces of tape over his forearm Cash did today. Knight raised his arm to show his kids' names running down it, and Brixby admired the work Harrison's sister had done.

Harrison whistled sharply, interrupting the flow of idle chatter. He was on his feet, next to a chair but not sitting in it. He waited for the room to settle, then waved his phone.

"I just heard from Dobransky," he said directly to Brixby. "He's looking to pick up Arlo and Kimi, so I told him he might as well come here. We've got a two-for-one deal on abducted subs tonight. But," he said, addressing himself to the room at large now, "that means we'd better get talking before the Feds show up."

"Who's Dobransky?" Knight asked.

"Like I said—the Feds. He's the agent assigned to the case."

"And you don't trust him?" Sebastian asked.

"No, I do," Harrison answered. "He spent a whole morning with me poring over my case files when most Feds would act like I didn't exist. But he's focused on San Francisco. DDD headquarters."

"And Hell's Bedroom is *ours*." Cash was passionate on the subject of the kink community having a responsibility to police itself. "Maybe San Francisco is behind this ring, but we've got a local conspirator. Mike didn't fly in from California. He was right here in Boston, waiting for Arlo or someone like him."

"So what are you suggesting?" Brixby asked Harrison.

"He's suggesting we keep working the case," Sebastian said. "But we don't all have to be involved, if some of us are feeling timid."

"Don't give Brixby shit," Harrison said. "He already got shit on hard enough by Captain Murphy. This is a voluntary operation. If anyone wants out, they're out."

"Out of what though?" Brixby didn't know what Harrison had in mind for them to do.

"Whatever it is, I'm happy to help," Francesca said. "I don't see how I could say no."

"And I'm game obviously." Sebastian waved his hand in a magnanimous gesture meant to imply everything he'd already done for them, which was provide money, not donate a kidney. He didn't need to be so full of himself, but that was his natural state. Sebastian was tall, handsome, rich—filthy rich—and a lawyer. He had a crowded slate of traits to be arrogant about.

Brixby was tall and—at least in his mother's opinion—handsome, but he hadn't been born with a silver spoon in his mouth, so he couldn't be cavalier about his job. Captain Murphy had told him he was off the case. Harboring Arlo for the last week was risky enough. If he got involved with Harrison's vigilante justice and Captain Murphy heard about it, Brixby wouldn't be quitting the force because he wanted to be out-and-proud or do more interesting, socially responsible work. He would be getting fired. Choice removed. Even the union wouldn't be able to save him if he disobeyed direct orders like that.

"You want to go back to Philadelphia with me, Harry?" Sebastian asked, using Harrison's undercover name because he knew how much Harrison hated it.

"Wherever Harrison is going," Cash said, emphasizing Harrison's full name, "he'll be going with me."

Sebastian raised his eyebrows in mock surprise. "But he and I had such a good thing going on."

"Ooh, ooh." Tripp raised his hand. "Take me instead. I want to go back to that club in New York. There was this *thing*, like a Saint Andrew's cross except—"

"The point wouldn't be to play," Harrison reminded him.

"I know. I'm just saying." Tripp flashed a grin in Sebastian's direction, practically begging Sebastian to string him up.

"I appreciate the enthusiasm," Harrison said, "but Cash and I are thinking we should concentrate our efforts here in Boston, see if we can smoke out the rat inside Hell's Bedroom. And as far as Hell's Bedroom goes," he added, cutting Tripp off before he could volunteer again, "we have plenty of resources without involving a teenager."

Tripp pouted. "Nineteen isn't a teenager," he said, somehow not hearing the teen part of nineteen.

"We've got enough folks that we don't need you either, Brixby," Harrison said. "So don't sweat it."

Brixby nodded, appreciating that Harrison was trying to let him off the hook, but the call-out only made him feel more like he had to choose a side. Knight was risking *his* job by being here. When Knight had realized Hell's Bedroom's management might be implicated in what was going on, courtesy of some deleted records in the security system, he'd sought Harrison out rather than look the other way. And he kept coming to their meetings even though he was a vanilla straight dude and they were a bunch of queer kinksters. Though that might be for the food.

Sebastian had ponied up more than a hundred thousand dollars; Francesca had allowed her reputation at the club to be destroyed by pretending to ignore a red call; and Harrison had worked Arlo's case for free, despite not having any other source of income. The only one who hadn't sacrificed anything meaningful was him.

"I'm still not sure what the plan is," he said, putting off making an actual decision until he understood what would be involved.

"We haven't got a solid one—just fan out and cover the space, watch for anyone who looks vulnerable and pay attention to who's watching *them*. I wish we had a sub to plant."

"Ooh, ooh," Tripp said, raising his hand again.

Sebastian lowered it for him. "You're the exact opposite of a lifestyle sub, darling, and everyone at the club knows it. A little brat like you—"

"But then you could punish me," Tripp suggested with far too much enthusiasm.

"Once again," Harrison reminded him, "this isn't about playing. And Sebastian is right. You're already known there and don't fit our victim profile. I don't suppose Kimi would be willing to—"

"You're not suggesting she expose herself to the same fate a second time?" Francesca asked sternly.

"Nooo, I suppose not. They'd probably figure out the connection anyway, realize they've sold her already."

Brixby raised his hand—hesitantly, because he hadn't actually made a decision yet. "I've never been to Hell's Bedroom. At least, not as a customer."

"But you're a Dom," Tripp said.

"So he claims," Sebastian said. "I haven't seen any proof of it, unless cuddling is a new form of domination I'm not aware of."

"Oh, fuck you," Brixby rejoined, but considering he had Arlo half in his lap, he wasn't really in a position to deny the charge.

"Shh," Arlo hissed. He pressed a hand to Brixby's stomach, trying to get him to settle down. "He's coming."

Who was coming? Dobransky? Well, good. Dobransky could take charge of Arlo, then Brixby could put this investigation behind him—go back to his normal work routine and not piss off any higher-ups. But before he could say that, he realized who Arlo was actually waiting for. Mr. Moo had stepped off his perch and was threading his way between chair legs, heading in their direction.

"Sebastian's just being an ass," Harrison said. "As always." He gave Sebastian a glare and got a shrug in response. "If you're up for it, Brixby, we could definitely use you. Not sure how vulnerable you look—"

Tripp snorted.

"Well." Harrison seemed to agree with Tripp's assessment. "Do your best."

"Being a sub isn't a matter of size," Cash said.

"Neither is getting taken advantage of," Brixby agreed.

Harrison had been a terrible plant when he'd tried to go undercover because his attitude screamed the opposite of victim. Brixby figured he could do a better job, if only because he understood the submissive mindset better. His strategy would be to come across as hardcore—driven so strongly by his kinks that he would agree to a dubious way of having them met—and desperately in need of something more than an hour's entertainment.

"All three of our known victims were homeless at the time they were taken," he reminded Harrison. "I'll play with that, ask people if they've got a place I can crash."

"So you're in?"

Brixby nodded. He hadn't consciously made a decision. Arlo, sitting in his lap cooing in Mr. Moo's direction, had made it for him. Arlo wouldn't be safe on the streets until

Mike was removed from them.

"Any other thoughts?" Harrison asked. "Hold on." He waved off comments as he looked at his phone. "Dobransky's here," he told Cash.

Arlo made a soft clucking sound, and twenty pounds of cat landed with a thud on top of them. Mr. Moo's claws dug uncomfortably into Brixby's thigh, but Arlo was beaming so widely he decided to bear it.

"That cat won't so much as acknowledge my existence," Harrison said. "And I live here."

"He likes me," Arlo said. "Can I keep him?" He glanced up at Brixby, but the answer was no. Arlo himself wasn't coming home with him. Never mind Arlo plus a cat.

"You'll never get Mr. Moo away from Cash," Harrison said, saving Brixby from having to answer. "They have secret cuddle times when I'm not looking."

Mr. Moo seemed happy to cuddle Arlo too. He tipped his head back, allowing Arlo to rub under his chin, then pushed it down, directing Arlo's fingers to a spot behind his ear. Bossy cat. But Arlo didn't mind. He just petted whatever Mr. Moo gave him to pet.

Cash came back in with Dobransky, who was dressed in a suit similar to the one he'd been wearing in Captain Murphy's office the other day, though it was past eight. Harrison made the introductions while Kimi and Ilona fetched him refreshments.

"So what have we got here?" Dobransky asked from the folding chair Cash had found for him. "A vigilante group?"

"A gathering of friends," Harrison corrected. "Who happen to have certain things in common."

"Hmm." Dobransky took a bite of the brownie. His eyes closed momentarily in approval. "I'm on your side," he said when he'd finished savoring it. "Your brass may have closed the case, but you can trust me to keep working it. I see who's being targeted. Underage gay men, Indigenous women, addicts and runaways. In other words, marginalized people. People the ringleaders think no one will care about if they go missing. But I care, and I promise you I'll find them. I don't share all of your, er, interests, but I do fall under your rainbow."

"It's not that we don't have faith in your investigation," Harrison said. "It's just that there's action that needs to be taken locally."

"And I can't stop you from taking it. But can I ask you to share whatever you learn?"

"Do we get the same favor?"

"Absolutely. Brixby is my local liaison. He'll have full access to my files. If there are any details I need chased down locally, I would expect him to help in return. His captain would expect it as well, I'm sure."

That wasn't even close to what Captain Murphy had said, but if Brixby got caught working on the case, maybe Dobransky could bail him out of trouble.

"This is Arlo, I presume," Dobransky said, turning in their direction. "And Kimi was the one who gave me the brownie, yes? Have you two been taken good care of?"

"Yes, sir," Kimi said.

Brixby prodded Arlo, who was too focused on Mr. Moo to realize he ought to answer. Arlo nodded.

"Good. We've got a spot in a local safehouse for you, Arlo. And Kimi, we have one for you back in Chicago."

"No!"

"Kimi?" Francesca put a fingertip to Kimi's nose.

"I mean 'no, sir,'" Kimi said, but Francesca's expression suggested that still didn't cut it.

"You don't make the decisions around here, do you? You turned yourself over to my care, which means you'll trust me to do what's best for you. Or would you prefer to terminate your contract?"

Contract? Francesca and Kimi had a contract? The last Brixby knew, Francesca was only housing Kimi until she had somewhere else to go, but the look on Ilona's face suggested she knew about the contract and couldn't wait to see it torn up.

"No, Mistress," Kimi said, her gaze pinned to the floor. "I don't want to terminate my contract."

"Then I don't want to hear another word out of you." Francesca waited a solid thirty seconds while Kimi's silence echoed around the room. Everyone was a little stunned, but most especially Dobransky. "I'm responsible for Kimi," Francesca told him, meeting his eyes levelly. "And the best thing for her is to remain in my charge. She's not under arrest, is she?"

"Definitely not." Dobransky shut his mouth and wiped it with a handkerchief he pulled from his trousers. "She's free to turn down protective custody if she doesn't want it."

"Then she'll stay with me."

"It's better if Kimi stays with Francesca anyway," Harrison said, which was a surprise. Harrison had made his opposition to Francesca's style of dominance pretty plain in the past. "That's where our traffickers expect her to be."

"But Arlo's not where they expect *him* to be," Brixby said. "I'm still concerned Terzini might come looking for him."

"About that," Dobransky said. "I have an update. The tap we placed on Terzini's phone paid off. He placed a call complaining Arlo had disappeared and demanding his money be refunded."

"Who did he call?"

"The business office at XXXtasy, his club in Philly. He spoke to the manager, who put on a convincing show of having no idea what he was talking about. Maybe she did, maybe she didn't. It took us a few hours to get a tap on her phone, so we might've missed it, but she didn't pass on the information about Arlo's disappearance that we were able to catch."

"But you think the information got passed on," Harrison guessed.

Dobransky nodded. He took another look around the room, as if judging their readiness to hear whatever he was about to say. Brixby wanted to put his hands over Arlo's ears.

"Terzini turned up dead."

"Master's dead?"

"I told you not to call him that. He wasn't your master. He was a kidnapper and an abuser and—" He became aware that the whole room was watching him lecture Arlo, who'd turned his face up with wide, hurting eyes. How many times had he told himself to stop policing Arlo on this subject? It was just that hearing Arlo call another man master bugged the hell out of him.

"Sorry." He gave Arlo's nose a quick nuzzle of apology and prompted Dobransky to go on. "You were saying?"

"We didn't have Terzini under physical surveillance, unfortunately, but when he hadn't used his phone in twenty-four hours, we went looking for him and found him laid out on his bed with a hole through his heart."

Dobransky helped himself to another brownie. Apparently the thought of Terzini's chest being blown open didn't affect his appetite, but it made Brixby queasy. He'd only been worried someone might try to recapture Arlo. Now he had to worry someone might try to kill him.

Ilona must've had an even more visceral reaction because she made a dash for Cash's bathroom, which was situated close enough to the living space that they all heard the sound of her retching through the door. Which didn't seem to affect Dobransky's appetite either.

"Dead men don't tell tales," Sebastian said as Francesca hovered on the other side of the bathroom door. "I don't like how smart these guys are. Every step they take is designed to make prosecuting them more difficult."

"Last I heard, murder was a prosecutable offense," Harrison said.

"If we find someone to pin it on," Dobransky agreed, "but I take Mr. Gage's point. Terzini was the link between Arlo and the people at the top. When he proved he couldn't be trusted to keep his mouth shut, they had him taken out

70

of the picture."

Ilona came back out, and Francesca guided her over to the sofa, sitting her on it rather than putting her on her knees.

Dobransky leaned toward them. "Didn't mean to upset the lady's stomach."

"It wasn't the gore," Francesca said as she smoothed a hand over Ilona's forehead. "It's a migraine. Why didn't you tell me one was coming on?"

"What you were talking about was important."

"Can I get a glass of water?" Francesca asked, but Cash was already standing over her with one. She pulled a vial from her handbag and shook out a pill, which she handed to Ilona. Then she held the glass up to Ilona's mouth for a sip. "I should've been paying more attention, pet. I'm sorry."

"It's the tension," Cash said.

"Very much so." Francesca pulled Ilona into her body. "She's had too many migraines lately." Her gaze rested momentarily on Kimi, who shrank away in response. "We have to leave. Ilona needs dark and quiet."

"Let me drive you." Knight popped to his feet. "I'll pull my car around."

"Guess the party's breaking up." Sebastian stretched himself onto his feet as if this were the normal end to a normal gathering, and Cash bustled about seeing them all out.

Dobransky stood up too. "Are you ready to go, Arlo?"

Arlo turned his head up to Brixby with a plea. "Mistress Francesca said Kimi didn't have to go."

"Kimi is staying with Francesca."

"And I'm staying with you. Please, Officer Brixby."

"You'd be safer with Agent Dobransky."

"Oh, keep him," Dobransky said. "If that's what he'd rather. Terzini's murder makes it highly unlikely anyone is out looking for Arlo. Who could he testify against other than Terzini?"

Only Mike, if they could find him. And Mike would be

even farther down the ladder than Terzini. Dobransky was right. In killing Terzini, whoever was running this human trafficking ring had severed their connection to Arlo.

"Please," Arlo begged. And God damn those big blue eyes, like giant cornflowers fringed in gold lashes.

"Fine," Brixby said, pretending his chest hadn't just loosened in relief.

Arlo might be safer in FBI custody, but he wouldn't be where Brixby could see him. Or touch him. And Arlo needed stability. Poor little thing, inhaling the scent of authority off Brixby's shirts whenever he got a chance. He wouldn't like being in an FBI safehouse with a vanilla guard who wouldn't cuddle him or understand him.

"If you're coming with me, then it's time I got you home," he said gruffly, but on the inside he was all smiles. Arlo was going to stay right where he belonged.

Chapter 8 Arlo

It was dark out, and the street was mostly empty. Arlo wasn't scared because he was with Officer Brixby, but it was cold too. He'd been warm in Cash's apartment with Officer Brixby and Mr. Moo, but Captain America wasn't doing much to keep him warm now. The evening had cooled considerably, and a breeze blew in off the bay carrying a hint of impending autumn. He shivered, the movement shaking him head to toe.

"You're cold." Officer Brixby hooked an arm over his shoulders.

"I'm all right," he said, but he moved in closer.

"I should've brought a hoodie for you." Officer Brixby ran his hand up and down his arm, ruffling some warmth into him. "I don't have a lot of experience taking care of someone. You might've been better off with—"

Arlo shook his head. Officer Brixby was going to say he would've been better off with Sebastian or Agent Dobransky, and Arlo didn't want to be with either of them. Agent Dobransky seemed like an okay guy, better than Sebastian, but he would choose Officer Brixby over anyone.

"I could call a Lyft," Officer Brixby offered.

"I don't mind walking. I haven't gotten any exercise in months. Master—" He choked himself off. Officer Brixby kept telling him not to say that word, and he kept forgetting. But Officer Brixby didn't yell at him this time. Maybe he knew how hard Arlo was trying.

"Are you upset about Terzini being dead?" Officer Brixby asked.

"I don't think so." Mostly he was surprised. He hadn't really believed anyone had done anything criminal to him, but if someone had murdered Master, then maybe Officer Brixby and his friends were right.

"For what it's worth," Officer Brixby said, "he doesn't deserve your sympathy. He was a lousy Dom, and you deserve a good one. If you still want one, that is. It's okay if you don't."

"Is it okay if I do?"

"Of course."

This morning, in the shower, he'd jerked off. It was the first time since he'd been released from the cage—and he'd *never* jerked off in the cage, because Master would've known—and he'd been surprised when his sweet fantasy of sucking Officer Brixby's cock had turned a little rough. Life with Master had been so bad he felt like maybe he ought to be over it, but Officer Brixby kept saying it would be different with a better Dom, and Arlo knew where to find a better Dom.

"Then could you be my Dom?"

"Me?" Officer Brixby squawked. "I don't think so, Arlo."

"Mistress Francesca kept Kimi. Why can't you keep me? Is it because I broke my contract with Master?"

"God, no. And I *am* keeping you. For as long as you want to stay."

"But not as your sub?"

"It would be a bad idea for you to enter into another D/s relationship so soon. You're young, and you've got trauma to process."

"But Kimi gets to."

"Honestly, I'm not sure Kimi should either, but she and Francesca get to make their own choices."

"Then how come I can't make a choice?"

"Because both of us have to make it, and I'm not taking on a sub who was locked in some shitty asshole's cage a week ago, I'm not taking on a sub who's still healing from the wounds that shitty asshole inflicted on him, and I'm definitely not taking on a sub who's got nowhere else to be except with me."

Well, that was clear enough. Arlo ducked out from under Officer Brixby's arm and started walking faster to get away from him. "I *do* have somewhere else to be," he said. "I could've gone with Agent Dobransky. I would've if I'd known you didn't want me."

Officer Brixby caught his arm and dragged him to a stop, making Arlo realize he'd been about to step into traffic. "I didn't say I didn't want you. I said it wouldn't be right. You're welcome to stay at my apartment, but I can't play with you while you're dependent on me."

Arlo shook his arm free, but he didn't rush off again. He stuck by Officer Brixby's side as they navigated down the steps to the T station, but when they got on the train, he took a seat one seat away from him. The vacant stretch of orange plastic between them felt lonely after being on Officer Brixby's lap at Cash's. If he slid over, probably Officer Brixby would let him, would put an arm around him and rub his cold skin, but Arlo didn't slide over.

He saw how it was. Officer Brixby was a nice man and a good police officer. He'd rescued Arlo, so now he felt responsible for him—for keeping him safe from Master and the people who'd killed Master. He treated Arlo nice because he treated everyone nice, but he didn't like Arlo. Not like that. And no wonder. Arlo had disappointed Master, then broken his contract. He'd run off, and Master had gotten killed for it. Who would want a sub like that?

They got off at Officer Brixby's stop in Jamaica Plain. Arlo was super cold now, eager to get back to the apartment where he could roll himself in Officer Brixby's sheets and pretend the smell comforting him was the smell of his own Dom, but Officer Brixby unexpectedly turned the wrong way.

Where were they going? Was Officer Brixby taking him

to the safehouse after all? He shouldn't have sassed like that. He was on the verge of tears—ready to beg as hard as he'd ever begged Master—when Officer Brixby stopped at a phone store.

It was warm in the store, at least. While Officer Brixby talked to the clerk, Arlo toyed with a Samsung phone out on display. A new model had been released while he'd been in the cage, and he'd never even known it.

"This is, um, not that," Officer Brixby said. He thrust a bag into Arlo's hands.

"What is it?"

"A phone, but just a prepaid one. Sorry. Sebastian could've gotten you a nicer one."

"Why would Sebastian get me a phone?" Arlo asked as he delved into the bag, remembering just in time to say Sebastian instead of Master Sebastian.

"If you were staying with him instead of me. He would probably let you sub for him too. But Arlo, that would be a really bad idea."

"Okay." He didn't want to sub for Sebastian. Sebastian was mean, even to other Doms. Sebastian would give him so many punishments. He wouldn't be forgiving like Officer Brixby who'd bought him a phone instead of being mad at him for sulking on the subway.

Officer Brixby was right about the phone not being fancy, but Arlo was so excited to have any phone at all that he threw his arms around him right there in the brightly lit store.

"It was only fifty bucks," Officer Brixby said with a shrug when Arlo thanked him for it over and over as they walked home. "You know, just for the month. And then we'll figure it out from there."

A month. That gave Arlo a target for how much time he had to get Officer Brixby to change his mind. Arlo would prove what a good sub he could be. No more being disobedient or sulky. He would be perfect. Perfect, perfect, perfect. He gave Officer Brixby another hug, trying to

76

convey how grateful he was for being taken care of like this. New clothes yesterday and a phone today. It showed how rewarded he would be if he behaved.

When they got home, Officer Brixby went to a drawer in the kitchen, the one where he kept all his junk like scissors and tape and weird pieces of things. Arlo knew every drawer in the apartment by now. It was snoopy of him, but he didn't have anything else to do during the day, sort of like when he'd been in the cage only bigger. But now he had a phone. He hugged it to his chest as Officer Brixby rifled through the drawer until he came up with a key.

"That's to the apartment." He set it on the table, then opened his wallet and took out a twenty-dollar bill. "I don't have a lot of cash, I'm sorry."

Arlo fingered the bill, but he didn't pick it up. "What do I need money for?"

"For whatever. For lunch. You've gotta be tired of what's in my cabinets."

Arlo shrugged. He knew what was in the cabinets for the same reason he knew what was in the drawers, but he hadn't eaten any of it.

"Or if you need to go somewhere. Maybe you'd like to see your parents."

"I'm allowed to go places?"

Officer Brixby sighed. "Dobransky doesn't think you're in any danger, and I can't keep you cooped up here forever. That would make me no better than Terzini."

Arlo shook his head, even though he'd just been thinking that the apartment was like a bigger cage. Officer Brixby was nothing like Master.

"But we need to establish some guidelines," Officer Brixby said. "I'd like to have you home by dark. Stay in public places. No sneaking into bars or BDSM clubs. Keep an eye on your surroundings. Any sign of Mike and I want you to call me immediately, even if you're not sure it's him, even if you just think it might be him. Understand?"

Arlo nodded.

"And the main thing is—don't go anywhere with any strangers, no matter what their story is."

"The way I did before, you mean."

"Now that you know what can go wrong, you won't make that mistake again." Officer Brixby kissed the top of his head, then went over to the dresser and opened the drawer where he kept his long-sleeved shirts. "We should've gotten you a hoodie while we were shopping the other day, but I've got a dozen of them. So stop shivering and come put one on."

Arlo liked it better when Officer Brixby warmed him with his hands, but he went over and took a grey hoodie from him and put it on because he was being obedient. Officer Brixby sat down on the couch with his phone, and Arlo sat next to him with his.

"What happened to your old phone?" Officer Brixby asked as Arlo got connected to the Wi-Fi. "Did Terzini take it?"

"I lost my backpack on the bus. It had everything in it. My wallet too."

Officer Brixby frowned. "Right. You need ID, don't you?" He sighed like Arlo was too much of a burden. "How'd you manage to lose your backpack on the bus?"

"I fell asleep."

"And?"

"And then I don't know. Mike bought me a cup of coffee, but it had the opposite effect coffee usually has. I think it might've been drugged." That was the only way he could explain it. And if Mike had drugged him, then maybe he really had been abducted. "I was so sleepy getting on the bus he had to help me, and then I woke up and the bus was in Philadelphia and my backpack was gone. Mas—"

He stopped because he knew Master was wrong, but he didn't know what was right. He couldn't refer to his former master as Terzini in the cold, blunt way Officer Brixby did, and he definitely couldn't refer to him as Zach. Zach sounded like a guy who shared his weed, not someone who would lock you in a cage. Not someone who would hit you and burn you and yell at you.

"That man I was staying with," he said vaguely. "He was waiting for me at the station. He said the police would look for my stuff, but I never got anything back."

"I sincerely doubt he reported it. Or that he would've given it back to you even if it'd been found."

No, he probably wouldn't have. Because if Arlo had had his phone in the cage, he might've called someone, and that someone might've come and got him, which Master wouldn't have liked. But Arlo had believed everything Master said in the beginning, which made him seem foolishly naïve even though he wasn't. He'd just wanted it to work so bad.

He looked down at the phone Officer Brixby had bought him and thought about the key sitting on the kitchen table. Officer Brixby was everything Arlo had imagined Master would be, except for not wanting him. It didn't seem fair.

"Are you going to use that phone?" Officer Brixby asked. "Or just stare at it."

"I don't know anyone's number."

"You can start with mine." Officer Brixby entered it himself. He saved it under the name Cade, which was what he'd said Arlo could call him. Arlo hadn't yet, but having that single word *Cade* in his contact list made him feel instantly more connected, like Officer Brixby was his in-case-of-emergency contact.

"I have your parents' cell numbers," Officer Brixby said, "but they're in my case files at work. I'll text them to you tomorrow."

Arlo shrugged.

"How about Tripp's number?"

That one Arlo took. He sent Tripp a text and got one back almost immediately. They texted back and forth until Officer Brixby stood up with a yawn.

"I've got an early morning, but you can stay up if you want."

But they always went to sleep together. Did Officer Brixby not want him in the bed anymore? Maybe the phone and the key weren't rewards. Maybe they were ways to make him go away.

"I can sleep on the couch," he offered.

"Why would you do that?"

"Because you don't want me?"

"Don't be manipulative. I explained why I can't be your Dom. That doesn't mean you should sleep on the couch. All this sulking is doing the exact opposite of convincing me you're emotionally mature enough to be in a relationship."

"So if I prove I'm a grownup, then we can?"

"Somewhere down the road we can talk about it. I can't promise you anything right now, but could you please just behave for me?"

Yes! Now Arlo had orders he understood. He dashed into the bathroom to brush his teeth, then made an obvious production out of flossing. He peed, even washed his hands after, and changed into the boxers Officer Brixby had given him to sleep in that first night. Those were his pajama boxers, big and soft like a hug.

"Ready for bed," he announced, spreading his arms wide to indicate his readiness. "Early to bed and early to rise. Just like an adult."

Chapter 9 Brixby

"Shh, Arlo. Don't cry, angel. It's okay." Brixby's own voice woke him. For a moment, he wondered if he'd been dreaming that Arlo was crying, but no, Arlo was really crying—still asleep but whimpering, curled on his side facing away from Brixby rather than half on top of him like usual.

"Arlo? Come on, angel. Wake up for me." He nuzzled a kiss behind Arlo's ear as he stroked soothing circles into the warm, bare flesh of his stomach. Arlo gave a wild jerk and then settled, the rhythm of his breathing letting Brixby know he was awake now. "Bad dream?"

"I don't remember."

Brixby could guess Terzini had been involved, but was Arlo haunted by what Terzini had done to him or sad about him being dead? Or maybe Arlo was afraid the people who'd murdered Terzini would come for him next.

"Well, whatever it was, you're safe now." He pulled Arlo into a spoon only to realize he was hard, probably from his own dreams. His cock was now firmly wedged between the pert globes of Arlo's ass. He started to ease away, but Arlo clung to him, holding him in place.

"Arlo." He meant no, but his tongue tracing over the shell of Arlo's ear sent a different message.

Arlo squirmed around to face him. "Please can we? You don't have to be my Dom, just..." He took a deep inhale, then let it out with a sigh of longing that went straight through Brixby's soul. "I just want to feel good."

It was too dark to blame Arlo's blue eyes or golden curls, but an image of how Arlo would look if Brixby could see him came unbidden. His cheeks would be lightly flushed and his mouth would be hanging open with soft vulnerability. A mix of lust and need would gleam in his eyes.

Brixby groaned in desperate refusal even as he leaned forward, surrendering to the inevitability of this mistake. His mouth found Arlo's unerringly. Arlo's lips were soft and sweet, so willingly parted and accommodating. Brixby licked over them, mapping their every curve. There was still time to stop this. He'd kissed Arlo before, gently and kindly. He could call a halt here—on the dangerous edge between caretaker and lover, between friend and Dom.

Or he could take.

Arlo trembled in his arms. He made a choked, whimpering sound, but he didn't press forward, and it was that—the obedience—that did Brixby in. He rolled, trapping Arlo beneath him in a decisive move. Arlo was soft and lean, but also firm and sinuous, like something resilient wrapped in something fragile. His body gave under Brixby's easily, the softness of his submission its own strength.

Brixby ground down against the only hard part of Arlo's body, that firm column of flesh that begged for what Brixby wanted to give it. They were both of one mind, sleepy-hot and caught in that midnight state where sex felt like an extension of dreaming. Arlo's arms looped loosely over his shoulders—soft, silky skin stretched taut over limbs that still retained a pleasing plumpness despite Arlo's hauntingly visible ribs. Arlo was part baby fat, and the thought made Brixby groan at the reminder that he shouldn't be doing this. Arlo was very young. Recently traumatized. And warm and nearly naked in his bed.

He tried to pull away, reason breaking through desire, but the movement made his hips grind harder into Arlo's. Arlo responded by tipping his head back, offering up his throat with a whimper, and Brixby's resolve fizzled. He leaned down to take the offered flesh, tracing wet, open lips up the column of Arlo's delicate throat until he found Arlo's earlobe, which he nipped gently.

"Arlo," he breathed into the boy's ear, needing to say his name.

Arlo's body screamed "more," and Brixby couldn't stop himself from giving it. Arlo was so hot—slightly damp, as though his dream had given him night sweats, his skin slick enough that Brixby's slid smoothly over it, no friction to stop him from frotting again and again against the lithe body beneath him. He took Arlo's mouth with a silent apology. He wasn't going to be able to hold himself back long enough to bring Arlo release without seeking his own. They rocked against each other as they kissed, open-mouthed and hungry, Brixby's tongue in Arlo's mouth, his teeth seeking out the plump lips, biting and sucking and thrusting between them.

"Arlo," he mumbled again, wanting a response but not sure what response he wanted until he got it.

"Sir."

Aw, fuck. Yes. It was... it was what he had to have— Arlo calling him sir, Arlo squirming hotly under him, Arlo shaking with the force of his orgasm, arching up to meet him, saying it again. "Sir."

Brixby buried his face in Arlo's neck and came, right into his boxers because that was how rushed, how impetuous their encounter had been. He shuddered with a combination of pleasure and shame until he realized he must be crushing Arlo's light frame.

He'd taken Arlo's compliance as submission, as willingness, but maybe Arlo had only been accepting what he hadn't felt able to reject. Because he had no home to go to, was possibly in danger, and Brixby was his housing and his protection in addition to being his moral support. And Brixby had taken advantage of that by practically forcing—

He pulled out of Arlo's embrace and pushed himself off the bed. "Let's find you something else to wear."

Arlo shimmied out of the boxers he'd orgasmed into and dropped them over the side of the bed. "Don't wanna," he mumbled.

Through the darkness, Brixby made out the gentle curve of Arlo's smile and the flutter of eyelashes as his eyes drooped shut. He went into the bathroom and came back with a cloth and cleaned up the traces of come that clung to Arlo's groin, but he left Arlo naked. He was asleep already, and Brixby didn't have the heart to wake him. He got back in bed, determined to leave Arlo untouched this time, but his intentions didn't matter. Arlo found him.

IT WAS EARLY WHEN BRIXBY SLUNK out of the apartment, careful not to wake Arlo so he wouldn't have to face him and equally careful to have a very thorough wank in the shower in hopes of staving off any repeats of last night's mistake. Despite the hour, his landlord was up, washing the sidewalk in front of the building, which she did with a regularity that could be counted on.

"Good morning, Mrs. Zhao." He greeted her with a tip of his uniform cap like he was a 1950s beat cop. She acknowledged him with little more than a grunt. Mrs. Zhao was the best type of landlord—the kind who left you alone. She owned several stately old houses that'd been remade into multi-family apartments along the street and did all her own maintenance despite her age and the general roundness of her figure. If there was a Mr. Zhao, he had different pursuits.

A greeting and a grunt were as far as their morning interaction usually went, but today Brixby lingered.

"I don't know if you noticed," he said, "but I've had someone staying with me lately."

"Your love life is none of my concern, Officer Brixby." She aimed a stream of water at the wild rose bushes on one side of the porch.

"He's not, um—" Yeah, okay. That'd been his love life last night. How did Mrs. Zhao even know he was gay? Or was she just assuming he was gay because he had an eighteen-year-old boy shacked up in his apartment? "He's a friend."

That only earned him another grunt.

"The thing is, he doesn't have anywhere else to stay, so he might be with me for a while, and I gave him a key, so you might see him coming and going. I'm not sure..." What he meant was, did he need to pay extra for having a semi-permanent roommate? He couldn't help totaling up how much having custody of Arlo was going to cost him. Food, clothes, phone, and maybe rent.

"Rent is by square footage, not by occupancy," Mrs. Zhao said, appearing to guess his meaning. "It's your name on the lease though. If he does any damage, you'll be the one paying for it."

"Definitely. He won't be any trouble. Thank you." He got in his cruiser before she changed her mind.

Determined to think about something other than how Arlo was spending his day and whether it involved him getting kidnapped at all, Brixby threw himself into work. He patrolled his usual haunts, even made a few stops to show some local street kids Jessica Chambers's picture in case she was in a shelter or a crack house right here in Boston and not missing after all, but he still couldn't find anyone who'd seen her, and he didn't dare spend too much time on it.

Around noon, he stopped in at the station house to check his department email and found one from Dobransky. The agent hadn't been fucking around when he'd offered to share information. He'd sent Brixby an email crowded with pictures and reports, most of which had been forwarded from the Philly PD. Pictures of the crime scene, details on Terzini's autopsy, even interview notes. It was a bonanza of information, more than Brixby ever would have gotten out of Philly directly, even if he were still assigned to

85

the case.

He went through it all in order—starting with the transcript of the call Terzini had made to XXXtasy to complain about Arlo running off. The office manager was a woman named Carla Loomis who seemed convincingly confused by Terzini's rantings, repeating several times that paid sex work wasn't allowed on XXXtasy property, as if she thought Terzini had hired a prostitute on the premises. Based on the transcripts, Terzini hadn't been the least bit disappointed in Arlo. He rather desperately wanted him back.

Next up was a report detailing the decision to execute a welfare check on Terzini. A uniform had knocked at his door, and when she didn't get a response, she eventually forced entry, at which point she discovered Terzini's body laid out on his bed with a bullet placed neatly through his heart. Blood evidence suggested he'd been killed just inside his front door and moved to the bed, though why they wouldn't have just shot him and run Brixby didn't understand until he looked at the photos of Terzini's bedroom.

There was no cage. Sure, Terzini might've gotten rid of it himself, but the way he'd demanded the return of either Arlo or his money suggested he hadn't given up hope he would have someone to keep in it. More likely, whoever had killed Terzini had also removed any sign of Arlo ever having been there.

For a dead guy, Terzini looked pretty neat, dressed in a dark grey power suit with his hands folded beneath that single wound. Only the brownish-red trickles leaking down from the powder-scorched hole suggested he was dead rather than resting.

A man like Terzini probably owned dozens of suits, but Brixby couldn't help seeking out the schedule attached to the autopsy report that listed everything that'd been taken off the corpse, and bingo. One St. Michael's medallion. The coroner had even noted that there appeared to be some sort of device soldered to it.

Brixby paged through the rest of the photos attached to the email. Aside from remembering why he'd decided against going into forensics, he didn't find anything helpful, so he logged off the computer. On his way out, he swung by the duty officer's desk to put his name down on the overtime list. He was so lacking in seniority he rarely managed to pick anything up, but he threw his hat in the ring anyway.

An overnight shift flagging traffic would pay Arlo's phone bill for a few months, and if Brixby weren't sleeping next to Arlo, he wouldn't be so tempted to fuck him. His next third shift rotation couldn't come soon enough, though leaving Arlo alone at night didn't sit well with him, and he hated the way his schedule rotated around every few weeks so that he never knew night from day. Which was another factor in favor of getting out of the Boston PD. More time with Arlo versus more money to spend on Arlo. It was a dilemma best solved by getting Arlo on his own two feet and out of the temptation of Brixby's bed.

His phone rang as he was heading home at the end of the day. When he saw it was Francesca, he pulled over so he could give her his full attention.

"I was thinking we should get our charges together for a play date," she said.

"Arlo and I aren't—"

"Sorry, I wasn't suggesting a scene. I meant let the kids interact with each other on their own level. I don't know how Arlo is doing, but Kimi is struggling."

"With what?"

"Is she a victim, or did she choose her fate? She can't call her abductors criminals because she feels like she signed up for it. Add in the fact that she still wants what she thought she was signing up for, and it gets complicated."

Yeah, Brixby could see that in Arlo too. Arlo hadn't gotten lucky the way Kimi had in finding the dominant of his dreams at the end of his bus ride, but what he'd found wasn't completely contrary to what he'd been looking for either. He needed to develop a more nuanced—and ethical—understanding of how BDSM worked and what exactly he wanted. Then maybe it would be all right for Brixby to give it to him. Until then, even fucking around with him in a vanilla way was taking advantage of someone still trying to process his trauma.

He was surprised to learn Francesca had similar concerns though. Maybe he'd gotten the wrong impression about her. Her form of domination was so cold and formal he hadn't imagined her caring about anything except her own will. But then he remembered how quickly she'd flipped the script when Ilona came down with a migraine, how suddenly she'd moved from being served to serving. It was a mistake to judge anyone's relationship based on what you could see from the outside.

He agreed to a play date later in the week, then called Harrison.

"Sounds like a good idea," Harrison said after Brixby filled him in. "Letting Arlo and Kimi talk through their shared experience might benefit them both. Sometimes it's easier to see in someone else what it's hard to see in yourself."

Yeah, the human mind was capable of some pretty good tricks. Like how he'd rationalized turning comfort into sex last night. He didn't tell Harrison about that, but he did tell him about Arlo having been drugged.

"Probably because the bus makes stops between Boston and Philadelphia," Harrison said. "An awake Arlo might've changed his mind."

"And not having a phone or wallet put him in a more vulnerable position. He wouldn't have had anyone to turn to when he got off the bus except Terzini. No way to call for help or buy a return ticket."

Harrison made a disgusted sound. "Well, Sebastian will like it. He's got something he can charge Mike with now. Petty theft, if nothing else. Speaking of Sebastian, is he signing you in as his sub on Saturday?"

"Not a chance."

Harrison laughed. "I figured. No worries. Cash and I will be there. Or Francesca can do it. We'll figure it out. Though if you'll recall, *I* had to deal with playing sub to Master Sebastian."

"I apologize for not sufficiently appreciating what you were going through."

"You want to borrow my booty shorts?"

"No, thank you." He wouldn't fit in Harrison's booty shorts, for one thing. "I have club gear. I can sub it down."

"Well, just say the word. Listen, I've gotta run. I've got a very interesting case of domestic theft to work this week. Grandma got her diamonds stolen, almost certainly by her own grandkid, and it's my job to get them back without anyone being arrested. Unless it turns out to be the maid because then who gives a shit, right? The things we do, Brixby." Harrison made an exaggerated kissy sound into the phone and hung up.

Brixby pulled back into traffic and headed for home, eager to see Arlo but determined not to repeat last night's mistake. *Older brother,* he told himself sternly. Guide, protect, care. Not fuck.

Chapter 10 Arlo

Arlo rolled across the mattress searching out Officer Brixby's body and then—failing that—Officer Brixby's scent. Cade, he told himself. He could really call him Cade now.

Maybe Officer Brixby didn't want to be his Dom, but Cade was his boyfriend practically after what they'd done last night.

Today was going to be a good day. He'd woken up in a bed that smelled like warm man with happy memories of hot sex, then got to take a shower with no time limit and no fear about what was going to happen when he got out, and now he could leave the house if he wanted. He hadn't decided where to go, but he was excited about going.

He dressed in the new clothes Cade had bought him, then considered a box of Cheerios. He'd eaten a lot last night, more than he probably should've, but he was hungry again now, and Cade kept telling him to eat. Cade usually meant what he said, not like Master, but he hadn't seen Arlo chubby. Arlo decided he would only eat when Cade was watching. That way he could stay small but also be obedient.

So instead of eating breakfast, he brewed a cup of coffee and drank it black. Even though the coffee was bitter without cream or sugar in it, he appreciated it. Master had never let him drink anything in the morning because he didn't like coming home to find the pee bottle overflowing. Arlo drank two cups, then used the bathroom. Because he could.

Maybe it was time to stop thinking about what Master wanted or what Master would let him do. He lived with Cade now, and Master was dead. Had Master really missed him enough to complain? It seemed unlikely. Master had always said he wasn't worth his keep, that if it weren't for the contract, he would throw Arlo out on the street. Then he would remind Arlo the contract couldn't be broken, not by either of them, and even though sometimes Arlo had really wanted to break it, it'd been reassuring, in a way, to know Master couldn't. So maybe that was why Master had called to complain. Not because of missing him. Only because he'd broken his contract.

Determined to be a good sub, or at least a good boyfriend—an adult one—he washed his cup and put it back in the cupboard. Then he tucked the twenty-dollar bill, the key, and his new phone into his pockets and left the house. Which was wild. He hadn't been alone outside in months. No one telling him where to go or what to do, no one checking to see if he did it. No one to protect him either, if the bad guys came for him.

He wasn't really worried though. He'd been homeless on the streets of Boston. He could walk down a sidewalk in Jamaica Plain. He knew how to get to the T, and from there, he could go anywhere. This wasn't new, and he wasn't a naïve child, whatever Cade thought. Not with parents like his.

He didn't care about his parents any more than they cared about him, which was practically not at all, but everything he owned, other than what had disappeared with his backpack, was at their house in Medford, so he took the T downtown then hopped a bus heading that way. He knew the route well from traveling back and forth before he'd given up on going home and decided to just hang out in Boston. Couch-surfing could make a guy feel unwelcome, but not as unwelcome as the empty disinterest of his own family.

It was a long walk from the bus stop with Harrison's sandals flapping loosely around his feet. Harrison had big feet for his height. Arlo wondered if that meant Harrison had a big dick too. He walked like he was about six inches taller than he really was so maybe, but he lived with Cash, the Dom with the chonky cat, which either meant they were two Doms together or meant something else Arlo didn't understand.

He would have to ask Tripp, who'd been his main source for kinky insights before Uncle Bob. Uncle Bob must've wondered where Arlo had gone off to that night and why he'd never called again. Arlo patted his pocket to make sure he still had the phone Cade had given. Much as he appreciated it, he would rather have his own phone back. It would have all his contacts and pictures, his old text messages and saved passwords—all the things that made your phone your life instead of just a piece of plastic. Plus, it was a much nicer phone.

His parents' neighborhood was quiet during the day, with almost everyone off at work or school. Arlo let himself in the side door, knowing it wouldn't be locked.

"Who's that?" his father shouted from the living room. Couldn't even be bothered to get up and find out.

"It's me," he shouted back as he crossed through the kitchen to the living room. "Arlo."

His dad was in the same place Arlo had last seen him—on a tan recliner stained by body sweat and food, watching television. Some of the empties surrounding him were probably from last night, but at least some of them were from this morning. When Arlo's mother got home from work, she would sweep them into a garbage bag, muttering the whole time as if it were an unexpected hassle instead of just what she did every day. That garbage bag would join a pile of others in the garage, waiting in vain for someone to cash them in for the deposit. Arlo wondered how many hundreds of dollars' worth of nickels were in the garage. It was like an alcoholic savings account.

His mother was only marginally more functional than his father. She went to work and cleared empties out of the living room once a day, but by six o'clock, she would be adding to the pile herself, the more drunk of the two, if anything. His father drank at a maintenance level. His mother drank to catch up. Neither of them ever got arrested or sent to rehabs. They just existed. Like this.

Arlo scuffed a foot through the cans. They tumbled like bad wind chimes, all the same note.

"Back, huh?" His father wiped a hand across his face, removing a trace of drool. Maybe Arlo had woken him. He slept like that—off and on in his chair. No day or night to it anymore, just the grey of a mild buzz. "There was a cop here looking for you."

"Yeah?" He headed down the hallway to his bedroom in search of shoes that fit and another change or two of clothes.

"He had a uniform. You'd have liked him."

"Probably." He held his breath as he opened the door, but his room was exactly the way he'd left it, which was a perfect metaphor for his relationship with his parents. They never hurt him and hadn't thrown him out the way some of the other kids Arlo hung out with on street corners had been thrown out. They didn't seem to care that he was gay except for a bit of ill-intentioned teasing like that crack about the cop—though if it was Cade who'd come looking for him, his father wasn't wrong—but for all the lack of harm, there'd been an even greater lack of interest. To hurt him, they would've had to notice him.

"He said you might've been kidnapped," his father called after him. Then he snorted like he didn't believe it, the same way Arlo had a hard time believing it. "You get rescued?"

"Something like that." It was too much to explain, and his father didn't really care.

Sure enough, there were no follow-up questions, just the sound of a pop-top puncturing the seal on another can of Miller Lite. Sometimes Arlo thought that what disgusted him most about his parents' addiction was their drug of choice. Meth, coke, fucking Popov even—those were respectable highs. How drunk could you get on Miller Lite? It was a wonder his father's kidneys hadn't floated away. He sure as hell wouldn't be able to make it through ten hours with a one-liter piss bottle, Arlo could guarantee that.

Since his good backpack had disappeared with Mike, the only one he could find was the one he'd carried in middle school. The zipper was fucked up, and it was hokey as shit, but it was big. He must've looked comical carrying it, as tiny as he'd been as a pre-teen. Not that he'd gotten all that much bigger since then.

He crammed the bag full of socks and underwear, t-shirts, sweatpants, hoodies, a pair of furry pajama pants he never slept in—no idea where they'd come from even. His grandmother at Christmas, maybe. When the bag was full, he put on a pair of sneakers that fit and felt like he'd gotten a part of himself back. But he was ready to clear out of this room that reminded him too much of all the years he'd spent holed up in it.

The house was so small there was no escaping the sound of the news—a steady drone of misery his father only pretended to care about—so Arlo used to hide in here. Door shut, earbuds in. It'd been another cage in a way, the bed nicer than a foam mat but not by much. He'd inherited it from his parents when they bought a new one, and it'd already been worn out by the time he took ownership of it, with a sag so prominent you could see where the covers dipped down.

His bedroom walls, which had once been white, were dingy and scuffed, dotted with holes from years of him hanging things up and then taking them down again. He'd hung movie posters originally. Band posters later. Then cheesecake pictures of men, some of which he'd drawn himself. And then nothing. At some point he'd given up, taken everything down. Pictures couldn't disguise the emptiness, so he'd stopped trying to disguise it and waited until he could escape it.

Which meant there was nothing here he needed.

He was about to shut the door on that chapter of his life when he changed his mind and went over to the drawer where his old art supplies still lingered to grab a sketch pad and some pencils. Everyone kept asking him what Mike looked like, and he couldn't explain it in words, but he might be able to draw it.

He left the rest of the room the way he'd found it and went back out into the living room to sit at the desk in the corner where their computer was set up. It was an ancient thing, slow to crank to life, and it insisted on running one update after another. Probably no one had used it since he left.

"I need a new phone," he told his father for form's sake. "I lost mine."

His father only grunted, so when the computer finished booting, he went to the Verizon site and ordered a new one. If he had any ID, he could pick it up at the store today, but he didn't so he asked to have it shipped. He needed a new ATM card too, but he couldn't get one without either some ID or access to the phone number his account was registered to.

"Where's my birth certificate?"

"Why would I have your birth certificate?"

"When you have a baby, they give you its birth certificate. Some parents treasure it."

"Ask your mother. She'd know."

Arlo didn't want to want to see his mother. It was worse with her because she tried to act like she cared. She would ask him questions, but her eyes would drift slowly over to the television as he answered until it became obvious she wasn't listening. If he saw her, she might fuss about how he'd gone missing, but she hadn't bothered to report it. So instead of waiting for her to get home, he went into his parents' bedroom and rummaged through their closet.

95

"What're you going through my shit for?" his father yelled from the living room.

"I told you. My birth certificate."

In a cardboard box marked "Important," he found an envelope marked "Arlo" and opened it to rifle through the contents of his life. Birth certificate, Social Security card, a smattering of report cards from his early years. He rubbed his thumb over an "exceeds expectations" checkmark in Art. Art just seemed so useless now.

He stuffed his Social Security card and birth certificate into his backpack and returned the box to the closet.

"Hey," his father yelled as he headed for the side door to make his escape.

"Yeah?" He stopped with his hand on the doorknob. Maybe...

"Can you grab me a beer?"

Arlo let the sound of the door closing behind him be his answer.

Back on the bus, he typed out a text to Tripp and got one in return. Tripp had just started his sophomore year of college and claimed to be in class, but he texted back and forth with Arlo anyway, proving he wasn't that much less of a fuck-up than Arlo was. Tripp had parents who'd helped with all the shit it took to get into college, that was all.

As the bus pulled into Boston, they promised to see each other in person soon—just the two of them without a bunch of Doms hanging over them. Arlo took the T back to Jamaica Plain where he found a grocery store and managed to stretch the money Cade had left him far enough to buy ingredients for dinner. He only knew a few recipes, things like chili he could make in a big batch and freeze. Sometimes when his mom hadn't been in a cooking mood, he'd lived on chili for a week at a time. Which meant he would be happy to never eat it again. But he wanted to show Cade what a good, grown-up boyfriend he could be.

When he got back to Cade's, loaded down with grocery bags and an overstuffed backpack, there was someone on the porch—a heavyset Chinese lady with short, black hair. She had to be in her seventies, but she was sweeping the porch with vigor. Unnecessary vigor, considering that the porch was perfectly clean. She turned to look at him, probably wondering why he was standing at the end of the walkway like some kind of weird gawker who got off on sweeping.

"I'm staying here," he said. "With Officer Brixby."

She nodded.

"I have a key." He consolidated the grocery bags into one hand and fished Cade's key out of his pocket with the other.

"He told me."

She didn't say anything else, so he climbed the steps leading up to the porch, wondering if he should wipe off the bottoms of his shoes first and suddenly worried that the key Cade had left him wouldn't work. Maybe it'd been a ruse to get him to go away and when Arlo tried to open the door, this lady would see Cade didn't really want him. But the key worked without any problem.

"Okay, then," he said. "See ya."

He scrambled up the two flights of stairs to Cade's apartment, which in a more romantic place and time might've been called a garret, but this was Boston in 2018 and it was an attic. The eaves hung down so low they blocked most of the light, but Arlo didn't mind. Cade's apartment was warm and safe—like Cade himself—and Arlo was glad to be back in it.

He went to the medicine cabinet and found his salve. His sores were pretty much healed now, but Cade would ask if he'd remembered to use it, so he did. Whether Cade was his Dom or not, he made Arlo feel important enough to be taken care of properly. The way he smoothed the ointment on Arlo's knee after dinner every night or tried to warm him up when he was cold—those were things you only did for someone who mattered to you.

Arlo wanted to matter to Cade, so he made the bed and

97

cleaned the bathroom, then mixed all the ingredients he'd bought in a big pot and set it to bubbling. It wasn't exactly gourmet chili—just cans of beans and tomatoes with ground beef added to it—but the smell made his stomach growl. Master had never fed him before dinner, but his stomach had gotten greedy since he'd come to live with Cade.

He smoothed a hand over it, testing it for flatness. He was pretty sure he was putting on weight. He wished Cade had a scale so he could check. Master had weighed him every morning, and if Arlo had gained even a little, that meant no food for the day, but at least he'd known. Now he didn't even know.

He was sitting at the table trying to draw what he remembered about Mike when he heard Cade's key in the door. He quick hid his sketch because it was awful and dashed over to throw himself at him. Cade hugged him back, but he didn't seem all that enthusiastic about it, and there was no kiss to go with the hug. He set Arlo away from him.

"Did you cook?" He went into the kitchen and removed the lid from the pot.

"I made chili." Arlo went over and looked into the pot too, even though he already knew what was in there. "I know it's a lot, but it'll freeze. We don't have to eat all of it right now." His stomach rumbled like he could definitely eat all of it right now.

"You didn't have to cook for me."

"I wanted to." He wrapped his arms around himself, chilled by Cade's reception. Had he guessed wrong? Should he have waited for whatever Cade brought him to eat? Maybe Cade would be mad about him getting different clothes too. Arlo looked down at his sneakers.

"Those are new," Cade said. "Where'd they come from?"

"Home?"

"I almost forgot you had parents." Cade laughed, but he didn't sound like he thought it was funny. "Now that

Terzini's dead, there's no reason you couldn't move back there."

Except he didn't want to. Medford was boring, and his parents made him sad. Right before Mike had picked him up, he'd been thinking about moving back home. Life on his own had been so tedious. Then Mike had offered him a better option, which had actually turned out to be a worse one, and now he was back where he'd been two months ago.

"I thought I could keep staying with you, now that we're boyfriends."

"Boyfriends? Arlo, we're not boyfriends. Last night was a mistake. We were half asleep, and we made a mistake. No, *I* made a mistake. I'm the adult."

"But I made dinner," Arlo protested.

"Is that what this is? Proof you're an adult?" Cade put the lid back on the pot. "Arlo, come sit down with me a minute."

He dragged Arlo over to the table and made him sit in one of the chairs. Arlo didn't want to sit in a chair. He wanted to crawl into bed and cry from thinking about how no one wanted him ever.

"I was doing my best," he said, but that had never worked with Master. His best wasn't good enough. He didn't know how to be a sub *or* a boyfriend.

"I'm sure the chili is delicious. I can't wait to eat it. And yes, you're being very adult, thank you. Cooking for me and going back to your parents' to pick up clothes. Very responsible."

"Then what did I do wrong?"

"Nothing. Not a single thing. It's entirely my fault—what happened last night. I shouldn't have taken advantage of the fact that you were asleep, especially considering you'd just woken up from a nightmare. I'm sorry."

Arlo didn't remember the nightmare, only that he'd been running and running and that when he woke up, Cade was there. He couldn't remember what he'd been running from, but he knew who he'd been running to. And then

Cade had kissed him and it'd been so nice with the two of them rutting against each other in the bed they shared, with the darkness around them like a curtain.

Sometimes Master had made him come, especially in the beginning when Arlo had still believed he would grow to love Master in time. Later, the sex had gotten more confusing because it was sex, and if Master wasn't hurting him in one of the ways he didn't like, it felt good. But there'd always been that tinge of fear that Master would *start* hurting him in one of the ways he didn't like, that he needed to hurry up and enjoy the interlude before it ended.

Last night hadn't been anything like that. No pain, not even the good kind, and no worries or guilt. Just sweet, sleepy pleasure with a good, kind man. It'd been like vanilla boyfriends, not kinky, but he wanted to do it again, and he didn't see why they couldn't.

"But I liked it. I wanted to."

Cade sighed. "You *think* you wanted to."

Arlo cocked his head. What was the difference between thinking he wanted something and wanting it? He'd wanted Cade right from the beginning when he was Officer Brixby in his hospital room, and he'd wanted Cade last night.

But Cade said, "You're too young to know what you want."

"How old are you?"

"Twenty-four."

"Like that's so much older."

"It's old enough. I have a job, a place to live. I'm not dependent on anyone the way you're dependent on me. So before we get into any kind of relationship, especially a D/s one, we need to get you on your feet."

"I can't sub for you unless I have all my shit together?"

"Don't you think that's a reasonable prerequisite before I top an eighteen-year-old who's been recently released from captivity?"

"No."

"No?" Cade repeated. His brilliant blue eyes flashed like

he was more amused than angry. "What do you think would be reasonable?"

"Do it now?"

Cade laughed. "You know I'm not going to. I've gone too far already."

"Because you don't like me?"

Cade blew out an exasperated breath as the mirth dropped from his expression. "I've told you how I feel about you being manipulative, Arlo. I'm only going to say this one more time. I like you very much. I find you very attractive. I would be happy to play with you and call you mine. I've said all that before."

Arlo shook his head. That was much more than Cade had ever said before. Hearing it felt so good he almost didn't realize Cade was telling him no.

"When you're ready for a relationship, we'll talk about it. Until then, we'll be friends."

"Friends with benefits?"

"Friends with kissing and cuddling benefits. Not sex benefits. Now stop sulking and serve me some of that chili. It smells wonderful, and I'm starving."

Arlo did as he'd been ordered. He wished he could figure out how to move things along more quickly, but this would have to do for now. Cade had said so.

Chapter 11 Bixby

Francesca's place was out in the burbs of Charlestown and huge. Brixby didn't know why he was surprised. She was in real estate, after all, and everything about her suggested money, from the premium membership at the club to her elegant outfits that felt like costumes to the fact that she was able to support two subs.

It was Ilona who answered the door, dressed in a white gauze dress that hardly qualified as clothes, her hair done up in ringlets and ribbons and her eyes demurely down. She looked like a classic Star Trek version of a sacrificial virgin with pink stained lips and powder blue eyeshadow, her legs and feet bare.

Brixby followed her through an open foyer featuring a spiral staircase with Arlo trotting next to him, his eyes as wide as Brixby wasn't allowing his own to go as he took in the opulence of the crystal chandelier hanging over their heads like a threat. He looked nice in a pair of skinny jeans he'd brought from home that were so faded they were almost white and a polo in the same light pink that brushed his cheeks The clothes fit—or would if Arlo didn't need to gain ten pounds. Close enough anyway that he looked like a young gay man instead of a refugee. A very glowing, very handsome young gay man.

Ilona opened a set of French doors at the far side of the foyer and ushered them into a solarium. The glass room overlooked a sloping backyard that was perfectly manicured but not large, and at the center of the room there was an honest-to-God fountain. Francesca was seated in a rattan chair, one of the many matching pieces of furniture scattered across the dark tile floor, but she rose as they came toward her.

"Nice place."

"Temporary," she said with a dismissive wave.

"Why temporary?" He was still taking in the sheer number of plants. It was like they'd walked into a tropical rain forest.

"It's not mine. This is one of my listings. I move in, make sure the place is adequately staged, and give it just the right amount of a lived-in look until it sells. Then we're on to the next place." She gestured at the seating area she'd risen from, and Brixby took one of the chairs. Arlo got down on his knees at his feet.

"Not on the floor." He could tell Arlo was mimicking Kimi, who was kneeling next to the chair Francesca had been in. Kimi was dressed in the same get-up as Ilona, though her darker skin and hair gave a different vibe to the costume. If this were the movies, Ilona would be stretched out across an altar and Kimi would be on the verge of getting thrown into a volcano. "Come up here."

Arlo rose in obedience and wormed his way onto Brixby's lap.

"I didn't mean— Fine." He just hoped the chair was sturdy enough to handle their combined weight. He didn't want to be responsible for the cost of anything in this house. "Sounds like a nomadic way of life," he said to Francesca over Arlo's head.

His little apartment might not be much, but he would hate for it to be a different one every few months. Not to mention all the packing and unpacking. Then Ilona appeared with a tray and he reminded himself that Francesca probably didn't do any of the packing and unpacking.

Ilona had tea, which she served in delicate china cups

103

on matching delicate saucers with a delicate finger of pastry tucked onto each one.

"You're going to have to get down," Brixby told Arlo. There was no way he could juggle a hundred and thirty pounds of squirming man-child with a breakable cup of scalding liquid. "And not on the floor, please. On that chair over there."

Arlo slid off his lap and made his way into the chair, managing to act like sitting in a chair was punishment. Brixby handed him the cup and saucer Ilona had given him.

"Eat the cookie." He fixed Arlo with a look that suggested there would be consequences if he didn't. Arlo sat up straighter and took the cup from him. Ilona immediately served him another.

Francesca had a cup too, but neither of her subs did, so maybe he'd fucked up by giving Arlo tea. Maybe tea was for Doms only. But Arlo wasn't his sub, dammit. When they got home, he would remind Arlo of that, but for now it was helpful to have Arlo obeying him.

"You said something about playing?" he asked Francesca. Were they going to play tea party? Arlo had already finished his sliver of pastry and was gripping his cup in a way Brixby felt sure was going to result in the handle snapping off.

Francesca smiled, her teeth perfectly even and white between the vivid red slashes of her lipstick. She was very fifties-pinup today, dressed in a full-skirted blue dress with her dark hair in gentle waves around her shoulders.

"Take Arlo into the TV room," she told Ilona. "You too, pet," she said, urging Kimi up with a light press between her shoulder blades. "You may have an hour of free time, but I expect you to be considerate hosts."

The three subs went off together, across the tiled floor and out through the French doors. Brixby followed their progress with jealous eyes. Watching TV sounded like more fun than drinking tea from a china cup while making conversation with a fashion-plate of a stranger.

Once Arlo was out of the room, Brixby turned his attention back to Francesca and found a different woman than the one who'd been sitting there a moment ago. She was wearing the same clothes and had the same precisely applied makeup and picture-perfect accessories, but her posture had changed, and so had her expression. She looked less like a mistress and more like Brixby's mother at the end of Thanksgiving—like she'd finally been given permission to sit down.

"How's it going having two subs?" Maybe the answer wasn't as positive as he'd been assuming.

"Chaotic. Ilona and I have been together a long time. We had our system in order. Now everything has to be negotiated, worked through. The balance has been upset."

"Would you rather we found somewhere else for Kimi? I thought you were... enjoying her."

"It's complicated." Francesca slipped her feet out of the towering heels she was wearing and walked barefoot to a cabinet in the corner. She came back with two highball glasses full of ice and a bottle of vodka, which she wagged at him in question.

"Straight up?"

"It's good vodka." She poured him an inch and passed it over. "My clients left their liquor supply." She toasted him, then took an impressive swallow.

Brixby sipped at his more tentatively. It was good vodka.

"Having Kimi here is a disruption, but I can't send her away. She's a human being who's had a rough life. Beyond that, she's kneeling at my feet, wearing my collar. It stirs up emotion."

Brixby could relate to that.

"But we haven't done anything intimate." Francesca took another generous swallow, as if to give herself courage. "She kneels for me, does service, that sort of thing. It grounds her, gives her a reason to be here. If I weren't in a monogamous relationship, I'd give her a try, but Ilona and

105

I *are* monogamous. I don't want a second playmate."

So Brixby was the only one who'd taken advantage of the victim entrusted to his care. Wonderful. He'd accused Sebastian and suspected Francesca, but neither of them had gotten themselves off by rutting against their charge in the middle of a dark and intimate night. That was only him.

"But you signed a contract with her," he pointed out, grasping at anything that would suggest Francesca had also gone too far.

"No, not me. She's very attached to that contract she signed in Chicago, despite not having read it and my not having signed it. It's real to her, and for now I'm letting her think of it that way. I'm not sure what else to do. If Ilona asked me to find another place for Kimi, I would. But she has enough sympathy for what Kimi's gone through that she's determined to be noble about it. Noble," Francesca repeated with a light shake of her head. "But not nice. It's exhausting, always keeping track of who's had more of what kind of attention from me. D/s used to be my solace. Lately it's been nothing but a burden."

"I'm sorry." He hadn't realized how much they'd imposed on Francesca, but he could see the strain clearly now that she had her shoes off and her feet tucked up, with more lipstick on the rim of her glass than on her lips.

"Not your fault," she said with a wave. "Tell me how you're doing with Arlo."

"I'm struggling too," Brixby admitted.

"In what way? You don't owe your loyalty to anyone else, do you?"

"It's not that. He wants me to top him, and I don't think he's in a condition to give informed consent."

"Perhaps not." She ran her finger around the rim of her glass in consideration, then picked up the bottle and poured herself a second shot. She offered it to him and he took more than a finger's worth this time. This conversation was too heavy to have completely sober.

"So it wouldn't be ethical, right?" He was basically

asking Francesca to contradict him, to give him permission to do what he wanted to do. What Arlo kept asking him to do. Despite the conversation they'd had the other day, in which Brixby had insisted he was nothing more than Arlo's friend, they kept ending up in situations like what'd just happened, where he gave Arlo an order and Arlo jumped to obey it.

Every night, Arlo made him dinner and served it up so eagerly, moving around Brixby's tiny kitchen to pull out dishes and silverware with surprising accuracy and setting the table with rectangles of paper towel folded under the forks. It was absolutely adorable and made Brixby feel like a king. Or like a Dom. He'd once envied Harrison for having a partner who cooked as well as Cash, but he would be happier eating Arlo's chili that was basically four cans of beans poured into a pot if it came with Arlo barefoot in his kitchen.

"I think I'm helping Kimi," Francesca said.

"I wasn't accusing you of anything."

"I'm merely answering your question about whether or not it's ethical to top our charges. I wasn't given a lot of choice in the matter. Kimi was determined to submit to me, as you'll recall, and letting her was easier for us both. But I see it as a service to her. I give her structure, stability, and time to consider her options in a safe space. Not to mention room and board."

Brixby snorted softly to himself. "Room and board" was an overly modest description for this kind of opulence.

"She came to me with nothing except the clothes on her back and a dream of what a D/s relationship could do for her—one that wasn't grounded in any kind of reality. Dominants are hero figures to these two, not people with their own tastes and flaws."

"Exactly." Brixby put down his glass. Now they were getting to the meat of it. "Arlo's still confused about whether Terzini was his master or his captor. Until he understands the difference, it doesn't feel right to play with him. He's starting to come around a little. He told me the guy who put him on the bus might've drugged him, and that seems to have woken him up to the idea that it wasn't all aboveboard. Has Kimi said anything about being drugged?"

"They'd been giving her a regular dose of Valium. It took me a while to wean her off it. She's not as complacent now." Francesca smirked. "Despite how lovely she looks in a collar, I'm not sure she's entirely suited to a submissive role. You think they drugged Arlo to make sure he got where he was going?"

"That and someone stole all his shit while he was out. Did Kimi come with ID?"

Francesca shook her head. "We've requested a copy of her birth certificate from the reservation where she was born. For now, she's cleaning for me, but I'm looking into getting her into some kind of certificate program once she's got ID—something she'll be able to earn a living at. Considering the way she'd been living in Chicago, I'm not surprised she was willing to exchange freedom for a mythical mistress who would save her."

"And yet here she is with a mistress who's saving her."

"Only because we interceded in the auction. Imagine where she might've ended up otherwise."

Brixby could imagine because Arlo had ended up there. But now Arlo was with him, and his job was to guide Arlo toward a better path. Which might lead away from him. But was it really so wrong if he enjoyed whatever time they had together? Arlo needed guidance and direction. He also needed to learn what to expect from a Dom, and Brixby could show him that. He couldn't call Arlo his sub. Even boyfriend seemed like a step too far. But maybe it was all right to act like a bit of both.

Chapter 12 Arlo

Francesca's place was *fancy*. Her subs were fancy too. And girls. Arlo didn't want to be sent off with them. He preferred to stay wherever Cade was, but Francesca's subs were also obedient. If he didn't go along, he would come off looking like a brat, so he followed the two women who were dressed like twins through the house until they came to a room with a screen big enough to be in a movie theater and a whole bunch of matching chairs with cup holders.

"This is the TV room," Ilona said. She was the chubbier one who'd had a migraine at Cash's, the one who'd always lived with Francesca. She took a few steps into the room, but he and the other one—Kimi—stayed right in the doorway. He was just trying to take it all in. Kimi was looking at him like she was trying to take *him* in.

"You want a Coke?" Ilona asked.

"Sure. Diet though." He stepped farther into the room, which was wallpapered in something that looked like cork—tan with little holes in it. Soundproofing maybe. Everything in the room was some shade of brown, which he decided he liked, and there weren't any windows. Ilona handed him a can of Diet Coke.

"You don't have to wait on me, you know." He carried the can over to one of the chairs and put it in the cup holder, then took a seat. He pushed back and, sure enough, the chair slid with him. Six enormous recliners with cup holders, all in a row like a private movie theater. Arlo rubbed the microsuede. Soft.

Meanwhile, the two women were just standing there, looking at him.

"I'm not a zoo animal."

"You're pretty." Kimi sat in the recliner next to him.

"Plus you got kidnapped." Ilona took the chair on his other side but she didn't recline in it like he and Kimi were doing.

"I didn't get kidnapped."

"Mistress says you did."

"Did *you* get kidnapped?" he asked Kimi.

"Not really." She went to the refrigerator and got herself a Coke.

"Mistress didn't say you could have soda."

"Are you gonna tattle?"

Ilona thought on it a minute, then shook her head. Arlo didn't want to be in the middle of whatever they had going on, which he figured was jealousy. He sure wouldn't want to have a brother-sub himself. Maybe Master hadn't been the best master, but he'd never brought anyone else home.

"So what happened to you?" he asked Kimi.

"Nothing. I stayed at a hotel by myself in a room. During the day, I cleaned, and at night, I watched television. It was boring."

"That's it? No mistress or anything?"

She shook her head. "I was waiting until Mike found me one."

"Mike? Hey, that was the name of my guy too. What did he look like?"

Kimi described a guy who could've been the same guy but probably wasn't. Kimi had met her Mike outside a club in Chicago, and Arlo had met his outside a club in Boston. Kimi's Mike had short brown hair and a beard. Arlo's had short brown hair *without* a beard.

"It's probably their code name," Ilona said. "Whoever the guy is, they call him Mike."

Kimi snorted. "All white guys are named Mike anyway."

Arlo was a white guy, but he still thought that was funny. There'd been a lot of Mikes at his school. He decided he liked Kimi, who was only a few years older than he was and seemed pretty chill. She was kicked back in the recliner with her legs splayed like she was wearing sweatpants instead of a doll dress, slurping away at her Coke. Ilona was a priss—sitting upright with her legs crossed at the knee, prim and proper. She had to be in her thirties. Francesca was probably forty, which was super old, as old as Arlo's parents.

"Let's put something on," he suggested. It would be a shame to waste a screen that big. Kimi handed him a remote, and he figured out how to turn on the television and scroll through the menu. He cued up an episode of *The Wire* and kicked his chair back a little further.

"We're not supposed to be watching TV," Ilona said. "You two are supposed to be talking about your feelings."

"I don't have feelings," Kimi said.

"You got kidnapped. Of course you have feelings."

"I didn't get kidnapped."

"You could've just walked out of that hotel room, right?" Arlo couldn't have gotten out of his cage, but he could've done something probably. Master was bigger than him, but Arlo didn't think that was what had kept him from running off. He'd never even thought about it, about how to manage it. He hadn't been waiting for anyone to rescue him either. He'd just been surviving, living in the bed he'd made.

"The hotel room was better than where I was before," Kimi said. "And cleaning rooms was better than what I'd been doing."

"What had you been doing?" Arlo asked her.

"Men. The club was always full of men, and they paid. But I didn't like them. I didn't like playing with them— letting them hit me and hurt me and saying 'yes, sir' and 'no, sir' and their hands all over me. I *hated* it."

"I get that." He couldn't imagine playing with a female

111

dominant. If it came down to being either gay or submissive—if he couldn't have a man who was a Dom—he would take vanilla sex with a man like Cade over BDSM with a Domme any day.

"I get that too," Ilona said. "And I'm glad you don't have to live like that anymore, Kimi, but there were better options than letting yourself be sold in an auction."

"I was already selling myself. At least Mike sold me to a woman. If he'd sold me to a guy, I'd have run away, but he didn't. He found me exactly what I was looking for, so how am I going to be mad at him?"

"He was taking advantage of you." Ilona sounded angry, but Arlo didn't think she was angry at Mike. She was angry at Kimi. "And you too," she said to Arlo. "They were taking advantage of you too."

"I wasn't hooking," he protested, though life away from home hadn't been going nearly as well as he'd expected when he'd decided to leave Medford behind him.

Turned out that the money he'd saved over two years of bagging groceries didn't go far, not when you needed two months' rent plus a security deposit to get a place to live. And even if he'd had the funds, he needed references, which he didn't have, and proof of income, which he didn't have, and to be eighteen, which he hadn't been. Most jobs didn't want someone under eighteen either, not to mention that you needed an address to apply.

That was why he'd borrowed his cousin's ID in a last ditch effort to find a Dom who would help him sort out his life. He'd needed an adult, and he'd wanted a Dom. Why couldn't they be the same person? Why shouldn't there be one fucking person who loved him enough to take care of him?

When Hell's Bedroom had thrown him out, it'd been the lowest point of his life. So Ilona was right in a way. He'd been taken advantage of when he most needed help. But Kimi was right too. He'd boarded that bus to Philly because it was heading to where he thought he wanted to go.

"The reason they were able to take advantage of you," Ilona said, "is because you were trying to shortcut the process." She stalked over to the refrigerator and came back with a bottle of water. Such a priss.

"Me?" Kimi asked, because Ilona was glaring at her in particular.

"Both of you. You thought you could buy a Dom."

"Hey, I was the one being sold," Kimi said. "I cost a hundred and twenty thousand dollars," she told Arlo proudly. He whistled. He wondered how much he'd cost.

"I don't mean you were buying a Dom with money," Ilona said. "Ugh. I don't know how to explain it. You were acting like a Dom is something you can get at a store—just pick one out. D/s is a *relationship*. It's not just sex, and you can't just—" She snapped her fingers. "You were a baby," she accused Arlo. "Still are. You shouldn't even have been having sex."

"Hey."

"And you just needed a job," she told Kimi. "A real job. You should've stayed in that hotel and kept cleaning rooms and found yourself a Domme the right way."

"Which is?" Kimi asked coolly.

"Which is the way I did it. I met people. Straight ones, kinky ones. I had dates and play sessions. I negotiated scenes. Some of them were good, but a lot of them were crappy. There were women who broke my heart and women who didn't do anything for me and women who wanted things I didn't want, and when I finally met Mistress, I worked at it. Made myself perfect for her so I could have the honor of submitting to her—of being the *only* one who submitted to her."

"And I ruined that. I get it." Kimi lobbed her empty Coke can at the recycling bin. When it bounced off the rim and landed on the carpet, she scowled at it but didn't get up to deal with it. "I butted in, so you now hate me."

"I hate you because you're spoiled." Ilona picked up the wayward can and deposited it in the bin.

113

"How am I spoiled when I've never had a damned thing in my life?"

"Oh my God, she's going to do the white oppressor thing," Ilona warned Arlo. "I never oppressed you."

"Yeah, well, plenty of people did. My life was shit compared to yours, so it's nice for you, having the luxury of doing it the 'right' way, but not everyone does."

"That's the only reason you're still here, you know. Because Mistress feels sorry for you. Because you don't have anywhere else to go. You're not her *real* submissive. You're just a pretty girl in a dress she feels sorry for. And you know what else? She told me if I wanted you gone, you'd be gone."

Arlo wished *he* was gone. The two women were about to start throwing things at each other, and the soda he'd drunk sat like a dark, acidic weight in his stomach, even though it was diet. He ran his hand over his stomach, checking for bloat.

"It's not true, you know," Kimi told Arlo. "Ilona doesn't get to decide whether I stay or go. I signed a contract. It says I belong to Mistress Francesca forever."

"People can't be slaves," Ilona said. "That's a lie Mike told you."

"You have a contract."

"That's different."

"No, it's not. My contract is the same as yours."

"Mistress didn't even sign yours!" Ilona shouted.

"I signed a contract too," Arlo said when the two women lapsed into silent glaring.

"What did it say?" Ilona asked.

Arlo shrugged because he hadn't read it. Mike had handed him some papers and a pen. He'd leaned against the wall of the club and signed by the light of a street lamp. "I think it just said I belonged to Master but in a lot of words to make it legal."

"See, this is what I mean about you two," Ilona said with a sigh. "You have no idea what you're doing. A contract isn't

114

you selling yourself. It's two people negotiating how a D/s relationship is going to work—what your responsibilities are, what their responsibilities are. What was your master's responsibility to you, Arlo?"

"To keep me."

Ilona shook her head. "You should want more than that for yourself. Have some self-respect. Being a sub doesn't mean being a doormat."

"Look who's talking," Kimi snorted.

"I'm not a doormat. I'm obedient."

From where Arlo was sitting, doormat and obedient seemed close enough. Running around fetching things didn't appeal to him in a sex way, though it was better than getting yelled at or hit. If Master had wanted Arlo to do easy things like serve tea, maybe he could've lived up to the terms of his contract. Whatever those were.

Ilona was right. He should've read it. But Mike had rushed him, and he hadn't really cared. He'd been tired of hanging around on street corners waiting for it to get late enough to go wherever he was crashing for the night and discouraged about having been thrown out of the club. Alone and unhappy and wanting to be somewhere safe where he was loved.

When Mike had popped up out of nowhere and promised him everything he'd ever wanted, as if Mike could read his mind, he'd believed. Believed that if he signed the paper and got on the bus, he would end up where he wanted to go. And at first, he'd thought he had. Master had been wildly excited to see him, really pleased, and though he was older than Arlo had been expecting and not exactly his type, the validation of being wanted that much had been enough. It didn't matter whether he wanted Master, as long as Master wanted him.

"You got lucky," he told Kimi. Imagine if it'd been Cade who'd met him at the bus the way Mistress Francesca had met her.

"It's not perfect," she said with a flick of her eyes in

115

Ilona's direction.

"Real relationships are never perfect," Ilona countered. "Only ones that've been made up like a story someone wrote. That's what happened to you two. Someone told you a story, and you believed it."

She was right. Mike had told Arlo a story, and he'd believed it. The story wasn't true—he was starting to understand that now—but still. It'd been a good story. He didn't know a better one.

Chapter 13 Brixby

"Because I need to be able to concentrate," Brixby told Arlo, explaining for the third time why Arlo couldn't come to the club with him. "I can't sign you in anyway. I'm not a member."

"Sebastian could do it."

Brixby scowled at himself in the mirror. Arlo wasn't coming to the club tonight regardless, but if there was one thing he didn't need right now, it was any suggestion that Sebastian would be a better Dom for Arlo because ugh. Brixby's reflection was telling him he wasn't a Dom at all.

The clothes don't make the man, he reminded himself as he adjusted the harness across his chest. And anyway, the whole point was to look like a sub. A vulnerable sub. He cast his eyes toward the ground, trying to get into the mindset and hating it. Especially hating that Arlo was watching him do it.

"Sebastian isn't signing you in," Brixby told him. "So help me, if you even ask him, there will be consequences." So much for a submissive attitude.

"Then why do *you* have to go?" Arlo whined. "We can play right here."

"Arlo." Brixby gave him a light rap on the nose and moved him out of the way of the mirror. He couldn't concentrate on his own reflection when he could see Arlo next to him being so much more automatically submissive than he would ever be. "You know why I have to go. I don't like that Mike is still out there. He's a threat to you. And who knows how many subs he's shipped off to illegitimate Doms. He needs to be stopped."

"I guess."

Brixby blew out a breath. He'd thought they were making strides in getting Arlo to understand that what had been done to him was wrong.

"You don't want another boy being sent to someone like Terzini, do you?"

"No." Arlo shivered—probably from thinking about Terzini, but Brixby wrapped him into a hug in case he was cold. His own chest was bare beneath the harness, but he had more meat on his bones. Arlo didn't seem to be adding any weight. His cheeks should be round and rosy, without any sharp edges of bone showing through the skin. Brixby kissed one of them. Plump or bony, they were adorable.

"All right, so I'm going to see if I can prevent that," he told Arlo as he set him aside again. "You'll be fine here. Lock the door behind me."

"But everyone else gets to go," Arlo complained as he followed Brixby to the closet where he pulled on a pair of loose sweats to cover the chaps he'd paired with his briefest black briefs. "Even Ilona and Kimi."

"Until Mike is found, you're not setting foot in that club. So if you ever want back into Hell's Bedroom, you'll stop fussing at me over this."

Not that he wanted Arlo in Hell's Bedroom even *after* Mike had been found, but he would have to allow it. If Arlo was going to learn about ethical BDSM, he needed to go places where ethical BDSM was practiced and search for a Dom who would practice it with him. Whoever that might be, the fucker.

"Call Tripp," he said as he leaned down to give Arlo a goodbye kiss that went on far too long. Arlo had been taking the kissing and cuddling benefits of their friendship seriously. Brixby lived in constant need of a cold shower. "Tripp can come over and keep you company, if you like. Be good for me?"

Arlo nodded, but he insisted on so many more hugs and kisses before Brixby could get out the door that it bordered on disobedience. Sometimes Brixby swore Arlo was pushing for punishment, checking to see how much he could get away with. If he were any other sub, Brixby would've put a stop to it by now—shown him exactly how much he could get away with, which wouldn't be much—but he was still treading lightly with Arlo, trying to walk the line of bossy older brother without veering into more dangerous territory.

At the club, he found Francesca and the girls waiting for him in the lobby. Francesca signed him in with a minimum of fuss and he took off his outerwear and ditched his phone, then went through the double doors that led to the playroom. He spent a moment surveying the room, finding it much more open and easy to assess with a single glance than the club in New York. Undoubtedly there were private spaces somewhere, but the main room was basically two concentric circles.

The middle circle was obviously where the showoffs went. He wasn't surprised to see Sebastian there with a bullwhip, cracking it at an empty St. Andrew's cross like he was doing target practice. Despite not having a victim, he'd drawn an audience. Brixby turned away from him to check out the outer ring, which was dotted in smaller setups with various pieces of equipment and attachment points available. The place was brightly lit for a BDSM club, making it easy to find a scene to meet your tastes.

Francesca took her girls over to a bondage station. Brixby didn't follow, since the point was to appear alone and vulnerable. He drifted around the ring, stopping to watch scenes that interested him, trying to keep his head bowed like a submissive while still keeping his eyes peeled like a cop. The club was orderly, exceedingly clean, and staffed with security guards at regular intervals. No music played in the background. The only soundtrack was the whistle of whips and the shrieks of subs.

Brixby could see himself here. As his true self—not this self—with a pretty sub at his side. Not playing necessarily, but being part of the scene, communing with his people. He hoped that when all this was over some kind of club remained, that when DDD got taken down, Hell's Bedroom survived.

Having completed a full circuit and identified the hallway down which the private rooms were located, he found himself in front of Francesca again. Kimi had been laced into an intricate rope corset, and Francesca was starting to bind Ilona into what looked like it would be an identical one until Kimi fussed about being itchy and Francesca went over to scratch her nose for her. Funny how subs could endure almost anything except an itchy nose.

"Well hello, handsome," a voice next to him drawled. "Was *not* expecting to see you here today."

It took Brixby a moment to figure out who he was looking at because the last time he'd seen Bob Jones, the guy had been fully dressed and sitting with a ladylike cross of his legs on a brocade chair as they discussed the night he'd signed Arlo into Hell's Bedroom. This Bob Jones was wearing booty shorts and a harness almost exactly like Brixby's with his hairy beer gut spilling out between the straps—unashamedly gay, male, and submissive. And very seriously giving Brixby the eye.

Jones knew he was a cop, but cops were allowed to be kinky too, right? He decided to play it that way. He was a sub, just like Jones, here to find a Dom. According to Tripp, Jones knew everyone in the scene, was a veritable database of information and almost certainly a gossip. Who better to convince of his undercover role?

But Jones pursed his lips into a pout when Brixby started pumping him for information about which Doms at the club might play particularly hard and deep.

"Master Sebastian, I suppose," he said with a wave toward where Sebastian was still putting on a clinic. "But come on, Officer, you're breaking my heart. A big, sturdy

120

guy like you? Please tell me you're a Dom." He put a hand on Brixby's bicep. "A switch, at least. I've got a fancy to get my ass whupped by a cop. What do you say, darlin'?" He kicked out his hip, nudging Brixby with the ass he was asking to have whupped.

"I'm not a switch," Brixby said as he pried Jones's hand loose. That much was true anyway. "I was hoping to get my own ass whupped."

"Well, you never can tell," Jones said with a doubtful shake of his head. "I knew you were in the scene, anyway. Not like that partner of yours. Completely clueless, isn't he?" Jones laughed, and Brixby laughed with him. Jones wasn't wrong. Even though Harrison enjoyed his own version of BDSM, when it came to other people's kinks, he could be pretty clueless.

"But there's no way I'd have pegged you for a sub," Jones continued. "I've usually got such good domdar too.

"Domdar?" Brixby laughed. He could see why Tripp and Arlo liked Jones. He was a campy bit of fun. "A friend of mine did say you were the one to ask about who to play with. So what's your recommendation?"

"Like I said, if you want someone who'll take you right to the edge of wrong, try Master Sebastian."

In front of them, Francesca seemed to be struggling to control her scene. Every time she went back to Ilona, Kimi would complain about something—it itched or it pinched or she was thirsty. Francesca had been dutifully attending to her, but Ilona was running out of patience, starting to fuss for Francesca's attention herself. Ilona was typically one of the most well-behaved subs Brixby had ever known, but right now she was giving Kimi a run for the money in needy disobedience.

Jones made a tsking sound. "Mistress Francesca used to be the most admired Domme in the club, but my how the mighty have fallen." He launched into a description of what'd happened the night Ilona had pretended to call red so they could set up Francesca as a customer for the

121

human trafficking ring, clearly relishing the tale. "And now look at her," he finished. "She's about to lose it with them, just like she did that night."

There was no doubt Francesca seemed flustered, bordering on angry. Her calm, controlled dominance had deteriorated into shrill commands, and a crowd had gathered to watch, all of them eagerly waiting to see if she would do something awful again.

"Enough." Francesca's voice rang out loudly enough to pierce the general din. "This stops now."

Brixby held his breath. Had they put her under so much stress she was going to do something unethical for real? But all she did was yank a pair of scissors from her belt and start slicing through the ropes holding Kimi in place. Ilona's bindings took less work because Francesca had never managed to get her all the way strung up, and soon both girls were standing denuded of rope, looking at each other with expressions that had morphed from bratty to concerned.

"Stay here," Francesca ordered. Then she pushed through the crowd—past Brixby and Jones and everyone else who'd come to gape—and out through the double doors.

Brixby was torn between following her and attending to the girls who'd been left alone, but neither action would be appropriate for his cover. When Security showed up in response to the scissors having come out, he figured Ilona and Kimi would be all right. They were both adults, after all. Ilona was nearly forty, for heaven's sake. She might be a sub, but she wasn't a child.

"I'm going to keep looking," he told Jones. The guy was entertaining, but Jones wasn't getting him any closer to enticing Mike into approaching him. He would stroll around some more and see if he could find a high-risk Dom to engage with *besides* Sebastian.

Then halfway around the circle, he spotted Popinjay, the other person who would recognize him as a cop. Damn, his luck was bad today.

Popinjay was peppering a woman with a crop, stinging her all over as she lay face down on a spanking bench with her lifeless eyes turned toward the audience. The woman looked so incredibly like the mugshot they had of Jessica Chambers—young, blond, stringy, and with the unmistakable signs of a drug problem—that Brixby had to do a double-take to make sure it wasn't actually her.

The way the blond moved in twitchy spasms suggested she was high right now. And not on an endorphin high either. A drug high. She probably shouldn't be here, and she definitely shouldn't be with Popinjay, who was the type of Dom who thought he was owed service without returning care, absolutely the sort who would keep a sub in a cage if he could get away with it.

Brixby didn't want to be recognized again, so he kept moving. When he ran into Cash and Harrison, he told them about Popinjay and the young blond woman. Cash went to ask Security to check in on them, which left Brixby and Harrison alone to confer.

"You should've borrowed my shorts," Harrison said with a pointed look at Brixby's chaps.

"They wouldn't have fit. My dick needs room."

"So I see. Well, you look very handsome. Any takers yet?"

Brixby shook his head. "Jones tried to point me at Sebastian."

Harrison snorted. "Exactly what I've always said. Cash swears by him, though, and you can't deny he's been a help."

"I suppose." In some ways, he'd be happy if Sebastian turned out to be involved, but he didn't have any real suspicions in that direction. Sebastian was a bit too obvious as a villain. "Jones didn't think much of Francesca either."

Harrison made a face. "Cash feels really bad about what we've done to her reputation."

"It's going to be worse now." He filled Harrison in on

what'd just happened.

"Well, it would be nice if we could find a suspect who wasn't one of our people," Harrison said. "And let's hope it's a guy because you don't make a half-bad sub, but no one's going to believe you're straight. Not in that get-up."

Brixby laughed, appreciating that he had a colleague he could joke with about something as fundamental as his sexuality. Yesterday in the squad room, one of his fellow officers had made an inappropriate comment about the department's female stenographer, then looked directly at him like it'd been a test. He liked to think he wouldn't respond to that kind of comment even if he were straight, but he'd felt like he was giving himself away when he only shrugged and changed the subject.

His plan of keeping his sexuality to himself until some perfect right moment had been wishful thinking. The sort of people who gave a fuck about other people's sexuality were bound to catch on to him eventually. And what would happen when he took a sub—a boyfriend, a partner, a husband? It wouldn't be fair or possible to hide his sexuality then. Either he had to be an out cop or he had to stop being a cop. And if it weren't for financial concerns, he knew which one he'd choose.

"I'm going to make a commotion," he told Harrison. "Get written up in the security system like Arlo did."

"For what? You're definitely not underage."

"For being extreme—for wanting more than the club allows."

The question was how, and the crack of a whip coming from much too close gave him his answer. It was the answer he'd been trying to avoid, but it was the only one he had.

"Sebastian," Harrison acknowledged coolly, as if Sebastian hadn't just flicked a bullwhip at them.

"How's sub life?" Sebastian asked.

"Slow," Brixby admitted. Good thing he wasn't really a sub. He hadn't been hit on once, not even by an ethical Dom, never mind a criminal one. "You want to help me out?"

Sebastian wrapped the whip sinuously around his naked arm, turning it into a snake that looked almost as deadly as Sebastian himself. "I could be convinced to take you on," he drawled.

Brixby rolled his eyes at him. "For purposes of the investigation, Sebastian. Not because your domly display totally changed my orientation."

"Give it a while."

Brixby couldn't roll his eyes any harder than he just had, so he didn't bother. "All I want is for you to reject me. Loudly."

"How's that going to attract the right kind of attention?"

"Because I'm going to be too sick for you to play with. I want too much, too deep, too risky. Tell the guards you can't handle me."

"Kind of a blow to my reputation."

"Listen, if Francesca can—"

Sebastian held up a hand to stop him. "I didn't say no. Tell you what, I'm going to go back to the cross. You come beg me to string you up on it." He strolled away, unwrapping the whip to give it another echoing crack as he made his way over to the St. Andrew's cross where the crowd had only just dispersed. A new one started to form.

"Are you going to let him hit you?" Harrison asked.

"He'll pull the plug before it gets to that point, right?"

Harrison shrugged. "We're talking about Sebastian here."

Fuck. Brixby squared his shoulders—not, perhaps, a very submissive thing to do, but he was walking into battle and needed to do it with his head held high.

Be more fucked up than Sebastian, he told himself as he parted the crowd, dodging bodies until he was in front of Sebastian. He bowed his head, took a deep breath, and dropped to his knees.

"Please, sir?"

"Please what?" Sebastian put a hand in his hair and

125

used it to tug his head back until their eyes met. The sadistic glee he saw on Sebastian's face wasn't faked. Sebastian was enjoying this.

"Please put me on your cross and whip me. I want to bleed for you, sir."

"A tough guy, huh?"

"Not for you, sir. I'll be so soft. I'll be anything you want. Please take me." He wrenched his head out of Sebastian's grasp so he wouldn't give in to the urge to punch Sebastian right in his firm gut and dropped all the way down to the floor.

"Show me how much you want me." Sebastian nudged his face with one pointy-toed leather boot. The fucker.

Brixby kissed the silver plate at the boot's tip, wondering as he did if Sebastian was rich enough and vain enough to wear real silver on his toes.

"So unimpressive," Sebastian drawled.

Brixby swallowed back how much he hated every aspect of this and went to work, licking and kissing Sebastian's booted foot, using as much saliva as he could work up in hopes of ruining the leather. At least these shoes had never been on the T. Sebastian wouldn't lower himself to public transportation.

"Please, sir? Flay me. I want to be ribbons for you."

Sebastian laughed. "You talk a good game."

"Try me." He grabbed Sebastian's leg, and Sebastian shook him off with a scowl. "I'll do anything. Anything. I want it all. I want you." He crawled after Sebastian, amused by the fact that Sebastian had taken a step back.

"You're kind of annoying."

"Noooo," Brixby howled. "Don't say that. You want me. I know you want me. I'll be good for you. Make me bleed."

Sebastian kicked him hard enough to actually hurt, but Brixby went with it, even thanking him for it.

"Bleed me, flay me, shred me." He sounded like a nutjob, but it was doing the trick. Not only was the crowd talking about him, but Security had shown up.

126

"Just a reminder, sir," a guard said to Sebastian. "Bodily fluids aren't allowed in public play spaces."

"I'm well aware," Sebastian said haughtily. "I've been a member of this club for fifteen years." Leave it to Sebastian to pull the don't-you-know-who-I-am-card at a BDSM club. "That's not my sub. He's not even a member. You should find whoever signed him in and talk to *them*. I don't want anything to do with him."

"Please." Brixby lunged forward and managed to catch Sebastian around both legs. He nuzzled his face into Sebastian's crotch, knowing he might be crossing a line but certain Sebastian had been planning to cross as many lines as he could get away with himself. Sebastian peeled him off, genuinely annoyed now, and the security guard wrestled him away.

"I'll get him out of your hair, sir."

"Get him out of the club altogether," Sebastian said. "I don't pay the kind of dues this place charges to be attacked by an undisciplined sub with a death wish."

Brixby let the guard tow him away, continuing to beg for someone to beat him and attracting attention the whole way until they were back through the double doors and out in the lobby. Then he straightened up and offered the guard an apology. Poor guy didn't deserve to have to deal with that. The guard ushered him into Knight's office, which was vanilla and familiar. Brixby had been there before, though not dressed like this. Knight looked him over but refrained from commenting until the guard had summarized the situation and left.

"Sorry," Brixby said about the fact that he was essentially in his underwear.

"I've seen worse." Knight swept a hand toward his guest chairs and Brixby sat in one, arranging the chaps to cover as much as they could. "You want me to log this?"

"Yeah, write it up. We know whoever's at the top of this ring monitors the reports. It might even be how they identify their targets."

Knight turned to his computer and, with Brixby's input, wrote up a report that made him sound like a submission-crazed masochist willing to put up with pretty much anything. If that didn't trigger interest, nothing would.

"Now what?" Knight asked.

"Now I go outside. Hopefully someone was watching." And would be waiting for him.

"What kind of backup have you got?"

"Harrison will be keeping an eye out, but if this goes down the way it did with Arlo, Mike's not going to nab me. He's just going to make me an offer I can't refuse. I promise I won't accept any refreshments from him."

It'd been fifteen or twenty minutes—long enough to give both Harrison and Mike time to get in place—so he left Knight's office and crossed through the echoing lobby to the bronze relief door that led outside. It was an ADA nightmare. Beautiful, but heavy.

The night on the other side of the door was cool, making him realize he hadn't stopped by the locker area to grab his stuff. He was standing on a Boston street in chaps, undies, and a chest harness. He turned to go back inside, but as he did, a flicker of movement caught his eye. Someone was coming toward him—someone tall and wide. Hopefully Mike.

No, wait. It was two someones, walking so close together they might almost be fused. One was tall and lean. The other was...

"Arlo?"

Chapter 14 Arlo

By the time they got off the T, Arlo was beginning to think this was a really bad idea. He shouldn't have let Tripp talk him into it.

"Maybe we should go back," he said as they started the walk to Hell's Bedroom. He'd only been to the club that one time, but Tripp knew his way. He strode confidently down the dark sidewalk, his long legs eating up ground, not slowing at all in response to Arlo's hesitation.

"Dude, it's the *best* idea. You didn't even get to see the place before. You're going to love it. And you're eighteen now. It's all legal."

"Yeah, but." It was true he had an ID in his pocket, freshly obtained from the RMV this morning with his own name on it and showing him to be legally eighteen. "Officer Brixby said I shouldn't. He gave me rules. Like, I'm not even supposed to be out of the house at night."

"He's not the boss of you. If he doesn't want to be your Dom, then he doesn't get to be your Dom. And anyway, Doms can't tell you not to leave the house."

"He's trying to keep me safe though. What if Mike's there?"

"I'm not going to let you run off with any Mike," Tripp said with a snort. "If I'd been at the club with you that day, none of this would've happened. Uncle Bob should've taken better care of you."

"I guess. He wanted to do his own thing. Aren't you

going to want to?"

"Well, maybe." Tripp admitted. "But you can watch. Or you find someone to play with and I'll watch you. We'll be buddies, like on a field trip at school."

"You really think someone will sign us in?"

"Oh, yeah. You look adorable. Doms are going to be all over it." Tripp swung an arm over his shoulder, which made him feel a little better about the pools of darkness between street lamps. If he were here with Cade, he wouldn't be nervous at all, but Tripp was so cavalier about the possibility of danger it made him feel like he needed to be the one watching out for it.

"Officer Brixby's going to know I disobeyed him though," he said nervously. "He's going to see me."

"Not if we see him first."

"But Francesca is there and Sebastian and Cash. All of them. We can't avoid everyone, and then they're going to tell Officer Brixby, and I'm going to be in so much trouble."

Tripp stopped walking. He turned to Arlo and grabbed him by both elbows. "If you're serious, we'll go back. I don't want you to freak. But come on, Arlo. You want a Dom, right?"

Arlo nodded.

"And Brixby won't do it, right?"

He shook his head sorrowfully. Cade was still refusing to even fool around with him in a vanilla way. They did a lot of kissing, but if Arlo tried to ramp up from kissing to something more, Cade always stopped him, even though Arlo could feel he was hard. Arlo wanted Cade's hard cock so bad he almost couldn't sleep at night. It wasn't fair that Cade thought he couldn't take it, that no matter how much Arlo cooked and cleaned and tried to be obedient, Cade never saw him as a sub or a boyfriend or even an adult.

"Wait until he sees you playing with someone else," Tripp said. "He'll change his tune fast enough."

"You think so?"

"Absofuckinglutely. Dude is so into you. He's like a

130

panting dog. You've just gotta activate his jealousy gene, let him know that if he won't top you, someone else will."

"But what if he tells me I can't stay with him anymore?" If Arlo was a bad sub, he would get put out on the street. That was what Master had always said.

"Then you'll go live with Sebastian. Sebastian would top you, I'll bet."

"I don't want Sebastian to top me."

"Then he doesn't have to. You could just live with him. Up in the sky over the harbor?" Tripp sighed. "I bet his place is mint."

"It was okay, I guess." Who cared if Sebastian's place was nice? He wanted to live with Cade. But not just as a roommate, and he didn't know how to get Cade to see him any differently. "You really think Officer Brixby will get jealous of me?"

"Positive. Come on." Tripp took him by the hand and tugged him down the block some more. "By the end of the night, you're going to have a Dom. One way or the other."

Oh, boy. That sounded drastic, like the kind of attitude that had led to him ending up with Master. But Tripp was so sure.

Arlo snuck closer to Tripp's body, still a little worried about Mike popping out of one of the doorways. They went past a guy taking a lady's car keys and handing her a ticket, but neither of the people involved paid any attention to him and Tripp. Beyond them, Arlo saw the Hell's Bedroom marquee, illuminated by a single overhead light. The marquee only read Private Club, no mention of Hell's Bedroom or BDSM at all. If you didn't know, you'd never guess.

A guy came out of the door to the club and stood silhouetted beneath the marquee. It wasn't until Arlo was much too close that he realized who it was.

"Arlo?"

Arlo squeaked as he froze into place on the sidewalk. Caught already, and he hadn't even made it inside. It was worse than last time.

"What are you two doing here?" Cade asked as he approached them. Tripp had kept walking, so Cade got to him first. "What the fuck were you thinking, bringing him here?"

"We were going to play."

Arlo didn't know how Tripp was managing to sound so calm. Tripp was tall, but Cade was taller, and Cade was broader too, looming over Tripp like Bruce Banner about to turn into the Hulk.

"Play?" Cade repeated. He was angry. So angry. Like how Master used to get. Arlo looked around, not knowing where to run. "You brought Arlo to the club he was abducted from so he could *play*?"

"Whoa, whoa, whoa." Harrison popped up out of nowhere. Arlo had never been so glad to see anyone in his life. "Stand down."

"I'm going to fucking kill him."

"You're not killing anyone." Harrison put a hand in the middle of Cade's chest and pushed. Harrison was shorter than either Cade or Tripp, but he wasn't afraid. Couldn't he see how angry Cade was?

Arlo wrapped his arms around himself, trying to disappear into the brick of the club's exterior, waiting to see who would get hurt first and when it would be his turn. But Cade stepped back when Harrison pushed him. He ran a hand over his hair, looking wild and terrifying but also stunningly handsome in that outfit he'd put on. Arlo knew Cade was trying to pretend to be a sub, but no one had ever looked less submissive.

"I told Arlo to call you so you could keep him company," Cade said, his tone a little more rational now, like maybe he wasn't going to hurt Tripp after all. He hadn't acknowledged Arlo yet, but when he did—that was when Arlo would get it. "Not so you could lure him into a dangerous situation."

"We were trying to do something here," Harrison said.

He sounded angry too, but only in a put-out way. "Tonight was about shutting down a human trafficking ring, not a couple of kids getting their rocks off. If you had to go out and pick someone up, couldn't you have done it somewhere other than here?"

"Arlo's not picking anyone up," Cade said ominously.

"Either way, the operation's blown. If Mike was going to approach you, he's been well and truly scared off now." Harrison blew out an exasperated breath.

"We didn't mean to fuck up the operation," Tripp argued. "We were just going to go in and look around."

"And how were you planning to get in?" Cade asked.

"Hit up the people coming in until someone said yes. I've done it before."

Cade's eyes grew even more murderous, if that was possible. "You were going to ask random people to sign you in? That doesn't sound at all like how someone might get kidnapped?"

"Dude, you're extreme."

"I'm about to show you extreme."

"Brixby. Chill." Harrison put his hand on Cade's chest again. "It's fucked up, but it's done. Arlo is fine. He's standing right there, and you're terrifying him."

Cade looked over at him, finally taking notice of him. Arlo ducked his head. He didn't want Cade to take notice of him. He'd made a horrible, horrible mistake, and now he would either get punished or banished.

"I'm sorry." His chest was so tight the words almost wouldn't come out. He wanted to explain that it was Tripp's fault, but Cade was already mad at Tripp and Arlo would be a terrible friend to make more trouble for him in order to save himself. He would have to bear whatever was going to happen, that was all. He'd borne so much. He could do it.

"Take him home," Harrison said. "I'll figure out what to do about Tripp. You want to put some clothes on first, maybe?"

"Fuck, my phone is in there too. Call me a Lyft, will

you?" Cade went into the building, flashing his ass, which was covered in nothing but a tiny pair of black bikini briefs, as he turned for the door.

While Harrison squinted at his phone, Tripp came over and stood next to Arlo along the wall, like they were perps who'd been lined up by the police. "You don't have to go with him, you know."

"Shut up." He was so mad at Tripp. He was almost as mad at Tripp as Cade was.

"Just saying." Tripp shrugged. "I'm not sure *I'd* go with him right now, personally. I like a wild ride, but there's gotta be seatbelts, if you know what I mean."

Arlo didn't know what Tripp meant, not at all. This wasn't a ride. It was real, and it was his life, and thanks to Tripp he'd fucked up whatever good there'd been in it.

Cade came out dressed like he could go to Target just as the Lyft pulled up in front of the club. He opened the door to the car and gave Arlo a look. Arlo crawled inside as Tripp shouted "call me tomorrow" after him.

"We'll talk about whether you're ever allowed to see Tripp again," Cade said as the car pulled away.

Arlo just sat in his corner and kept quiet. Tripp was his best friend, but right now Arlo was too angry at him to consider him much of a loss. Arlo had faced a lot of punishments during his time with Master, but he'd never dreaded anything worse than the possibility that Cade might throw him out, and it had nothing to do with Cade's soft bed or warm hoodies. It was because he'd thought— stupid him—that he might have a future worth looking forward to if he played his cards right, but now—stupid, stupid him—he'd screwed it up. How could he have listened to Tripp when he'd known—he'd *known*—that the only way to make Cade like him was to be perfect?

He was trying to be quiet, but he couldn't keep from crying, not even when his sobs got so obvious that the driver checked on him in the rearview mirror. But Cade didn't so much as glance his way—not in annoyance or concern or anything. Cade didn't pull him onto his lap or ask him why he was crying. He just sat in the other corner and looked out the window until the Lyft pulled up in front of his house.

Arlo got out of the car. He wasn't sure he was supposed to, but he didn't know what else to do, and when Cade headed for the porch, Arlo trailed along behind him. Cade opened the door and flicked on the light at the bottom of the staircase, then started up—slowly and steadily, his footsteps reverberating in the narrow corridor like doom. Arlo's footsteps were a lighter echo of doom as he stayed carefully three steps lower until they made it to the third floor and into Cade's apartment.

Well. Arlo was in the apartment, at least. But he didn't know what to do next because Cade wasn't talking. So he stood near the door and watched as Cade stripped off his sweatpants and then the chaps beneath them and then the briefs under that so that for a moment he was standing there naked and handsome and Arlo briefly imagined him opening his arms, how Arlo would run into them and they'd hug and kiss and fall onto the bed together and be safe and happy again.

But Cade didn't open his arms. He put on a pair of boxers, then the same sweatpants from the club. He threw his briefs in the laundry basket and folded the chaps up into a neat square, which he stored on the top shelf of the closet.

Now he would say something, right? Tell Arlo whether he had to be punished or go away or what was going to happen next. But he didn't say. He took out his phone and sat down on the couch and started typing on it, like he was sending a text. A minute later, his phone buzzed and he typed a text back, then he set it on the arm of the couch and leaned his head back and put his hand over his eyes.

Arlo was still by the door. He didn't know what to do. Why didn't Cade tell him what to do? He edged into the living room, step by step, until he was right next to the

135

couch, then sat on his end of it with his legs curled up onto the cushion, like he would if they were hanging out after dinner, both of them looking at their phones. Arlo would show Cade a funny thing Tripp had said or Cade would rant about something in politics and then they would get to talking about what it'd been like for Cade growing up in Jersey or what Arlo might like to study if he went to college.

Tonight, Arlo didn't take out his phone, and Cade's was sitting on the arm of the couch face down, but there they were, next to each other, like always.

Was this it? Was Cade going to just not talk to him? That wasn't what your Dom did when you were bad. Arlo didn't even think it was what your *boyfriend* did. It was what someone who didn't care about you did, when they were hoping you'd leave but were too nice to throw you out and now they were sorry they'd let you stay in the first place but they were still too nice to throw you out so they were going to ignore you. Just like your parents always had.

Arlo started to get mad. Mad and scared, all rolled into one. That same feeling came over him as when Master would lock him in the cage, where he would rather be hurt than lonely. If Cade wouldn't react, Arlo would make him. He stretched his foot across the cushion until it tapped Cade's thigh. When Cade didn't look at him, he pushed. And when Cade *still* didn't look at him, he kicked.

Cade rolled his head in Arlo's direction. "You're really asking for it tonight, aren't you?" His eyes were bright blue and tired, and Arlo almost changed his mind about poking the tiger, but he couldn't.

"I'm just stretching."

"I ought to stretch you over my lap and give you the spanking you deserve."

"You wouldn't."

"You think I wouldn't?" In an unexpectedly fast move, Cade pulled him up and over, so that Arlo was basically kneeling on Cade's legs and their faces were right in front of each other. Cade's was screwed up in anger, and his hands were tight around Arlo's upper arms, tight enough to hurt, and Arlo felt fear and hope all warring together. But then Cade's grip lightened and he moved like he was going to dump Arlo off his lap again.

"I knew you wouldn't," Arlo said, his voice bitter with accusation. He'd been afraid of being punished, but this was worse. This was rejection. "You won't punish me even when I deserve it because you're not my Dom because you don't want me. Master didn't want me either, but at least he tried. He tried to make me be good."

Cade sighed. "You *are* good, Arlo. Not so much at the moment, but usually. I don't understand why you went to the club tonight. You disobeyed me, you put yourself at risk, you disrupted our investigation, and you scared me half to death. Why, Arlo? Tell me why."

"Because I want a Dom." Arlo's breath caught in his chest. "I don't miss Master, but I miss..." He missed his dream, even if it'd turned out to be a nightmare. "It's not fair. Kimi gets to be Francesca's sub. She got everything in her contract, everything she wanted. If you won't be my Dom, I'll find someone who will. I'll go back to Sebastian's," he threatened. "Master Sebastian will do it."

Chapter 15 Brixby

Brixby could tell he was being manipulated, but he couldn't stop himself from rising to the bait. The need to turn Arlo over his knee and teach him how to behave was growing with every manipulative—and totally working—thing Arlo did.

Part of tonight's disaster was his fault. He recognized that. If he'd ignored Arlo, left him for Cash or Sebastian or Francesca to deal with inside instead of causing a scene outside, Mike wouldn't have been any the wiser. But the combination of fear for Arlo's safety and anger over having been so thoroughly disobeyed had made it impossible for him to think the situation through. He'd reacted, pure and simple.

He'd already texted Harrison to apologize and had almost calmed down enough to talk to Arlo rationally when Arlo started this temper tantrum. Hearing the words "Master Sebastian" come out of his mouth had Brixby's blood boiling all over again.

"You'll live without kinky sex for a few months," he said, trying to keep his tone reasonable, but his hands involuntarily clenched tighter around Arlo's arms.

"It's not just sex. It's a lifestyle. It's part of who I am. That's why I went with Mike. That's why I signed the contract. That's why I went to the club tonight. If I deserve to be punished, then punish me. Either be my Dom or someone else will."

He could tell Arlo was absolutely serious. If he didn't take Arlo in hand, Arlo would find someone who would. Like Sebastian. Or worse.

"How should I punish you?" He moved his hands from Arlo's arms to his hair, tangling them through the blond curls to tilt Arlo's head back and force some eye contact. If he was going to punish Arlo, he needed Arlo to say how. Because they hadn't discussed this, hadn't discussed any of it.

"Master says what the punishment is."

"I'm not your fucking master." He blew out his breath when Arlo flinched. "But I *am* going to punish you. Because you do deserve it." And because he needed to do it. Arlo was safe, right here in his lap, but Brixby's body was still on high alert. "So tell me what it should be."

"A spanking?" Arlo's voice was soft and breathless. Brixby couldn't tell if Arlo was aroused or scared or a combination of both. His own cock had chubbed up a little as his mind transitioned from problem to solution. Arlo had been bad. Very, very bad. But once he'd been punished, Brixby could forgive him.

"A spanking." He ran his nose up under Arlo's ear, into the froth of blond curls at the back of his neck. He smelled like warmth and anticipation, like softness. Brixby shuddered out a breath, suddenly overwhelmed with arousal, all his anger and fear finding a better outlet in dominance and lust.

"Stand up." He lifted Arlo off his lap and put him on his feet between his legs. "Tell me why you're being punished."

"For disobeying you."

"How did you disobey me?"

"I went out after dark."

Brixby nodded. "That's five swats for going out after dark."

"And I was trying to get into the club when you said not to."

"That's a big one, Arlo. The club is a dangerous place

139

for you to be. I'm giving you ten swats for that. What else?"

Arlo shook his head like he couldn't think of anything else. Maybe he didn't know, but maybe the swat count was getting high enough to scare him. Brixby couldn't hold back though, not if Arlo was going to learn his lesson.

"For kicking me?" he prompted.

"Oh, right."

"Five for that. And then there's the matter of manipulation. Bringing up other Doms, threatening me with them. While you're under my care, you are never, ever to call another man master. Do you understand that?

"Yes, sir."

And fuck. There it was. Brixby had laid down the law, and Arlo had called him sir in response. If he proceeded with this spanking, he was acting as Arlo's Dom. He couldn't deny it any longer. But he couldn't deny the need to do it either. He loved hearing Arlo call him sir as much as he hated it when Arlo called anyone else master.

Him. It should only be him. His cock was growing harder with Arlo's every submissive response, and the anticipation of laying his hand across Arlo's bottom had him wanting to add more and more strokes to the punishment, but he choked that back. He had no idea what Arlo was capable of taking or where the line between punishment and abuse would fall.

"I'm not going to add any punishment for that last one," he said, "because I never gave it as an order before, but remember it for the future."

"Yes, sir." Arlo nodded eagerly. "I promise."

"All right then. Twenty swats. Let's get those jeans off you."

Arlo opened the button on his jeans with a motion more like a caress than a flick. He parted the zipper slowly, using a single hand, and suddenly Brixby had had enough. It was more manipulation, pure taunting. He took Arlo's waistband in both hands and yanked until his jeans were around his knees, then flipped him easily over his lap so he was looking at a stretch of navy blue cotton. Short boxer briefs, the leg bands loose around Arlo's thighs where red marks still lingered from those sores Terzini had left.

Arlo squirmed on his lap, and Brixby brought his hand down once with a satisfying smack.

"Stop it. I'm checking on how you're healing." He landed a second swat because the first one had rendered Arlo so still. Obedience was intoxicating. Brixby's head swam with everything he wanted to do to the boy, everything he'd been telling himself he couldn't. But couldn't or not, he was going to.

"You're getting this bare-assed," he warned as he tugged the blue cotton down to reveal the most perfectly symmetrical rosy-pink ass he'd ever seen. His cock pulsed, desperate to be released, but he made no move to free it. He had a punishment to deliver.

The slap of flesh against flesh cracked through the room like thunder, like a blow straight to Brixby's chest. It made his heart ache, he wanted this so bad.

"When I tell you to do something, you do it," he scolded, following the admonition with another slap. "You don't listen to Tripp." Slap. "You don't listen to *anyone*, except me." Slap. "And when you're in trouble, you don't try to manipulate your way out of it." Slap.

"I didn't," Arlo wailed.

"You did." He tightened his grip around Arlo's waist to anchor him. "You think you can top me from the bottom?"

Brixby would make him sorry for it. A *little* sorry. Already Arlo's ass was turning a pleasing shade of bright pink. Arlo had expressive skin, rewarding Brixby with a red handprint wherever he struck. He doubled his efforts, giving Arlo a quick volley of smacks until all twenty had been administered and he felt nothing except forgiveness and lust.

He pulled Arlo's underpants up over his rump but pushed his jeans all the way off, then turned him over so he could cradle him in his lap. He loved how Arlo fit there,

141

how he seemed made to tuck into the crook of his arm.

"It hurts." Arlo squirmed, sliding his ass across Brixby's cock.

Brixby doubted it hurt much. He'd gone far harder on other subs, using a variety of implements, and had an idea of how much punishment an ass could take, which was far more than what he'd just doled out. But he bopped Arlo on the nose and said. "It's supposed to hurt. What do you say to me?"

"Sorry."

"For what?"

"For doubting you."

He'd been expecting an apology for the charges Arlo had been punished for, but that answer struck home with far greater accuracy. Arlo had been counting on him to give him what he needed, and Brixby had almost failed him.

Arlo snuggled into him now, content, despite his obvious hardon, to let Brixby decide what happened next, trusting him to make the right choice. Brixby didn't know what the right choice was. He knew what he wanted to do, but he still wasn't sure he ought to. Except that Arlo needed the same things he needed. Pleasure. Relief. Connection.

"You're forgiven, angel." He gave Arlo a very short kiss, just a nip at those plump lips. "You took your punishment, and now it's over. But if that spanking had really hurt, I don't think you'd have this." He dropped his hand into Arlo's lap and squeezed what he found there.

Arlo let out something between a whimper and a giggle. He gyrated his hips, brushing his ass over Brixby's erection again, and Brixby stifled his own response.

"I wonder if you've been good enough to deserve a reward."

He expected enthusiastic assent, but Arlo only looked up at him, sweet and patient. The poignancy almost killed him.

"Such a good boy," he murmured. "You're being so good for me now."

The demure flutter of Arlo's eyelashes was breathtaking. Lord, those eyelashes could ask for the world, and Brixby would hand it over. He kissed Arlo, taking his mouth possessively, pouring himself into him. The narrowness of the couch wasn't allowing him to get close enough so he picked Arlo up and carried him to the bed.

All the lights were on with the supermarket shine of CFL bulbs, a light no one could be flattered by, but Arlo's body didn't need flattery. It was perfect—every inch of it precious. His eyelashes made silken fans on the soft curves of his cheeks, and his lips parted with his breath as Brixby slid Arlo's boxers off and discarded them over the side of the bed. He scooped his hands under Arlo's ass to lift his hips and sucked one of Arlo's balls into his mouth.

First one ball, then the other, then a leisurely trip up Arlo's shaft and a tour around the head of his cock, which peeped out demurely from an intact foreskin. Brixby was circumcised himself, but he approved of the growing trend toward not circumcising boys at birth, especially when he got to play with the results. He caught the soft fold of Arlo's foreskin in his teeth and tugged just enough to threaten before releasing it so he could probe beneath it with his tongue, chasing down the essence of Arlo where it was concentrated.

Arlo whimpered, calling Brixby's attention back to his face. He had his bottom lip between his teeth, as if trying to stifle the sound. Brixby grinned wickedly. He intended to make staying quiet very difficult to do. Without any warning, he swallowed Arlo's cock, sucking it deep into his throat. Arlo inhaled sharply, then a low moan issued from him, at odds with his small frame and angelic face. This wasn't a child. It was a man being pleasured. But still so soft, so surrendered.

Brixby lifted Arlo's hips higher so he could work back behind his balls to tease at his hole, which was as pretty and pink as the rest of him. Arlo reacted to the intrusion of Brixby's tongue with another throaty groan. Brixby wanted in there, and he had no doubt Arlo wanted it too. Arlo wanted Brixby to take him. It was what he'd been asking for this whole time.

He lowered Arlo's hips to the bed and went to the nightstand to grab his supplies. As he coated his fingers in lube, he wished he had something fancier and more expensive than Astroglide, something as luxurious as Arlo deserved.

"Want these?" he asked, waggling his shiny fingers in Arlo's face.

"Yes, please."

"Then flip." He gave Arlo a gentle swat on the thigh and Arlo flipped so fast Brixby would've laughed if he weren't in the grip of a different emotion. Arlo pulled his knees up under him. His red-painted ass being offered up for the taking was the most beautiful sight Brixby had ever seen.

"So pretty." He leaned down to apply kisses to Arlo's shoulder as he worked his fingers slowly into his ass—first one, then two—gliding with the same cadence as his kisses, not focusing on Arlo's prostate but catching it every few strokes to send an extra shiver through him. Arlo held position perfectly, a lovely arch to his back as he displayed himself like an offering, his chest pressed against the bed and his face turned to the side so Brixby could see the acceptance washing over it.

When he couldn't make himself wait any longer, he shucked his clothes and reached for the condom. Arlo whimpered, so he steadied him with a hand between his shoulder blades as he finished rolling the condom down his shaft. The glide of his own hand was almost more than he could bear. As he set his cock against Arlo's hole, he offered up a prayer for fortitude, for the endurance to make this experience everything Arlo would want it to be.

The head of his cock popped through Arlo's sphincter, and then it was like running downhill—momentum took him. Arlo moaned, the sound drawn out and edged with relief, as if he were already as pleased as Brixby hoped to make him. Brixby echoed the sound, joining his voice to Arlo's. It was so fucking good.

Arlo was tight and hot around him, beautiful spread out before him. Exactly perfect. Brixby heard himself saying so—saying "you're perfect" and "you're mine" and "take me, take me" until Arlo was sobbing beneath him. Brixby wormed a hand under Arlo's body to find his cock, and it was so hard. So hot and wet and ready for him. Arlo convulsed with a high-pitched scream, and the control Brixby had been trying to hang on to dissolved like cotton candy in a hot mouth as Arlo's orgasm gave him permission to release his own.

God, he just wanted to collapse. But he managed to withdraw with proper consideration for Arlo's shivering body and remove the condom. *Then* he collapsed. Arlo lay right where Brixby had left him, his ass tilted to the sky, but when Brixby reached out, Arlo came—pressing up against him in a squirmy, eager rush, kissing him everywhere.

"So sweet," Brixby murmured, barely able to form words through the impending onrush of sleep. "Such a good boy."

It seemed to be the right thing to say because Arlo's mouth turned up in a smile, and a happy angel fell asleep on his chest.

Chapter 16 Brixby

"Just the man I was looking for," Dobransky called as he waved to Brixby across the squad room. Dobransky was dressed in a suit, as always. He gave Brixby a brisk handshake when they met in the middle of the room. "I'm heading back to San Francisco tomorrow. My financial forensics team traced the money you paid for Kimi back to DDD headquarters, and that should get me the warrants I need to go in and grab their data. Hopefully that'll tell us who's behind this."

"You think it's someone in headquarters?"

"Almost definitely. One or more of the folks right at the top, I'd say. Anyway, I need to wrap things up on the east coast and was hoping to have one last chat with Arlo before I go. Is he still at your place?"

Brixby nodded, feeling a little caught out. Though of course there was no way Dobransky could know what they'd gotten up to last night. That'd been... well. It'd been a hell of a scene. Hot and kinky and indescribably wonderful. But also everything Brixby had been telling himself not to do since he first took Arlo under his wing. He and Arlo were going to have to have another one of those talks about why they really, really couldn't do that. Even though they'd already done it.

Brixby brought Dobransky home with him, filling him in on the way about what'd happened at the club last night—everything up to the part where he'd spanked and fucked Arlo.

"So I guess we go back to the club next weekend," he finished. "Hopefully the security report Knight filed on me is ringing bells somewhere. At any rate, I made myself noticeable."

Dobransky laughed. Brixby hadn't gone into detail about the scene with Sebastian, because that was the sort of thing Dobransky would probably rather not know, but he'd told him about ending up on the sidewalk in chaps and a pair of briefs. Dobransky told him an embarrassing story about one of his own raids gone awry, and they swapped policing mishaps back and forth until they arrived in Jamaica Plain.

Apparently he should've texted Arlo to warn him he was bringing company because as soon as he opened the door, Arlo was on him—jumping into his arms wearing nothing except a pair of running shorts and slobbering kisses all over his face. At least Arlo wasn't naked and kneeling, but Dobransky could probably guess what was going on.

Dobransky cleared his throat, and Arlo finally noticed they weren't alone.

"Oh, hi. Lemme just, uh..." Arlo slunk deeper into the apartment where he rummaged through the closet and produced one of Brixby's shirts. It was a long-sleeved, button-down flannel in a brown plaid that looked incongruous with Arlo's pink running shorts and bare feet, especially since the shirt's tails came down far enough that only the bottom of his shorts peeked out, almost as if he weren't wearing anything beneath the shirt at all.

"Can I get you something to drink?" Brixby asked Dobransky to distract himself from the sight of Arlo swimming in his clothes.

Dobransky shook his head. "This won't take long."

He went through Arlo's story with him again. Brixby had heard it all before, but Dobransky had a methodical approach to his questioning that managed to pry a few new details loose.

147

"So you were outside of the club," Dobransky said. "Then what?"

Arlo shrugged. He was sitting in one of the kitchen chairs with Dobransky in the other. "I was just hanging out, not in a hurry to get anywhere, and this guy came up to me. I thought he might be a john, you know? Which I never did that." He cast a guilty glance at Dobransky, then a guiltier one at Brixby.

"We would understand if you did," Brixby said. He gave Arlo's head a comforting pat. His hair was so soft.

"Not for money," Arlo insisted. "Sometimes where I was staying, a guy would kind of expect.... I didn't mind, mostly. I like sex."

Dobransky cleared his throat again. "Did you see where Mike came from?"

Arlo shook his head. "But when I said I'd go with him, he had a car right there, so I guess he came from his car."

Dobransky had Arlo describe the car, but Arlo wasn't very knowledgeable about cars. Dark, expensive, and new was about all they could get out of him.

"Too nice for him," Arlo said. "Mike was ratty. Not rich like the car."

Dobransky flipped back a few pages in his notebook. "Ratty," he repeated thoughtfully. "Unkempt?"

Arlo looked like he didn't know what the word unkempt meant. "Ordinary," he clarified. "Not like Sebastian, all in brands and groomed up. Mike was more like me." Arlo hesitated a moment. "I have a picture."

Arlo had a picture of Mike? How had Brixby not known that? The revelation distracted him from how annoying that description of Sebastian had been as Arlo went over to the drawer Brixby had given him to keep his things in and pulled out a pad of paper. He flipped through the pages as he returned to the table, then handed it to Dobransky.

Brixby looked over Dobransky's shoulder at a sketch of a white guy with short hair and a long nose. His ears stuck out a little, and his chin was weak. He wasn't someone who would jump out at you in a crowd, but the detail in the sketch was far more than they'd managed to get out of Arlo verbally.

"It's not very good," Arlo said. "I used to know how to draw better, but I'm out of practice."

"It's excellent," Dobransky corrected. "You really remember him this clearly?"

Arlo nodded. "We were in South Station together for a while. He called someone to find out where I should go. I couldn't hear what he was saying, but we had to wait until they called back before he bought the ticket."

"They were finding a buyer," Brixby observed to Dobransky. "Doesn't seem like enough time to pull together an auction, though."

"I suspect they had a waiting list of gay male Doms. Terzini transferred a hundred thousand dollars to an offshore account a month before Arlo's disappearance, then another hundred thousand immediately after."

"A hundred grand just to be on a waiting list?" Brixby whistled. Human trafficking paid.

"Wait," Arlo said. "He paid two hundred thousand dollars for me? How am I worth that?"

"Aside from the fact that people can't be bought and sold," Brixby reminded him, "you're worth every penny of that and more. There's nothing I wouldn't pay for you."

Arlo jumped up and flung himself into Brixby's arms. His eyes were squinched shut, and his eyelashes were damp.

"Are you crying?" Why was he crying?

Dobransky had been taking photos of Arlo's sketch. Now he got to his feet. "I think I have what I need. Thanks so much for this picture, Arlo." He put a brief hand on Brixby's shoulder, then made his way to the door and let himself out.

"Hey." Brixby ruffled Arlo's hair. "I need you to talk to me. I can't help if I don't know what's wrong."

"I don't know what's wrong," Arlo sobbed into his chest.

"I said I wasn't selling myself, but I let someone else sell me, so I feel cheap but also expensive and you said I was worth it, but sometimes I think you're only putting up with me, and Mas—Mr. Terzini paid a lot of money for me, but he wasn't ever happy with me and you said I did good, but—"

"Okay, shh." He got it now, or most of it. He tilted Arlo's chin up so their eyes met. "Listen. I'm not putting up with you. I'm adoring you. And Terzini only said you were doing things wrong to control you. It wasn't you who was wrong. It was him."

"You'll see," Arlo said with a sigh. "I'm going to disappoint you, too."

The fact that Terzini had managed to convince Arlo he was a disappointment was fast becoming the thing Brixby hated him most for, which was saying something. But Arlo would recover from burns and malnutrition, given salve and food. His lack of confidence and the way his dreams had been shattered—those wounds were doing to take longer to heal.

"You couldn't disappoint me," Brixby promised him. "Because it's my job to take care of you, to discipline you with love if you need to be disciplined, and to work within your limitations. You don't owe me anything in return except honesty."

Which sounded like they were in a relationship. A power exchange relationship. How had that happened when he'd been so positive it shouldn't? Topping Arlo "just a little" in order to give him a sense of security had turned into "he's mine" without conscious intent on his part, but he couldn't argue with the feeling anymore.

"Let's talk about last night. If we're going to do this thing, which apparently we are"—Arlo brightened up at that, and Brixby let some of his guilt slip away—"then we need to set some ground rules."

"A contract?"

God, Arlo and his contracts.

"I don't know if we need to be as formal as all that. This

is only temporary. For now, it's temporary," he said when Arlo's face fell again. "We agreed, remember, that you aren't in a place for a permanent D/s relationship yet."

"*You* agreed that."

"All right, well, that hasn't changed. Come sit at the table with me."

Arlo slouched over to the table and sat in one of the chairs. "If we're not really in a relationship, then why do we have to talk?"

"Because there are a lot of ways I can top you, and you might be into some of them and not others. For example, Ilona is always submissive to Francesca, whereas Tripp—"

"Tripp doesn't have a Dom," Arlo said, his tone conveying both sympathy for his friend and a presumption of superiority.

"Not a permanent one, but he's played with Doms before. I have a feeling Tripp wouldn't be terribly obedient even if he had a regular partner. He seems like the bratty type to me. You know, like, bratty on purpose," he clarified when Arlo looked ready to defend his friend. "That's a thing some people enjoy—playing at disobedience—unlike Francesca who wouldn't find disobedience fun. And then in some BDSM relationships, there's no expectation of obedience at all. Like with Cash and Harrison."

"Harrison is a sub?" Arlo asked, as if he couldn't believe it.

"Well, he's a bottom anyway, and Cash is his top. At least when they play. But when they're not playing, you've seen how they are. They're equals. So those are all choices. I know the contract you signed with Terzini was for a fulltime thing, but aside from Terzini..." He trailed off, suddenly not sure how much "aside from Terzini" there'd been. "You *have* played with other Doms, right?"

Arlo had suggested as much before, but now he hesitated. "I wasn't a virgin or anything. I told you about the guys I stayed with."

"Right, but I'm talking about BDSM. Power play."

"Does online count?"

God, no. Online didn't count. Shit. The only practical BDSM experience Arlo had ever had was with an unscrupulous creep who'd kept him locked in a cage and *him*. Him ordering Arlo around whenever it seemed convenient. Him punishing Arlo without discussing limits or safewords. Him taking advantage of Arlo's vulnerability and naivete to hold him in what was essentially a second hostage situation.

Brixby felt sick to his stomach. He got to his feet and staggered away from the table, unable to face Arlo's innocence directly. He groped his way to the couch and dropped onto it to bury his head in his hands. What had he done?

"I can learn," Arlo's little voice said from beside him. "I'll get better, I swear. Please?"

"Please what, angel?" He drew Arlo into his lap, not sure he had the right to do even this much but needing to ease the pain he heard in Arlo's voice. Arlo felt so right in his arms. Brixby inhaled deeply, letting the familiar scent ease his troubled stomach.

"Please don't send me away."

"I'm not, I won't." He couldn't. "I'm not mad at you. I'm mad at myself. I knew you were inexperienced. I just... I kept saying you had choices, but you didn't even know what those choices were, did you? Did you think having a fulltime master was your only option?"

Arlo pondered the question for a moment. "I want a Dom," he said at last.

"But what does that mean to you?"

"That I would belong to him, and he would take care of me."

"That's a parent. You just want better parents." He didn't blame Arlo for wanting better parents—Arlo deserved them—but it made Brixby sick all over again to think he'd taken advantage of a kid needing love and shelter.

Arlo burst out laughing. "Not a *parent*. Ick. I want sex.

Maybe I should've said that part first."

"Okay." That was better. "And you want the person who takes care of you and the person you have sex with to be the same one?"

"Uh huh. And the sex should be..."

"Yeah?"

"Bossy. And maybe sometimes it hurts a little."

"But not a lot?"

Arlo ducked his head. "Mr. Terzini hurt *too* much," he said in a low voice, as if there were someone else there to hear him.

Brixby tightened his arms. The urge to find Terzini and kill him raged through him until he remembered Terzini was already dead.

"When I spanked you"—God, he didn't want to regret having done that—"did it hurt too much?"

"It was perfect." A small smile crossed Arlo's face, then disappeared quickly. "You didn't like it?"

"No, I did. I really did." But this wasn't supposed to be about him. He was there to give Arlo what *he* needed, so he added up the pieces. "I think you might be looking for a Daddy Dom. A little correction, a lot of spoiling, a moderate level of obedience, and no cages. You'd make a perfect Daddy's boy."

"That's what you are, right? A Daddy Dom."

"I... I don't know."

He'd always reserved the term Daddy Dom for men old enough to be *his* daddy, men who had full beards and grey chest hair, maybe a paunch. A Daddy Dom wasn't *him,* at only twenty-four.

But when he thought about how he felt toward Arlo, how he needed to take care of him, how automatically Arlo ended up in his lap when anything the least bit traumatic happened, and then about how much he'd enjoyed spanking Arlo's plump little ass, making him cry and drying his tears, he realized that Daddy Dom was exactly the role he'd been playing.

He didn't want a pet who had to be fed by hand, but making sure Arlo ate gave him a thrill that was part sexual and part something deeper than that. As if he'd found his purpose. And if he had to handfeed Arlo to make sure he ate, he would. Arlo should be healthy enough to feed himself most of the time, but when he wasn't? Brixby wanted to be there, holding out a spoonful of soup.

He didn't want to whip Arlo or leave marks on his pretty skin, at least none that wouldn't fade in an hour. And when he added all that up, he arrived at the same answer for himself he'd arrived at for Arlo. Daddy Dom.

"I could be a Daddy Dom for you."

Arlo attacked him with kisses, so gleeful that the last of Brixby's resistance to topping Arlo—at least for now, until Arlo got on his feet—blew away like dandelion fluff.

"Do I have call you Daddy though?" Arlo asked. "My dad is *nasty*." He wrinkled his nose in an expression of disgust.

"That's one of those things we're allowed to negotiate," Brixby told him. "I don't want to write out a formal contract because contracts have been used against you too much, but let's get back to that conversation we were having."

Chapter 17 Arlo

Arlo would prefer to stay right where he was, snuggled into Cade's chest. If they had to have a conversation, this felt like a safe place to do it. But Cade stood up and carried him over to the table and deposited him back in the chair he'd been in a few minutes ago when he'd accidentally said something that had made Cade really upset. Arlo didn't understand exactly what he'd said wrong, but they seemed to be through it now. Cade was going to be his Daddy Dom, and nothing could be more perfect.

Cade came back to the table with a notepad and a pen and sat down across from him.

"This isn't a contract," he said sternly. "You're not bound to it. No signatures, no forevers. Just a list of bullet points about what we both want and expect. You get to make as many points as I do, understand? We may play specific roles, but when it comes to negotiating those roles, we're equals. So please be honest."

Arlo licked his lips nervously. "Be honest" was something people said when what they really meant was "tell me what I want to hear and make me believe it." Like how he'd had to pretend to enjoy it when Terzini fucked him. Honesty hadn't had anything to do with it.

"So first thing," Cade said, holding the pen over the notepad. "You don't want to call me Daddy, so what *do* you want to call me?"

"Cade?" That was what Cade had said before.

"I like hearing you call me Cade." He wrote his name down on the pad. "How about when we're playing?"

"Sir?" But also... "Officer Brixby?" The term harkened back to when he'd been in the hospital and everything had been uncertain and awful and then there'd been Officer Brixby. Also, the uniform was hot.

"Officer Brixby," Cade repeated with a grin. "Only when we're in scene mode, though, okay?"

Arlo nodded and Cade wrote a slash next to his name and then "Officer Brixby" after it.

"And what should I call you? Boy?"

Arlo flinched. He couldn't help it. Just hearing that word made him want to look over his shoulder to see if Master was coming for him.

"Okay, obviously not. You can tell me that, Arlo. Say 'I don't want you to call me boy.'"

"I don't want you to call me boy," he repeated, finding the courage to say it because Cade had told him to. Cade wrote down "boy" and put a big X through it. The X made the tightness in Arlo's chest fade. He touched the paper like the X might be tangible. It seemed so powerful.

"I've been calling you angel," Cade said with a laugh. "I didn't exactly ask your permission for that."

"I like that one," Arlo said quickly, before Cade changed his mind and stopped doing it.

Cade wrote down *angel* and circled it. "Now let's talk about how much you have to obey me when we're not playing. I don't want what Francesca has with Ilona. I'd rather you were free to do as you please for the most part."

Arlo nodded. That was what Cade wanted, so that was how it would be.

"Tell me what you're thinking," Cade insisted, which was kind of funny.

"I like obeying you. When you tell me things, it feels..." He touched his chest.

"Like I care about you. Right." Cade tapped the pad with the other end of the pen. "I'm concerned about your general welfare, so I'm allowed to take charge of it as necessary. And you treat me with respect, like you would a parent. A *good* parent," he corrected. "You defer to me, but you also have autonomy, and if there's a big gap between what I want and what you want, we stop and talk it out. How's that?"

Arlo could agree to that. He didn't want Cade to stop telling him to do things in that steely-soft voice that meant he'd been paying attention, but Cade couldn't pay attention to him every minute, and Arlo knew how boring cages got.

"So this is important to me," Cade said. "We talked about it before, but I have to say it again. You need to be independent—find a way to support yourself and a place to live."

Ooh, he did *not* like that one. "Why can't I stay here?"

"You can't depend on me for everything—for sex and love and money and housing and food. It's not safe for you, and it's not fair to me. I'm not a machine. I have needs too. And Arlo, I don't have a lot of money, not like Sebastian or Francesca. So if it's financial support you're primarily interested in..." Cade looked around the apartment as if to ask why Arlo would want to live there, but it wasn't about square feet or granite countertops.

"Kimi gets to stay with Francesca."

"Only until the investigation's over."

So Kimi wasn't as well off as she thought she was. Arlo felt bad, thinking how sad she was going to be when Francesca made her move out—as sad as he was at the thought of moving out of Cade's. Every time it seemed like he and Cade were making progress, he ran into a brick wall again.

"I thought subs lived with their Doms."

"Some do, some don't. But this is only temporary, remember? We can talk about making it more permanent later."

"Later when?"

"Later after you've gotten your feet under you and you're a little older," Cade said like that was the end of that

157

conversation. "Let's talk about punishment. Do you like pain?"

"Not very much."

"You don't like pain very much? Or you like pain, but not very much of it?"

"It was okay when you spanked me."

Cade wrote down *spankings* and ticked it off with a checkmark.

"But the spanking didn't hurt," Arlo said in an effort to be honest.

"Are you sure it didn't hurt? I turned your ass a nice shade of red."

"It didn't hurt *much*," he corrected. Only exactly the right amount. "I liked it."

"Sure you did. Because it was ritualistic and parental and only hurt a little."

Arlo flushed, embarrassed about how Cade was saying all his secrets out loud like that.

"What else would push those same buttons for you?" Cade's voice dipped down intimately, pulling Arlo's eyes to him even though Arlo couldn't bear to look. His face felt as hot and red as his cock, which had come alive, squirming its way up to full arousal. "You like *this*, don't you? Having your dirty little desires called out. You want to be my plaything, Arlo?"

The pen had fallen from Cade's hand. He leaned back in his chair, his arms crossed in front of him and his shirt stretched taut across his broad shoulders, exuding authority.

"Yes, Officer Brixby." The smallness of his own voice turned him on as much as the certainty in Cade's. This was hot, so hot that drops of sweat broke out across his stomach and the insides of his wrists. He reached for the top button of his shirt, but Cade stopped him.

"Did I tell you to take your shirt off?"

"No, Officer Brixby." Only he was so hot he was going to melt right there on the kitchen chair. Just ooze to the floor in a gooey puddle at Cade's feet.

"Shit." Cade raked a hand through his hair. "We're supposed to be making a list, not playing. Let's see, um, safewords?"

Arlo shook his head. He didn't want to make a list. He wanted what Cade's eyes had been promising.

"Safewords aren't optional, but let me guess. You didn't have any with Terzini." Cade sighed. The dominant gleam in his eyes flickered out. "Okay, so the standard safewords are red, yellow, and green. Green means go. Red means stop. Yellow means—"

"Red."

"What?" Cade glanced up from the pad where he'd been drawing a little picture of a traffic light.

"I don't want to make a list right now. I'd rather do something else." He scooted forward on his chair until his knees touched Cade's.

"This is important."

"But I said red. Red means stop."

Cade shook his head with a laugh. "Little devil. That's not how this works, and you know it."

"I don't know anything," he lied. He didn't know much, but he knew about safewords, though it was true Master had never given him any. "You have to teach it all to me, remember?"

"I'm about to teach you something," Cade threatened.

That was what Arlo wanted, so he pointed to the spot on the list where Cade had written down spankings with the checkmark next to it.

"For someone who supposedly doesn't know anything, you're sure good at it." Cade sounded proud. He wrapped a hand around Arlo's wrist and gave a yank and Arlo let himself be dragged into his lap. "What am I going to do with you?" Cade said against his hair. "You have too much power over me already. They're going to take away my Dom card."

"Dom card?"

"Just a joke," Cade said, but he wasn't laughing.

159

"Sebastian will say I'm too easy on you."

"I don't like Sebastian."

"Which is why I'm the lucky guy who has you in his lap. *But* I'm not so smitten that I can't make you sit here and finish this list. So be good, and then you'll get a reward."

"What if I'm bad?" Arlo asked, his head swimming from hearing Cade say things like "lucky" and "smitten." Maybe he still had a chance of making Cade's home his forever home.

"Then you'll get your punishment, but either way, you're not going anywhere until we're done." Cade tightened the cage of his arms, and Arlo relaxed back into them. He would make the stupid list if he got to do it from Cade's lap.

"Let's get it over with then."

"Little brat," Cade said, all amusement. "Guess you're heading for a punishment, so let's figure out what punishment looks like."

Arlo was really sorry about fucking up the investigation last night. Sorry about being a brat afterward, too. He didn't ever want Cade mad at him. But he had liked how Cade had told him what he'd done wrong. His words had been stern but also warm, as though Arlo could be forgiven. And the punishment had been easy to take. By the time it was over, Arlo's cock had been as hot as his ass.

Being punished by Cade had been like how he'd imagined punishment being. If someone punished you, it was because they cared about you, not because they wanted to hurt you. And when your Dom punished you, it was also because it was sexy. Because it turned him on and turned you on and then he fucked you, the way Cade had fucked him last night, and you felt like the most important, most precious person in the world.

The first time Master had punished Arlo, which was only the second day he was there, he'd thought Master was joking. He'd tripped going up the stairs, and Master had called him clumsy. Arlo had expected him to kiss his booboo and give him a lecture about taking better care of himself, but there'd been no kissing, and the lecture hadn't had an oh-my-precious vibe to it. Only wrath and a sort of sadistic glee. "You'll be sorry," Master would say, and Arlo always was.

Master had never asked him how he would like to be punished, that was for sure. Arlo wouldn't even have known what to answer. But Cade described different things he might to do with one hand on the pen and the other on Arlo's cock, joking that he didn't need Arlo to answer because he could guess which ones Arlo liked from how hard and squirmy he got.

Truth was, most of what Cade suggested sounded pretty good, even things Master—no, *Mister*—Terzini had done that Arlo hadn't liked at the time. And Cade never mentioned any of the really bad stuff—like fire and blades. Or the hood.

The hood was the worst. A black leather thing—solid except for a tiny patch of mesh to breathe through, heavy enough that sounds came through all muffled. Mr. Terzini would put it on, then fasten leather mitts around Arlo's hands and cuff them to the side of his neck. Then he would put Arlo in the cage and leave him there for however long he wanted to with no sight, no sound, no human interaction, no way to touch anything, not even himself.

Cade didn't say anything about hoods or mitts or chains, but he did say corner time. Arlo shook his head at that one so vehemently that Cade wrote it down and put another one of those satisfying X's through it.

"Shh, it's all right. No corner time. I thought you might like it, that's all."

"I don't like being left alone."

Cade was silent for a moment. Then he drew a second X through the words. "I wouldn't have walked away while you were in the corner. I would've been right there, watching. But we won't use it."

"You can if—"

"Shh, no. Honesty, remember? No punishments where

161

you can't see me. I get it. Even if I'm really mad at you—not just for pretend—I won't walk away. You have the right to insist on these things, Arlo. Do you believe me?"

Because it was so important to Cade that he be honest, Arlo shook his head. He didn't understand. When someone took care of you, you had to do what they said. It might not be a perfect trade, but it was a fair one. Cade kept trying to give Arlo all the benefits of submission without ever taking anything back for himself, and if Cade didn't get anything from him, Cade wouldn't keep him.

"I think we've done enough of this for today." Cade dropped the pen and stood Arlo up on his feet. "We need to work on the basics. Power Exchange 101."

"You don't have to teach me that. I know how." He dropped to the floor, going into one of the positions Mr. Terzini had trained him in, the one where he had his knees spread wide and his hands cupped behind his back with his forehead touching the ground.

"Mm," Cade murmured appreciatively. "That's not what I meant, but I'll take it."

"What did you mean?" He'd thought that this, at least, he knew how to do.

"I meant that you need to believe you have power in this relationship, that it's not a one-way street where I command and you obey."

"But I like when you—" Arlo started.

"Shh." Cade pressed a finger against his mouth. "I know. Believe me, I know. You're so precious, but so young and so easily swayed. It worries me."

Arlo almost laughed. His chance to be young had ended too soon, and he wouldn't mind having it back. "I obey because I want to," he insisted. "Because I *like* it."

And because Cade was worthy of it. Cade saw him as soft and small, and Arlo so desperately wanted to be soft and small. If only Cade would let him.

"Can I?" He nuzzled into the space between Cade's thighs, inhaling deeply to pick up the scent of warm flesh beneath Cade's uniform pants. He pushed in deeper, wriggling forward on his knees until his body parted Cade's legs. His nose and mouth found their way to the bulge between them.

Cade was hard—another compliment. Arlo loved every nice thing Cade said or did. The spoken words, the unspoken reactions. Loved how those compliments expanded in his chest until the knowledge that he was wanted obliterated every past feeling of being unwanted. He didn't know everything about BDSM, but he knew this—how to make Cade hard for him.

Cade's hand rested on the back of his head, a light but firm presence, only the ghost of what Arlo wanted as he mouthed Cade's erection, turning his head so he could trace it up and down with his lips parted wide to capture the width of it. He left a trail on Cade's trousers as he moved, wetting the fabric until it was soaked through and Cade's fingers tangled into his hair the way he liked.

Cade said Arlo had power, that he had a right to say no, but his hands said Arlo belonged to him. His hands commanded. They twisted tight, pulling until Arlo's scalp tingled. He remembered how Cade had asked him about hair pulling and then written it down on the paper when Arlo squirmed in response. It was so right when Cade did it, the sensation just on the edge of pain and more about control than anger, not at all the way Mr. Terzini had sometimes pulled him around using his hair like a steering wheel.

As Arlo looked up into Cade's hooded eyes, a flash of understanding went through him. He could ask for what turned him on. Those fantasies he used to have as he scrolled through websites—those could happen. Not because BDSM was automatically wonderful, and not by accident. They could happen because he *asked* for them and because he had a partner willing to listen. Cade was perfect for him because Cade *wanted* to be perfect for him. And Arlo didn't just like him. He loved him.

Chapter 18 Brixby

Brixby had given Arlo permission to start spending time with Tripp again because he couldn't be the kind of Dom who cut his sub off from his friends, but he hadn't expected to find Tripp in his living room when he got home from work. He hadn't expected to find Arlo so flustered either. He was in front of the oven with a bright orange box in his hand, and he jumped about a mile high when Brixby came up behind him.

"Sorry, did I startle you?" He wanted to give Arlo a kiss, but Tripp was there and he still felt like he shouldn't be having the sort of relationship with Arlo he was actually having. But Arlo was upset about something, so he put an arm around his waist and drew him into his body, just to settle him.

"I'm sorry." Arlo slumped back against him, his head drooping to present a field of blond curls for Brixby to brush his nose through.

"Sorry for what?"

"I didn't know it would take an *hour*." Arlo lifted the box, which Brixby saw was for frozen enchiladas. "I thought it would go in the microwave for, like, ten minutes. And the brownies need eggs." He gestured at a mixing bowl that had a pile of brown dust in it.

"We probably don't have eggs."

"I *know*. But I didn't know I needed them. I thought everything was in the box. So I can't make you brownies, and dinner's not ready. The oven hasn't even pre-heated yet." He kicked the oven, which rattled in protest.

Brixby considered whether or not he knew brownie mix needed eggs, then decided it didn't matter. "So we'll pick up some eggs," he said. "The mix will keep. And I'm glad you didn't put dinner in the oven because we're going to Cash's, and you know he'll have a feast laid on." He kissed the irresistible skin of Arlo's cheek. "I should've texted to let you know not to worry about dinner."

He hadn't gotten to the point of expecting Arlo to cook for him yet. He hadn't even gotten to the point of expecting Arlo to be in his apartment yet. It was still a happy remembrance at the end of every day—that he wasn't just going home. He was going home to Arlo.

"You're having dinner at Cash's?" Tripp asked as he watched the two of them with something like suspicion.

"We're getting together to talk about how to proceed after the way you two fucked up last week's plan."

Arlo looked guilty, but Tripp looked even guiltier.

"Does that mean I don't get to be part of the team anymore?" Tripp asked.

Brixby almost wanted to tell him yes, but the Dom in him couldn't beat up on someone who was feeling down. "Didn't anyone text you?"

Tripp glanced at his lock screen, then swiped at a notification. "We've been busy." Which meant someone had texted him, which meant he could've warned Arlo and saved him the meltdown over dinner.

"Since you're here, you might as well come with us. I just need to change."

"You're not mad about dinner?" Arlo asked, tagging along with him as he collected clean clothes from the dresser.

"I'm not ever going to be mad about dinner, Arlo. You don't owe me dinner." He dithered between jeans and shorts. Technically, it was autumn, but the weather hadn't gotten the memo. "I like it when you cook, but it's not something you have to do." He tilted Arlo's chin up and gave him a quick kiss, Tripp be damned, then pulled out a pair of jeans. It would be cold by the time they were coming home.

"Do you have to change?" Arlo's pretty eyes had that look in them. Brixby momentarily forgot that yes, he needed to change.

"I'm off duty, and I've been in these clothes all day. But we could, um... another time, okay?" He shot a glance at Tripp who was making an unconvincing attempt at pretending not to listen, then went into the bathroom to change into the jeans and short-sleeved shirt he'd selected.

The shirt hugged him just right, and he took a moment to admire himself before going back out to the living room where Arlo did an even better job of admiring him. Brixby flashed him an equally appreciative look. Arlo made a gorgeous package with his pert ass snuggled into a pair of slim-fit jeans and a deep blue t-shirt that highlighted just how light his eyes were.

When Arlo smiled at him, Brixby's heart almost burst with fondness. He was getting in much too deep with this kid he'd been given temporary charge of. As soon as they wrapped up the investigation, he needed to concentrate on getting Arlo settled somewhere more permanent, somewhere with a future, but until then, he was glad they had this time together and fuck Tripp or anyone who thought he shouldn't make the most of it. He pulled Arlo tight against his body and gave him the kiss he'd wanted to give him when he first came in—a commanding, possessive kiss that said: "Dinner is nothing. It's you I want."

Arlo melted into him, surrendering his mouth with such sweet willingness it took everything Brixby had to draw away.

"I could wait outside," Tripp suggested. "Or watch."

Tempting. The waiting outside part, not the watching part, but they had somewhere to be. Brixby snagged a hoodie from the dresser for Arlo to wear on their way home, stopping on his way back across the apartment to take in a sketch Arlo had made of Tripp that was sitting on the coffee table.

"How come you never mentioned you could draw?" he asked as he followed Arlo and Tripp down the stairs.

"I can't draw good."

"He's *so* good," Tripp said. "That was totally me up there. I never even knew he could either. How come I didn't know?"

"It's not like it matters," Arlo said as they all clattered out onto the porch. "What's the use of it?"

"You could study art," Brixby suggested. They'd been talking about what Arlo might major in if he went to college, but somehow art had never come up.

"Art doesn't make money," Arlo said dispiritedly. "I have to get on my own two feet, remember?"

"Don't be manipulative," Brixby warned him. "And art can make money. Cash is a graphic designer. You should talk to him about it."

But when they got to Cash's, Arlo went straight for the cat. The three of them were the first to arrive. Even Harrison hadn't made it home yet, and Cash looked like he'd just landed and was still flapping.

"Sorry we're early. Tripp's fault." Because if Tripp hadn't been there, Brixby would've let Arlo take his uniform off for him.

"No worries. Want something to drink?"

Brixby waggled the six pack he'd picked up on the way, letting Cash know he was all set. He grabbed one and stashed the rest in the refrigerator, then found a pitcher of iced tea and poured a couple of glasses for the kids.

Tripp wrinkled his nose at it. "I can't have a beer?"

"You're nineteen."

Arlo ignored his iced tea in favor of trying to lure Mr. Moo down from his window perch. Brixby had a feeling he was going to end up getting Arlo a cat. He'd caved on every other subject. He sipped from his bottle, dividing his

167

attention between what Arlo was saying to Mr. Moo and what Cash was doing in the kitchen. Making something amazing, no doubt, but Brixby could be happy with frozen enchiladas.

"Hey, your tattoo's uncovered." He grabbed Cash as he flitted by so he could check it out. "A goldfish?" The fish was more red than gold, but it was basically a goldfish.

"A red molly," Cash corrected.

"Like the one Harrison had?" Poor thing. Brixby remembered the fish swimming alone in a barren tank in a nearly barren apartment.

"Like the one *we* have." Cash pointed over Brixby's shoulder, and Brixby swung around to see the tank sitting on a bookshelf. It was sparkling clean now and decorated with greenery and a purple castle. "Her name's Molly."

"Molly, the red molly?"

"Harrison didn't name her so much as end up with her, but she's got a home now, don't you, babe?" Cash stuck his face in front of the tank and damned if the fish didn't swim over like it had something to say.

"She probably just wants to take a bite out of you. Harrison says she's murderous."

"She is." Cash tapped a few dashes of food into the top of the tank. "Doesn't *look* murderous though, does she? Just a little thing who needs a lot of love, but she'll fight whoever she has to fight."

"So that tattoo is basically Harrison?"

Cash winked at him. "Don't tell him. He thinks it's just a fish."

"Don't tell Sebastian either, I suppose."

"I don't give a fuck what you tell Sebastian. I'm not afraid of his judgement." Cash stomped back to the kitchen a little too loudly for someone who didn't care. "The irony of this investigation is Sebastian's exactly the sort of Dom we're looking for."

"Unethical?" He'd thought Cash was vouching for Sebastian.

"Well, no. Not that part." Cash cracked his neck one way, then the other. "But he's got the arrogance. I could see him deciding which sub ought to be with which Dom and making it happen, stepping over a line here and there because he was so sure he was right."

"How serious are you?" Brixby had only known Sebastian for about six weeks and wasn't prepared to call him a friend.

"I'm a hundred percent serious about him being an asshole who thinks he knows better than everyone else, but if you're asking if I think he had anything to do with the abductions, the answer's a definite no. You're not really going there, are you?"

The arrival of Harrison, followed shortly by Francesca and her girls and then Knight, distracted Brixby from answering the question. The space grew crowded when Sebastian himself joined them in the kitchen, and Brixby escaped out to the garden. He ended up sitting next to Francesca while the four subs lounged on the grass together with Ilona and Kimi in more comfortable poses than Brixby was accustomed to seeing them. Francesca was practically ignoring them as she pressed Brixby for updates on the case.

"So there's a chance this will be over soon?" she asked when he told her about Dobransky's warrants.

"I hope so." He squeezed her hand, and she flashed him an appreciative glance. "Things still rough? They seem to be getting along all right now."

"They both like Arlo. They think he's pretty. Like a doll."

He wasn't *their* doll though. Brixby scowled at the way Kimi was toying with one of Arlo's curls. Those were *his* curls.

"Could I ask you a favor?" Francesca asked, catching his attention again. "I really need to get away for a day or two. Would you keep the girls for me?"

"I have a studio apartment. It's overfull already. And you know Kimi and Ilona are adults, right? I'm not going to play Dom to them, and they don't need a babysitter."

"I'm not asking you to top them, and yes, they're technically adults, but if I leave them alone with each other, neither one of them will have any hair left by the time I get back. With you and Arlo around, they'll behave better. Like how they're behaving now." She gestured at the group of subs who were all laughing at something on Tripp's phone. He was leaning halfway off the bench to show it to them and the other three were gathered around him with Arlo's bright blond head in the middle.

"You could stay at my place," Francesca suggested. "Bring Arlo and spend the weekend. I'd really appreciate it."

Brixby nodded his agreement. It was probably beneficial for Arlo to spend time with other subs. Important even. And it wouldn't be a hardship to move into Francesca's mini-mansion for the weekend. Why argue with luxury?

"HAD ENOUGH TO EAT?" CASH ASKED as he collected empty plates after dinner.

"It was lovely." Francesca rose from the bench to corral Ilona and Kimi who she'd allowed to feed themselves tonight.

Arlo drifted over, and Brixby pulled him into his lap. Together they watched Francesca groom her girls back to perfection with wet wipes and brushes and lipsticks. Arlo was a soft, quiet weight in Brixby's lap, smelling of shampoo and soap. He wasn't wearing anything fancy or showy, but he was perfect.

"Did you eat?"

Arlo nodded, his curls making soft contact with Brixby's chin.

"Enough?"

This time Arlo only shrugged.

"There's probably dessert."

Arlo turned his face up with a grin.

Brixby set him on his feet and gave his ass a tap. "Let's go inside. It's time for business."

Harrison already had most of the gang corralled in the living room, and once Brixby and Francesca and their subs had all found places to sit, he jumped straight to the heart of the matter.

"All right, so we know last weekend was a cock-up, and we know why. We're not going to rehash it, but it looks like we need a round two this weekend."

Francesca raised her hand. "Brixby said the FBI would be serving warrants on DDD headquarters Monday. Doesn't that mean our work is done?"

Sebastian shook his head. "Once DDD gets raided, they'll know we're on to them. They'll shut the operation down."

"Seems like a good thing," she responded with a shrug.

"Except charges always flow up," Sebastian explained. "First, you catch the little guy. He squeals on a bigger guy, who squeals on a bigger guy, and so on. Which is what you want, normally. But what *we* want is to catch whoever's behind the disappearances in Boston, and the FBI isn't going to offer a bigwig in San Francisco a deal to turn State's evidence on a bit player back east. Mike might fall through the cracks."

"Oh, no," Cash said. "We're finding Mike. That fucker turned our club into a crime scene. He's going to pay for it."

"Then if we want to smoke out the rat in our pipeline, we need to do it this weekend before focus shifts to San Francisco."

"Shame about last weekend," Knight said. "But I think we had the right idea, and Brixby's in the system now. If he comes back this weekend, they might be prepared to jump on him."

"Yeah, those incident reports are key," Harrison said. "Good chance Mike has access to them."

Knight grimaced. "I hired everyone who works for me,

171

but I'm not going to swear there aren't any bad eggs in there. One of my guys went home early the night Arlo got turfed—clocked out around the same time, said he wasn't feeling well. His name's not Mike, but we can assume that's an alias, right?"

Brixby nodded, though he wasn't as certain as Harrison that they were looking for a guard. Yes, Arlo had been logged into the system, but Mike had known more about Arlo than the fact that he was underage. He'd known Arlo was a sub and that he was gay. He'd known Arlo would be interested in a fulltime contract too. And none of that had come from the security system.

"I still think Brixby is too big, too old, and too"— Sebastian waved his hand vaguely—"clean-cut to attract their attention. Why not use a plant who's more what they're looking for?" He indicated Arlo, who was sitting cross-legged on the floor next to Brixby's chair.

"No way," Brixby said immediately. "Arlo has no business being in that club and definitely not as bait."

"He's eighteen now."

"Which means he wouldn't even trigger an alert."

"His face is an alert. Once they realize their escaped sub is back at the scene of the crime, they'll send someone running."

"It's a fair point," Harrison said.

Brixby shot him a glare. "Arlo would have to appear to be alone, and he's not doing that."

"He wouldn't really be alone though," Harrison said. "One of us would be inside the club, the other outside. Cash and Knight would both be there as backup. He'd be plenty safe."

"I don't like it."

"I'll do it." Arlo started to rise to his feet.

"No. Sit down. I said *no*, Arlo." Brixby spun Arlo to face him and forced all the command he could muster into his expression until Arlo sat back down, then he turned to Harrison. "No."

"All right, let's table that," Harrison said with only the slightest lift of his eyebrows. "Let's assume Brixby is playing victim again. We need another incident."

Sebastian threw out ideas for scenes the two of them could engage in, all of which Brixby hated. He knew Sebastian was goading him, intentionally coming up with the most humiliating scenarios possible, but he didn't feel like he could veto them because he'd used his veto power to keep Arlo out of it.

"Maybe we could involve Francesca instead," Harrison suggested, God bless the man. He was a good friend. Brixby flashed him a grateful smile.

"I wasn't planning to be there," Francesca said. And shit, Brixby had forgotten that part. "I'm heading down to DC this weekend to spend time with an old college friend. I figured I'd visit DDD's DC club while I'm there. Jessica's still out there too, remember."

"Good point," Brixby said. Arlo being only seventeen at the time of his disappearance and having such cherubic good looks made him a sympathetic victim compared to a nineteen-year-old drug addict with a criminal record, but Jessica had almost certainly fallen into the same hands Arlo had, and even though no one had hired them to look for her, they owed her some effort. "Now that you mention it, Sebastian should do the same thing. Maybe go to New York."

"Then who's going to scene with you?" Sebastian asked. "Cash? He's not going to do anything that'll get you kicked out of a club, I assure you."

"I'll figure something out. I'm supposed to be a sub in search of a Dom, not somebody who already has one."

"Can I go to New York with you?" Tripp asked Sebastian with a flirtatious sideways glance at the Dom he'd wedged himself in next to. "Maybe someone will try to kidnap me." He sounded like he wished they would.

"No one's going to kidnap you," Brixby told him. "You'd be there to look for Jessica, and even if they picked you out

173

as a potential victim, they'd just talk to you."

"And yet you think they're going to kidnap Arlo," Sebastian said.

"Totally different situation. Tripp would be a new recruit. Arlo is an escaped victim. They won't bother talking to him. They'll just grab him."

Which was why there was no way Arlo was going to Hell's Bedroom, no matter how much he sulked. He was kneeling now, as if to make the point that Brixby had played Big Bad Dom to him, but too bad. He would order Arlo around all day if it kept him safe.

"Sebastian and Francesca patrolling the other clubs for Jessica makes sense," Cash said, playing peacemaker. "I can sign Brixby in this weekend, and Harrison will back him up. How's Saturday?"

"Works for me." Knight got to his feet with a stretch. "I'll be ready to read you the riot act, Brixby, whatever you get yourself written up for." He made his goodbyes, and Francesca was quick to follow.

"We didn't even have dessert," Cash protested.

"Another time," she said graciously.

Brixby went over to her while the four subs gave each other a group hug on the floor. "Are you really planning to look for Jessica, or are you just escaping?"

"If I didn't look for Jessica, I'd feel guilty about escaping."

"Sorry." He put an arm around her shoulders and she leaned into him a bit. "We'll get this wrapped up. Then you'll have your life back."

"Soon, right?"

"Soon." Soon he'd have his life back too. And Arlo would be... somewhere.

"I want dessert," Tripp said once Francesca and her girls had left. "What is it?"

"Fruit compote over angel food cake."

"Fruit?" Tripp wrinkled his nose.

"Compote. You'll like it. Come help me get it dished up."

Cash went into the kitchen with Tripp and Harrison following eagerly behind him.

"Can I go too?" Arlo asked.

Brixby frowned at him. "You know you can do whatever you want."

"Not *whatever*," Arlo said significantly before heading for the kitchen, which left Brixby alone with Sebastian.

Brixby crossed his arms. He had an idea what was coming. "I didn't exactly intend for this to happen," he said, heading Sebastian off.

"Don't worry about it. You're perfect for him."

What? The last thing Brixby had been expecting was support. "You think so?"

"Sure. He's not ready for a Dom, like you said. But you're not really a Dom, are you? More of a mom." Sebastian laughed—an amused cackle that made the hair on Brixby's arms stand up. "I've heard of Daddy Doms, but Mommy Doms are a new one. It could be a whole thing."

"It's the same role, regardless of the gender of the person playing it. Mommy Dom is just misogynistic bullshit."

Sebastian waved his hand dismissively. "Chicken Soup Dom then. You kiss his boo-boos and wipe his ass."

And spoon feed him soup when he's sick. Wasn't that exactly what Brixby wanted to do? Why was he letting Sebastian make it sound negative?

"Taking care of your sub isn't new. Maybe you should try it."

"Oh, I take care of my subs, if you know what I mean." Sebastian winked, then stood up. "Think I'll skip dessert. Gotta stay in shape for swinging that whip." He called goodnight into the kitchen, then left. Meanwhile, Brixby sat on the couch with his fists clenched so hard he could almost feel his bones breaking.

"You're not letting Sebastian get to you, are you?" Harrison asked as he took a seat next to him. Harrison had a fork in one hand and a plate in the other. "Must be a Dom thing. You're all so insecure."

"I'm not insecure," Brixby said, trying to choke back how incredibly insecure he was. All that mattered was Arlo. Keeping him safe. Getting him established. Making him happy.

Stupid Sebastian. He had no idea what Arlo needed.

Chapter 19 Arlo

Arlo slunk into the kitchen where Tripp was hanging over Cash's shoulder urging Cash to add more whipped cream to the plate in his hand. Harrison already had a plate, piled high with cake and whipped cream and maybe a little fruit. He brushed past Arlo with it, forking a bite into his mouth as he left.

Arlo didn't really want cake. He'd eaten too much for dinner. He'd only asked if he could come into the kitchen because he was grumpy at Cade. Why did everyone get to be involved in the investigation except him?

Tripp turned with the tower of whipped cream Cash had handed him and noticed Arlo lurking in the doorway. "Hey, you're here. You can talk to Cash now."

"What about?" Cash asked as he set to making another plate. Arlo shook his head. He didn't know what about.

"About the art," Tripp prompted. "Arlo's an artist. Did you know that?"

"I didn't." Cash stopped serving to turn and beam at him. "Something we have in common then. What kind of art do you do?"

"I just draw things. Not in a while. I don't know." He felt ridiculous calling himself an artist. Drawing had once brought him a lot of joy, but somewhere along the line, life had gotten too hard for joy.

"He thinks it's useless because he can't make money at it," Tripp said through a mouthful of dessert. "But artists make so much money."

Cash snorted merrily before schooling his features back into a more thoughtful expression. "Sorry. I shouldn't laugh. Some artists do make a lot of money. Not me, but some."

So see? Arlo had been right to give up on it.

"But you have this great apartment," Tripp said. "It's not waterfront like Sebastian's, but it's all right."

"I like it better," Arlo said. "It has a garden and a cat and cool paintings." All the art in Sebastian's apartment looked like it'd been bought at the same store on the same day. It was *good*—his eye was trained enough to see that—but boring. "Did you paint those?" he asked Cash.

"A lot of them. Some of them are from my friends. We used to swap canvases back in art school, in case one of us ever got famous."

"Did anyone get famous?"

"Not yet. If you're going to go into art, it's important to have realistic expectations. I do draw for a living. I just don't get to draw what I *want* to draw. Though, you know, I should get my paints out. You're making me realize I've let that side of me slide. Being an adult is tough that way."

Arlo nodded. He'd tried being an adult before he'd even legally been an adult, and it'd been tough, all right.

Cash handed Tripp the plate he'd been working on. "Why don't you bring this to Brixby? Arlo and I can chat."

Tripp held out his own plate with a silent plea, and Cash added another slice of cake and some more whipped cream to it. Then Tripp took both plates into the living room. Arlo sidled in closer to watch Cash dish up another serving. Maybe a small piece of cake would be all right.

"No whipped cream though," he said. "More fruit."

"Very healthy of you," Cash said, even though Arlo could see the fruit was slick and syrupy and probably not healthy at all. Still, he accepted the plate Cash handed to him.

"So you might be interested in an art career?"

"Cade says I have to do *something*. He wants me to move out."

"It doesn't seem like he wants you to move out."

Arlo shrugged. "That's what he says. But if he wants me to move out, art isn't the way to do it."

"No, not in the short term." Cash had finally served himself some cake. He always left himself last. "Is there a big hurry?"

"Kind of." Arlo toyed with a shiny, plump blueberry, then forked it into his mouth. It was as sweet as he'd expected it to be. "He says I can stay as long as I want, but then he says we can't be boyfriends until I leave."

"Ah."

"Why ah?"

"He's a good guy. Thinking about what's best for you."

"It's *not* best for me." Best would be Cade and Iceman sheets and a cat of his own. Soft cuddles and rough blowjobs and sometimes a spanking. Cade calling him angel like he was the most important thing in the world. Sure, he would need to have a job of some sort, and art would be a cool job to have, but why did he have to go away?

"Let me see if I can explain," Cash said. "I have this friend, Mr. Jackman."

"If he's your friend, why do you call him mister? Is he a Dom?"

Cash laughed. "I don't think so. But he's eighty-three, so he deserves some respect."

Arlo whistled. Even his grandparents weren't that old.

"He told me this story once," Cash went on, "about how his wife saved her whole life for what she called a flee fund, in case she needed to escape from him."

"Did she need to?" Arlo asked, suddenly very interested in Mr. Jackman and his wife.

"No, Mr. Jackman is a stand-up guy. She bought a watch with it, actually. A gold Rolex," Cash said like Arlo ought to be impressed. Arlo knew what a Rolex was, of course, but he'd never worn a watch and didn't understand

179

why anyone would bother. He'd been more interested in Mrs. Jackman needing to flee, which was something he could relate to.

"Anyway," Cash went on, "the point is that Mrs. Jackman was saving that money because her mother had told her to—said a woman ought to always have a way to get free. Which is a little antiquated in terms of gender roles, but the concept applies to all genders, I think. We should always have a way out."

Oh. So this *was* about him.

"Cade doesn't keep me in a cage," he said, just in case Cash had some kind of wrong idea. "There aren't any locks anywhere. I can walk right out the door."

"But where would you go? That's the point. Brixby's trying to make sure you aren't stuck. You know what Mr. Jackman did when his wife gave him that Rolex? He worked overtime until he'd earned enough money to pay her back for it so she would have a flee fund again. Not because he was going to hurt her. Because he loved her and wanted to know she would always be safe."

"That was nice of him, I guess."

But Arlo didn't need a flee fund because he didn't want to flee. What he'd tried to explain to Cade the other day still sat heavy in his chest. Sometimes Mr. Terzini had almost seemed to hate him, he'd been so cold and cruel, but he'd paid two hundred thousand dollars for him, which was wild to think about. All Cade had to do was not throw him out of his apartment. It didn't seem like too much to ask.

"I TALKED TO CASH," HE TOLD CADE as they walked back to the T after dessert. He'd been given the assignment of talking to Cash and wanted credit for having completed it.

"What did he say?"

"That you can make a living as an artist if you don't mind selling out."

That was what it'd boiled down to, but it didn't sound so bad. Arlo didn't consider himself talented enough to be a purist. Drawing things, even if it was on a digital tablet according to specifications, would be a hell of a lot better than bagging groceries.

"I'd have to go to school though," he told Cade. "For four years. There's so much to learn. Logo design, web design, animation. And all this software, like Photoshop and other stuff I've never even heard of. And to get into school I'd have to have a portfolio, examples of things I've made. I haven't made anything."

"You've got that picture you drew of Tripp. And the one of Mike."

Arlo grimaced at the reminder. He preferred to keep the sketch of Mike hidden where he wouldn't have to see it, but Cade took it out every night and looked at it as if he could find Mike by ESP if he stared at it long enough.

"Haven't you drawn things before?" Cade asked.

"Yeah, but I got rid of it all. Besides, it was just kid stuff." To get into art school, he probably needed to draw something important, something colossal and stunning. Not superheroes or pencil sketches of his friends or naked men.

"Well, let's pick you up some supplies," Cade said as they boarded the T. "You can start working on your portfolio. It'll give you something to do during the day."

Arlo rode next to Cade in silence, not exactly agreeing with the plans Cade was making for him. He'd always enjoyed school—not like Tripp, who half-assed his way through it—and art school sounded amazing, like the kind of dream he'd given up on having, but Cade was talking about Yale, as if Arlo could possibly get into Yale, or UCLA, which was way on the other side of the country where he would never see Cade again.

"I don't think I want to go to art school."

Cade's face dropped. He'd been more excited about Arlo going to art school than Arlo ever could've been himself.

"Why not?"

Arlo shrugged. Because it was too hard. Because he didn't want to leave Cade. Because he wanted Cade to take care of him, not send him away. But he knew those were wrong answers so he didn't say them.

"You have to do *something*, Arlo."

"I *know*." He slumped down in his seat and stretched his legs out until the bottom of his sneakers touched the metal pole in the middle of the car.

"Now you're acting like a child. Sit up."

It was a dilemma. If he was a child, then Cade didn't want him, but being grown up meant having to leave. Nevertheless, Arlo sat up because he'd been told to, and he could hear from the tone in Cade's voice that he was pushing it.

When they got back to Cade's, he went over to the sketch he'd made of Tripp and looked at it, trying to decide if it was any good or if Tripp had only said so because they were friends.

"Even if you don't decide to go to art school, you have a talent and should use it." Cade hooked his chin over Arlo's shoulder to look at the sketch with him. "Let's pick out some stuff online. What kind of supplies do you need?"

He sat down on the couch and Arlo sat next to him and watched him search for art supplies and pick random, low-quality things because he didn't know what he was doing. Not that Arlo was an expert exactly, but he finally took over, adding items to the cart and checking with Cade after each one to see if it was enough.

Cade started to look uncomfortable, which maybe meant it'd been too much? Arlo removed some things. This all seemed pointless since he wasn't going to art school, but Cade had been so excited about it earlier. Now he only seemed worried.

"Can we do this later?" Arlo asked, not able to figure out what the right answer was.

"Getting sleepy, angel?"

"Yeah." That was better. Cade was smiling again. He put his arm around Arlo, and Arlo cuddled into it, glad he'd managed to postpone his inevitable departure one more day.

Chapter 20 Brixby

Harrison was supposed to be interviewing the security guard who'd left early the night Arlo was abducted, but he called Brixby right before his appointment to beg off.

"This new case I've got is burning through a lot of hours, and considering it's actually billable.... You can handle the interview, can't you?"

Brixby was out on patrol here. Putting up Arlo in his own home was borderline. Going to Hell's Bedroom during off-hours to pursue a case he'd been explicitly told not to work on pushed that line further. Working the case while he was on patrol went so far past the line he couldn't even see the line anymore.

Nevertheless, he told Harrison he would handle the interview. The sick security guard was a good lead, and Harrison probably really needed the billable hours after all the non-billable ones he'd put in on the investigation while Brixby had been collecting a steady paycheck from the Boston PD. Though at the rate he was going, he wouldn't be collecting it much longer.

At the club, he pulled his hat down over his eyes and hoped there wasn't anyone around to make the connection between this officer of the law and the sub who'd been kicked out on Saturday. A uniform served as a pretty good disguise. Few people saw past it. But once he was in Knight's office with the door shut, he stripped off his sunglasses and allowed himself to relax.

"Dobransky's investigation hasn't gone unnoticed," Knight said. He was kicked back behind his desk, splayed wide in an informal pose. "Got this memo today." He slid a piece of paper across his otherwise empty desk.

"Did this come to you specifically?" Brixby rotated the page right-side-up.

"No, not me specifically. It was addressed to All Security Personnel."

Brixby scanned the memo. "In other words, cooperate as little as possible," he summarized.

"That's the gist of it. DDD complies with all local regulations blah blah blah, but privacy is of our utmost concern blah blah blah. There's nothing in there you could fault."

Brixby shook his head. "Sebastian keeps saying these people are smart." Sometimes Sebastian sounded like he outright admired whoever was behind this thing. "That memo reads like something he'd write."

Lawyers. Brixby understood the need for them. No point in arresting criminals if they couldn't be brought to justice. But lawyers had their own priorities, their own agenda. And it wasn't always justice. Sometimes it was just showing off how clever they could be. If Sebastian were going to funnel vulnerable people into virtual slavery, he would know how to skirt the legal lines exactly the way these people were doing.

"You still up for letting me interview the guard who followed Arlo out of here?"

"Denzel. And I never said he followed Arlo. I said he clocked out early that night. I thought Harrison was handling this."

"Something came up. How about the night Jessica disappeared? Did Denzel sign out early that night too?"

"He wasn't even on the roster. Personally, I don't think he's your guy." Knight was the one who'd brought Denzel up in the first place, but he seemed oddly reluctant to let Brixby talk to him now. Was it the memo?

185

"I trust your instincts," Brixby said in an attempt to soothe whatever had Knight's feathers ruffled. "But it can't hurt to ask him what he remembers about that night."

"Yeah, all right. Let me grab him."

Brixby had guessed Denzel was Black from his name, but it wasn't until Knight ushered him into the office and Brixby saw the dreads and the diamond studs through both ears that he understood why Knight had been hesitating. No doubt Knight knew what kind of prejudice existed on the force and would rather not expose Denzel to a uniformed officer. He seated Denzel behind the desk in his own chair—a power move Brixby appreciated.

"I do something wrong?" Denzel asked. He wasn't a big guy, but he shrank in on himself like he was trying to make himself smaller.

"Not at all," Brixby assured him. "I'm just wondering if you have any information that might help us out. There was a young man here—underage. He got reported."

"By me?"

"No, not by you. But we're looking for anyone who might've seen him that night, and it turns out you went home sick around the same time he got tossed out."

"I ain't been out sick since May," Denzel protested. He threw a concerned glance up at Knight who was hovering over him.

"This isn't about your job record, son. It's just what the officer said. Maybe you saw him as you were walking out."

Brixby pushed his phone across the desk, showing off a photo he'd taken of Arlo a couple of days ago. Arlo had been smiling, and his eyes were so big they seemed to take up half the screen. "Look familiar?"

"I was really sick," Denzel said without even glancing at the picture. "Threw up in the bathroom and everything. My wife had to come pick me up."

Brixby tapped his phone and Denzel gave it a quick look like he'd rather not know what was on it, then gave it a second, closer one.

186

"Yeah, I seen him. I didn't talk to him, but I remember that hair under the streetlight."

"Then what?"

"Then nothing. I didn't even know he'd been thrown out. I was just waiting for my wife, trying to hold it together and not barf right there on the street. She pulled up and I got in the car. I wouldn't even recognize him except for the hair."

"Anyone else come out of the club around the same time?"

"People are always in and out. Ask the valet, maybe. He wasn't about to die." Denzel cut his eyes over to Knight, seeking permission to leave, and Knight gave it to him.

"The valet's not an employee," Knight said when Denzel had cleared the room. "Just a dude who takes tickets and his friends who park cars. They handle a couple of restaurants on the block, and we don't stop them from approaching our patrons. He's only here on weekends, but you must've seen him Saturday night."

"I didn't drive Saturday." And he'd been way too busy dealing with Arlo to notice anyone else who might've been lurking around, but the valet was worth talking to. Mike had had a car, which meant he might've used the valet service.

Knight had contact information for Patrick, the guy in charge of the operation, so Brixby swung by what turned out to be his home address. Patrick was quintessentially Boston Irish with fair freckled skin, bright red hair, and an attitude. He didn't recognize Arlo's picture, claiming he saw "like two hundred people a night, c'mon man, that was months ago" and his system was completely manual. He wrote the license plate number and a quick make, model, and color on one half of the ticket, then handed the other half to the owner. When the car was claimed, the two halves of the ticket were matched and thrown in a box. Literally in a box.

"Are these filed by date?" Brixby asked as peered into a

cardboard box swimming in tickets like Patrick was about to hold a raffle.

"They're not filed by anything. When I fill up a box, I get a new box."

Brixby fished out a few tickets. They were dated but not time-stamped. The most they could tell him was which cars had been parked near Hell's Bedroom on the days Arlo and Jessica had been there, but it was something.

"Can I take these?"

"I don't even know why I have them. Can't litter, so they just stack up."

Brixby wrote out a receipt for a pair of cardboard boxes—one from around the time Jessica had disappeared and the other from the general timeframe of Arlo's abduction—and packed them into the back of his squad car. He would ask Arlo to go through them as a sort of peace offering for refusing to let him be part of the sting this weekend. Make him feel like he was contributing.

When he got back to the precinct house, a completely different sort of box was waiting for him. This was one small and wrapped in brown paper.

"Someone proposing?" the desk sergeant joked as Brixby signed for it.

The box *was* about the size of a jeweler's ring box, but nowhere near fancy enough for a diamond, and what Brixby found inside was his own medallion. He flipped it over to verify it was actually his, not a random St. Michael's medal, and saw the raised disc of the GPS tracker Gina had soldered to it.

"Figured I'd get this back to you," Dobransky had written in a gracefully looping hand.

Brixby's fingers closed around the medallion. Then he opened them again, just to make sure it was really there. Stupid to be so emotional over something that had probably cost his mother fifteen dollars, but now that he had it back, he could admit how much he'd missed it. He started to fasten it around his neck, then remembered the attached tracker didn't belong to him and carried it down the hall to Gina's office. She was there with her partner, Lance—the two of them drinking from matching travel mugs with an array of pastries laid out between them.

"Sorry to bug you," Brixby said from the doorway. Gina waved him in. Her hair was down today in a mousy brown tangle, and she was wearing what looked like a radiologist's apron. Was it a bib to protect her from crumbs or a shield to protect her from random explosions? Brixby had learned better than to ask.

"I wanted to give you back your device." He handed over the medallion, not excited about having to part with it again considering he'd just gotten it back.

"You want me to swap out the battery?" she asked as she pried at one edge of the weld with a fingernail.

"No, thanks. The investigation is closed." Officially that was true, and anyway, he intended to hang the medallion around his own neck. He didn't need to track himself. "Go ahead and take it back."

"All right, gimme a minute." Gina fished through a drawer and came out with a chisel. Brixby winced.

"Um, while I've got you guys," he said, trying not to watch what she was doing to his medallion. "Let me pick your brain about something." Going with his theory that they were looking for an insider—someone who knew the players as well as the club—he'd been trying to figure out how a guest would get access to the security system.

"They'd give it to him," Lance said with a shrug.

"Right, but guests can't have phones on the floor, so how are they going to know if someone got pinched fast enough to be out front with a car before the victim leaves the building?"

Lance perked up. He spent a moment pondering the question, then used Gina's whiteboard to diagram a system involving database alerts, Apple watches, and signal boosters. It made Brixby's head spin.

"Or you've got two people," Gina said, taking an eraser

189

to her husband's masterpiece. "One who knows the players, one who has access to the security system. One inside the club, one outside the club. Keep it simple, stupid." She bopped Lance on the head with her eraser. "Tech isn't always the answer."

So there might be two Mikes? Not the greatest news, but it made sense. A club member to point out potential victims, an employee waiting to grab them.

Gina returned the necklace, and he fastened it around his neck, the familiar weight of the medallion settling against his chest like a hug. He put his hand over it and felt bulletproof. Call him superstitious, but this medallion had done its job.

Chapter 21 Arlo

Cade always managed to slip out without waking Arlo up, even though the apartment was tiny. Arlo figured it must be because he slept so well in this comfortable bed. No sagging mattress and no cold bars. It was as if he didn't have any prior experience with sleeping in comfort and was making up for all the time he'd missed.

He rolled over and stretched luxuriously, his body soft and lax except for his cock. Last night, Cade had sucked him to sleep, and his cock was remembering that—how Cade's dark hair had looked between his thighs and the flash of pleasure that'd ripped through him when he came. But his mind was remembering that he'd fallen asleep without reciprocating, which meant he hadn't done anything to earn his place in Cade's bed—this wide, soft space he never wanted to leave.

He pushed his dick down with the heel of his hand and thought about being in the cage until it softened, then showered and made a pot of black coffee. Cade had left another twenty on the table, and he fingered it as he drank his coffee, feeling like he hadn't earned that either. Cade must be tired of frozen food and chili.

He was making the bed—doing his best to prove he was an adult—when Tripp called.

"Let's do something," he said. "I've only got one class today, and I'm going to skip it."

"You shouldn't."

191

"Yeah, but I'm gonna. It's boring. The way the professor drones on makes me want to gouge my eardrums out with a melon baller."

"I don't think you can gouge your eardrums out with a melon baller."

"Then I'll stick a pencil through them. Or just slice off the outside like Vincent Van Gogh."

Arlo giggled. This was why he still liked Tripp even though Tripp had gotten him in major trouble. "Go with the pencil. I don't think you need the outside part to hear."

"Then what's it for?"

"I don't know. You're the one in college."

"I'm not an anatomy major. Anyway, instead of mutilating myself, I'm going to cut class. Cut with me."

"I don't have class. I have a chore." He explained about the valet tickets Cade had brought home. He was determined to do well with it, to make Cade proud of him.

"I'll help," Tripp offered. "I'm on the case too, you know."

Yeah, Arlo knew. Tripp got to go to the club in New York with Sebastian this weekend. Not that Arlo wanted to go anywhere with Sebastian, but he wanted to be part of the team.

By the time Tripp made it over, Arlo had figured out the best way to tackle the project. Step one was to separate out the tickets for the days in question, making one pile for the day he'd been there and another for the day Jessica had been there.

"Then what?" Tripp gathered his legs under him to sit on the floor next to him. There was a mountain of unsorted tickets in front of them.

"Then we compare the two," Arlo said. "We're looking for cars that were there both nights, especially black sedans." Because that was what he remembered Mike driving.

Tripp hadn't started sorting yet. He was too busy fiddling with his phone, cuing up some music Arlo didn't recognize.

"I have Geometry with the lead singer. His shit is super sick."

"He sounds all right."

"Come on, he's awesome. I don't know why he's bothering with Geometry."

"Thinking about his future, I suppose. Cade says I need a future."

Tripp laughed as if Arlo had said something funny. "Dude, you're going to have a future one way or another. Futures aren't optional."

"You know what I mean. He doesn't think I'm ready for a relationship yet."

"Aren't you already in a relationship? He was sure as fuck acting like your Dom the other day. If you aren't getting any sugar, you ought to complain. Come on, you two are fucking around, right?"

"Yeah, but it's temporary, only while I'm stuck here. I sort of forced him into it because of showing up at the club last weekend."

"Told you it would work. And you were all mad at me. Fist bump." Tripp held up his fist and Arlo bumped it rather than let him hang. He wasn't happy about the investigation getting messed up, but he couldn't help being happy about what had happened after. Even if Cade wasn't ready to take him on for real—for forever—at least he was getting a chance.

"So how is he?" Tripp asked. "Does he wear his uniform when he tops you? I would want him to wear his uniform."

"He usually changes when he gets home," Arlo said with a regretful sigh.

"I suppose it's his work clothes, not a costume. Still." Tripp winked knowingly. "How is he?"

"Good."

"That's not exactly a ringing endorsement. If you don't want him, I'll give him a try."

"I want him." No way he was letting Tripp have him.

"Well, all right. I thought so. You were crushing on him

from the get-go, and I don't care what BS he's been feeding you, he's crushing on you right back. So I'm happy for you. You could try to look happy for you too."

"I'm just worried it won't last."

"Nothing ever lasts." Tripp stretched, making his t-shirt ride up over his stomach. "Let's get a pizza."

"There's still a lot of tickets."

They weren't even halfway through the first box, but Tripp said they could keep working while they waited for the pizza to be delivered, and Arlo's mouth watered at the thought. Hot and cheesy, spicy and greasy. But very full of calories.

"I'm not really hungry," he lied, but Tripp was already on the phone ordering. When he hung up, he turned the music back on.

The song was haunting, the tone mournful, the words moaned out with anguish. It would've been a good playlist for his time in the cage. He twisted into a new position, as if he could escape the music by moving.

"What do you think of Sebastian?" Tripp asked as he let a pile of tickets sift through his fingers. Not really looking at them, just playing with them.

Arlo shook his head.

"He's handsome though," Tripp said wistfully. "And rich. Brixby's sure as hell not rich." He looked around the tiny apartment in obvious judgement.

"He's a police officer. Are you going to work on those tickets?"

Tripp went back to sorting with a huff, like it was torture. "Sebastian's a lawyer."

"So you like him?"

"I wouldn't mind doing a scene with him. He's wicked. Everyone wants to play with him because it's the biggest mind fuck going, but he always tells me no. Because I'm too young, supposedly."

"You're older than I am."

"Did he play with you?" Tripp sounded like he was

about to be angry.

Arlo shook his head. "I didn't want to play with him."

Sebastian reminded him too much of Mr. Terzini. Having escaped from that sort of cruelty, he didn't ever want to return to. *Escaped.* He shuddered, the word having more meaning to him than it had before. He'd been held prisoner, and he'd escaped.

The pizza came, and they took a break to eat it. Arlo tried to remind himself that Cade liked it when he ate, but he only made it through a piece and a half before that awful bloated feeling that told him he was going to get fat crept into his stomach. Tripp just shrugged when he said he didn't want any more and said, "More for me."

Arlo went back to sorting tickets on the floor in front of the coffee table, ignoring the smell of hot grease from the table behind him. Eventually, Tripp sat down next to him and started to help again. Between them, they made it through both boxes by mid-afternoon. Then they compared the two piles, searching for matching license plates. They found a dozen of them—four where the car had been black. Arlo took pictures of the matches and texted them to Cade. He got back a kissy face emoji that made him stupidly happy. He'd spent almost six hours sorting tickets, but a single emoji felt like sufficient payment.

"Oh my God," Tripp said when he stood up. "I may never walk again. Dude, that was brutal."

Arlo climbed gingerly to his feet. He wasn't as cramped as after a day in the cage, but it was a similar feeling. His limbs needed to learn how to move freely again.

"Let's go somewhere," Tripp said.

"Where?"

"Anywhere. Fuck. Is it still daytime?"

Arlo rolled his eyes. It was only three. But Cade would be home in a couple of hours, and he hadn't even started thinking about dinner.

"I have to go grocery shopping." He picked up the twenty Cade had left him and retrieved the key from the top of the dresser.

"What? Why?"

"So I can make dinner."

"Oh my God, you're turning into such a service sub."
Tripp draped an arm over his shoulders, his lean frame
surprisingly heavy. "I'll never be a service sub. Can you
imagine?"

"But..."

"But what?"

"If your master says to do something, then you'd do it,
right?"

"First of all, I'm not having any master. A Dom, sure.
Especially if he's a sadistic fuck like Sebastian." Tripp
wiggled his eyebrows. "But no master. Can you see me
letting someone tell me what to do every minute of my life?
Obviously not."

No, but maybe that was why Tripp didn't have a Dom—
because he was a sucky sub, which Arlo was trying not to
be.

"Cade's letting me stay here. I'm making him dinner to
pay him back. He didn't *tell* me to."

"Then say no more. Let's do it. Two dudes going grocery
shopping together, as they do."

Now he felt like Tripp was making fun of him, but he
didn't care. Tripp could suck it. He only cared about making
Cade happy. He locked up carefully and led Tripp down the
staircase and out onto the porch where that woman was
sweeping, like always. As if a porch could get that dirty
every day.

"Who was that?" Tripp asked as they headed down the
sidewalk.

"The landlady, Mrs. Zhao. I think she's spying on me."

"Why would she spy on you?"

"I don't know, but she's always watching me." He cast
a glance over his shoulder and yep, she was watching him.
"She said it was okay for me to stay here, but now she
probably thinks you're staying too."

"Ooh," Tripp said. "Officer Brixby and his bevy of boys. I like it."

At the store down the street, which was a small place jumbled with one of everything so that potholders hung in front of gravy mix and a salad spinner sat on top of the shelf above the lettuce, Arlo poked dispiritedly through the aisles.

"I don't know how to make very many things," he admitted to Tripp, who was trailing along behind him, picking up every package and squeezing the produce as if he would actually be able to tell a good tomato from a bad one.

"I don't know how to make *anything*," Tripp said. "I've got a meal plan at school. But that's what recipes are for, right?" He scrolled through his phone and came up with a bunch of recipes that would take hours—and probably skills—to cook, not to mention more than twenty dollars' worth of ingredients.

"So go with the frozen food option again," Tripp said. "Those enchiladas came out okay, right?"

"I guess." It wasn't ideal, but a glance at the time said he'd better do something, so he picked up a frozen lasagna and eggs for the brownie mix that was still sitting in a plastic baggie on the counter. A homemade dessert would make up for a frozen dinner, right? Although maybe brownie mix didn't count as a homemade dessert. Maybe he just wasn't cut out for this sub business.

"What's got you so down again?" Tripp asked as they walked back to the house. "You're like a roller coaster of emotions lately. Is it because you're traumatized?"

"I don't think so." More like he'd been woken up to reality and didn't care for it much.

Mrs. Zhao was weeding one of the flower beds when they got back, even though Arlo couldn't see any weeds there. She looked up as they climbed the steps, acknowledging their presence with a grunt. Tripp nudged him as if he ought to do something.

"Um, hi, Mrs. Zhao. This is my friend Tripp. He's not staying or anything."

In fact, Tripp should probably leave instead of come inside with him. He needed to get dinner ready. But Tripp stopped and extended his hand to Mrs. Zhao like he wanted to shake. She glanced at her dirty gloves, then slowly peeled one off and extended a hand in return.

"Is this your house?" Tripp asked her.

"And that one." She indicated the house on the left. "And that one," she added, indicating the house on the right.

"Wow, that's a lot to take care of. Seems like you've got it under control, though."

She nodded. Arlo tugged on the hem of Tripp's t-shirt to try to get him to move along, but he didn't budge.

"Hey, I bet you know how to cook."

"Because I'm a woman or because I'm Chinese?"

"I didn't say you knew how to cook Chinese," Tripp protested. "But I'll bet you do."

"Maybe," she admitted with something like a smile.

"Arlo needs cooking lessons." He pulled Arlo in front of him, as if Arlo weren't standing right there in plain sight. Well, maybe he'd been cowering behind Tripp just a little. Mrs. Zhao always looked so serious and disapproving.

"I'm sure you're busy," Arlo said.

"Do I look busy? I sweep the porch every day." She snorted, laughing at herself. "I retired last year. Now I've got nothing to do except take care of my property."

"No kids?" Tripp asked in a totally nosy way. "You should adopt Arlo," he suggested when Mrs. Zhao shook her head. "He needs a mother."

"Who says I want kids? If I wanted kids, I'd have kids. Your friend has antiquated ideas about women," she told Arlo.

"Sorry."

"How about you?"

He shook his head. His main approach to women was

to not think about them very hard one way or another.

"Then I could teach you to cook."

He said thanks even though the idea made his heart beat too fast. Mrs. Zhao had smiled at Tripp, but Arlo still couldn't tell whether she liked *him*.

"You can do it tomorrow," Tripp called over his shoulder as Arlo shoved him through the doorway. "Now you're all set," he told Arlo as they climbed the stairs together. "You can be service sub extraordinaire, assuming that's what you want."

"I'm more of a Daddy's boy." It felt like an awkward thing to say, but he and Cade had spelled it out in that contract the other day, so he got to claim it.

"Dude, that's so you," Tripp said without any judgement at all. "I'm glad you've got everything figured out."

He didn't have everything figured out. Not by a long shot. But he was starting to figure out some of it, and those were the parts he wanted to keep.

Chapter 22 Brixby

Brixby ran the license plates Arlo had sent him, wincing at yet another use of department resources for this non-department investigation, but his search turned up a couple of familiar names.

"Nicholas Popinjay," he told Harrison over the phone. "Black Cadillac, there both nights. Not surprising he drives a nice car." Rich fucker.

"Maybe not a surprise he was there both nights either," Harrison said. "I asked Cash about him back when we were looking for Arlo. He's down there most weekends, apparently. No particular sub, just whoever he can get his hands on, but Cash says he does all right. Straight women have no taste."

"Well, obviously he warrants a closer look."

"Who else you got?"

"There's a dozen names on the list, but only one other I recognize. Bob Jones. Drives an electric blue Kia Cerato."

"Huh," Harrison said, which summed up how Brixby felt. Of course Jones had been there both nights. He was practically an institution. And of course his car was electric blue. "But Jones can't be Mike," Harrison said. "Arlo knows him."

No, Jones couldn't be Mike, and Brixby couldn't imagine Popinjay ferrying anyone to the bus station, but he was still looking for that inside connection.

"I feel like this is our own people," he told Harrison.

"Maybe DDD is using the security system to coordinate the kidnappings, but someone in the scene has to be sussing out the victims' kinks. Otherwise Mike's offers wouldn't be so convincing."

"Send me the list," Harrison said. "I'll run it past Cash. He can at least sort out which of them are Doms for us."

Brixby forwarded it over, then signed out and headed home, hopeful they would find Mike this weekend even though it might mean getting called on the carpet again. Or worse than getting called on the carpet. But when his door popped open before he could put his key in the lock and a warm, curly-haired boy flung himself into his arms with a flurry of kisses, he couldn't be sorry about continuing to work the case. The people who'd preyed on Arlo had to be caught and punished.

"You're home!"

He was definitely home—this place where Arlo waited for him. "How was your day, angel?"

"It was good. Tripp helped me with the tickets, and then I made lasagna. Well, the frozen kind. But it's not ready yet."

"That's fine. It'll give me time to shower and change."

"Yeah, but, um, remember how you said we could do it with your uniform on someday?" Arlo toyed with the buttons on Brixby's shirt, looking up at him through his eyelashes like a flirt.

Brixby glanced down at his uniform. It wasn't the sexiest thing in his own mind, but if it made Arlo hot, he could work with it. His cock was already hardening, and everything he'd been worrying about on the way home had flown right out of his head. Arlo on his knees was the solution to any problem.

He brought Arlo over to the rug that marked off his living area, so Arlo's precious knees wouldn't get bruised, and snapped his fingers.

"Let's see what you can do."

Arlo hit his knees fast. He reached for Brixby's fly,

grinning as if Brixby's cock was the best treat he could imagine being offered. He cooed as he pulled out two handfuls of cock, the smallness of his fingers showing off Brixby's cock to its best advantage. Arlo opened up to swallow it down, but Brixby held him back with a palm on his forehead, making Arlo wait with his mouth and eyes wide while he traced a thumb around those plump lips.

"You have such a pretty, cock-sucking pout."

Light humiliation of the complimentary kind was on the table, and what he'd just said was no lie. Those pillowy lips were made to cushion a cock. There was even a strand of drool forming at one corner of Arlo's mouth, as though he couldn't contain himself. Brixby caught it with his thumb and fed it back to him, separating Arlo's lips wider as he did.

"Like a filthy angel."

Innocence ruined. It was gorgeous. Arlo was gorgeous.

"Wait for it," he warned as he shifted a hand onto his cock and tilted it in Arlo's direction. "Only take what you're given."

He fed just the tip in and let it rest on the bed of Arlo's outstretched tongue. It fit perfectly there, cupped and supported, tingling against the warm, wet flesh. He eased it in and out, teasing himself as much as Arlo.

Arlo was hard, his erection unmistakable in the silky fabric of his track pants, pressing straight out at Brixby like a police baton, and the longer Brixby made him wait with his mouth open, the more he drooled. He was like a puppy dog, his hair wild like he'd been rolling around in a pile of autumn leaves and his eyes big and wet. He was as eager as a puppy too, but behaving so beautifully that Brixby had to lean down and press a kiss against the wide stretch of his mouth.

"Such a good boy." His approval had Arlo happily opening his mouth again, asking for the cock Brixby had taken from him, so Brixby gave him a bit more this time— the head and a few inches of shaft until he brushed against the back of Arlo's throat.

"Can you swallow?"

Arlo didn't respond except to obey. The muscles of his throat massaged the head of Brixby's cock until Brixby was deep enough he felt like he ought to draw back, but Arlo grabbed him by the hips and pulled him even deeper.

Fuck. Brixby steadied himself with a hand in Arlo's hair, which produced a moan that had Brixby swearing again as it vibrated up and down his shaft.

"Go on, Arlo. Suck me dry." He stopped trying to control the blowjob, other than by keeping his hands in Arlo's hair to give Arlo that touch of pain he'd said he enjoyed. He didn't want to think about why someone Arlo's age was already so good at deep throating. He was too busy enjoying it, and Arlo seemed to be enjoying it as well.

"I love your cock," he said as he slobbered all over it. "I love *you*."

If Brixby were in a more rational state of mind, he might call a halt to this so they could have a talk about what Arlo had just said. He was eighteen and had been recently traumatized. He couldn't be in love. And Brixby shouldn't allow him to imagine he was. Or to believe Brixby loved him in return, even though he did. This boy had only been in his life a matter of weeks, and already Brixby couldn't tolerate the thought of letting him go. Everything he'd told Arlo about their contract being temporary—and not really a contract—was a lie. He wanted to lock Arlo up for good.

Ugh. No. Not lock him up. That was why he kept fighting the part of him that insisted Arlo belonged to him, that he was more than Arlo's temporary caretaker or a good introduction to ethical kink. Arlo ought to go out and explore a variety of D/s relationships, learn what worked for him, become part of the community and understand its guiding principles. Definitely he needed to develop a sense of self-worth strong enough to believe he had the right to state his preferences. Brixby didn't ever want to look back on their time together and see himself as a marginally better version of Terzini.

But his dick was hard, Arlo was kneeling at his feet, and Arlo's words had shot straight from his ears to his heart, coloring his world with the awareness of loving and being loved in return. Arlo's hopeful eyes looked up at him like he was a hero, and he wanted to be Arlo's hero. Fate had dropped the perfect partner right in his lap. Was he supposed to resist? Or could he, maybe, just enjoy?

"Too much talking," he said, since he couldn't respond to Arlo's inappropriate declaration. "Put your mouth back on my cock."

Arlo's grin lit up the tiny apartment. "Yes, Officer Brixby."

Arlo swallowed him down again, taking more than Brixby would ever ask him to take. He tried to monitor Arlo's reactions even as his own went through the roof, until there was nothing in the world beyond this space where they came together. Street noises faded, lights dimmed. Only the soft silk of Arlo's hair and the warm suction of Arlo's mouth registered as he came buckets down Arlo's throat.

Arlo spluttered, and Brixby switched instantly from a controlling grip to a supportive one as he cupped Arlo's chin, tilting it up so he could look into Arlo's eyes and make sure he was all right. He found Arlo a little hazy but otherwise unharmed with come dripping down his chin. He smudged it into Arlo's mouth, and Arlo accepted it with a grateful swipe of his tongue.

"You look good covered in come. One of these days I'll have to tie you down and come all over you."

"Is that on the list?"

"It could be." He smiled, glad Arlo understood it was okay to joke with him. There was an impishness in his eyes today, coexisting with that innate obedience Brixby couldn't resist poking at.

"You can get up now. I'm all done."

Arlo looked down at the lump in his pants, then glanced

back up with a scowl.

"Oh, did you want something too?" Brixby asked innocently. "I don't remember putting reciprocation on the list."

Arlo stalked over to the wall where their not-contract had been tacked up and wrote "Arlo comes too" in big letters under the last bullet point.

"When Officer Brixby says so," Brixby added, because he might want to play that game someday.

"What does it mean if I write something and you just contradict it?"

"It means we negotiate. For instance, I could torment you for a while."

"I guess that's okay." Arlo said with a pout.

"Or I might not want you to come at all—to be a good little angel who obeys me."

"I can obey you. I want to." Arlo placed a wavering check mark next to "when Officer Brixby says so" then dropped the pen.

"But tonight, I'm going to let you come." Brixby moved in until he had Arlo's back pressed against the wall. "Probably. If you can manage it."

"I can manage it."

"Shouldn't you be calling me Officer?" He liked this flustered version of Arlo—neither docile nor bratty, just horny and eager.

"Yes, Officer Brixby. Do you want me to kneel for you?"

"I'll tell you what I want you to do."

Maybe he'd been too lenient with Arlo up to this point, spoiling him because of the hardships he'd been through, thinking he was too precious to be pushed. But Arlo was coming alive in front of him now, as though those words Arlo shouldn't have said and Brixby shouldn't have wanted to hear had unlocked something in him. Arlo was really playing—into what they were doing, not appeasing him out of fear but not resisting either. He was everything Brixby had ever imagined in a sub, effortlessly submissive, sliding into the role like it was a comfort to him to fill it. All Brixby had to do was take charge.

"This is how you're going to come. Right up against me like this."

Arlo dropped a hand toward his cock, but Brixby caught it.

"Not with your hands."

"With *your* hands, Officer Brixby?"

"Not with anyone's hands. Just like this." He urged Arlo's groin into his thigh.

Arlo stiffened at the contact but he quickly caught the motion, humping Brixby like they were on a dance floor and he'd taken a big dose of Ecstasy and maybe done some poppers.

"Can you come like this?" His own cock was hardening again, enjoying the byproduct of Arlo's frenzied churning.

"I don't know," Arlo huffed. He threw his head back, jutting his hips more prominently forward. Brixby dipped his head to find Arlo's earlobe with his teeth, giving Arlo a splash of pain to spike his pleasure. Arlo keened, his tone ratcheting higher as his torso gyrated faster.

"So hot," Arlo mumbled.

Brixby didn't know if that meant Arlo was enjoying the scene or if he was complaining about the warmth their bodies generated against each other. They were sticky with sweat, but he wanted Arlo sticky with come too, so he pulled him in tighter and ground back harder until Arlo gave a ferocious whine and started jerking with the throes of orgasm.

Brixby let Arlo grind out every last bit of pleasure until he slumped, exhausted and limp in his arms. He was still whimpering, little aftershocks hitting him, and they were so hot against each other, so intimate—Arlo wet with perspiration and come after having humped himself to climax against Brixby's leg like a wanton animal. It was glorious. So good that Brixby had to have him again.

He carried Arlo to the bed and took his time undressing

him, enjoying every damp piece of clothing he removed, then rolled Arlo onto his knees in a tucked position and smoothed a hand over his trembling back.

"I'm going to fuck you, angel."

"Yes, Officer Brixby."

He'd only been inside Arlo a few times before, but when he slid inside tonight, it feel like coming home.

"You want to come again?"

"Uh huh."

"What do you say?" Brixby prompted.

"Uh huh, Officer Brixby."

Brixby grinned. Fuck, he really did love this boy, could imagine having him under him always. He drilled Arlo faster. Arlo's body unfurled as he started to push back, chasing his own pleasure instead of just serving pleasure up. Brixby slid a hand under Arlo to find his cock, which was sticky from his last orgasm and hard with his impending orgasm. Arlo squealed as Brixby fucked him until they rocked their way to another climax. Mutual this time, leaving them both left drained.

Brixby peeled off his uniform and threw it in the basket for the laundry service, then tossed his boxers into the regular laundry basket. Dimly he wondered if it would be rude to show up at Francesca's with laundry tomorrow.

Arlo was languid, spread out over the top of the blanket because Brixby hadn't taken the time to push it out of the way. They were a pair, the two of them. At moments like this, he remembered he was only six years older than Arlo, hardly an adult himself. What business did he have keeping someone who needed as much guidance as Arlo did? Not much, if he were being honest.

"You're wearing a necklace," Arlo said when Brixby pulled him into his chest. Arlo's cheek had come to rest on the medallion. Brixby fingered it, touching both the cool metal and the silky warmth of Arlo's skin.

"My mother gave me this when I graduated from the police academy. It's Saint Michael, the patron saint of law enforcement. It's supposed to keep me safe."

"Do you think it works?"

"Worked for you." He told Arlo the story of how they'd tracked him.

"I can't believe so many people were trying to find me. It's nice Tripp missed me, but all the rest of you..." Arlo ducked his head into Brixby's chest.

"You were worth finding. Everyone is, but especially subs because they've entrusted us with their well-being. That's why this investigation is so important to Cash, and why Sebastian helps even though he's sort of an asshole about it. The trust subs give us is sacred. It should never be abused."

Arlo lay silent, the soft fan of his eyelashes gold against his cheek. He curled his fingers around the medallion, joining them to Brixby's. "I don't want anyone else to end up in a cage like I did. I don't want them to be taken advantage of like I was."

"We're going to make sure of that," Brixby promised. He just hoped it was a promise he could keep.

Chapter 23 Arlo

Arlo woke up in another happy haze, his body lax and his mind full of memories, but it didn't take long before negative thoughts intruded. In the heat of their encounter last night, he hadn't noticed that Cade hadn't said "I love you" back, but he couldn't stop fixating on that now. Cade didn't love him. Cade wouldn't keep him. Arlo had been doing everything he could think of to convince Cade to let him stay, but it hadn't worked. He hardly knew what more to try.

After he'd finished his cup of black coffee and used the bathroom twice, he tromped downstairs. Mrs. Zhao was out in the front yard, as always. She raised a hand as he approached—the first sign of friendliness he'd ever gotten from her—but once the two of them were facing each other, he couldn't figure out what to say. Tripp made talking to people seem so easy. Arlo didn't know how to ask for the cooking lesson he'd been promised, and Mrs. Zhao didn't volunteer anything, so he ended up walking away.

First he went to the bank. He'd been saving every penny he got since he was fifteen in hopes of someday being able to live somewhere other than with his parents. He'd tried to avoid using any of it while he was living on the street, hoping to have enough left to put down a security deposit once he turned eighteen, but he withdrew some of it now. Maybe if he took Cade out for dinner with his own money instead of using Cade's money to make dinner, he would seem grown up enough to be in a relationship.

Back at Cade's apartment, he slunk past Mrs. Zhao who was in the process of shaping a bush into a perfect square, as if bushes were meant to be square, and up the stairs where he collected all the dirty clothes he could find into a basket piled so high he could hardly see over it. He managed to get it downstairs without killing himself, out past Mrs. Zhao's attempts at topiary, but he didn't get far before he realized he had no idea where the closest laundromat was.

"You, boy!"

Of all the people he didn't need calling him boy, Mrs. Zhao was way at the top of the list. He picked up the basket he'd put down so he could Google laundromats and resolutely continued marching.

"Boy! I forgot your name. Come back, boy!"

He came back. Most of the way. "Arlo," he told her. "My name is Arlo."

"It's a funny name. I forgot it."

"It's not funny. It's just... uncommon." Unless you were a folk singer. Or a dog. "What do you want? I'm on my way to the laundromat."

"Officer Brixby sends his uniforms out." She nodded at the basket, which was overflowing with navy blue shirts and pants.

"I was going to wash them for him," he said, but she shook her head sternly enough that he understood he'd been about to make a mistake.

Uniforms probably needed to be dry cleaned or starched or something. With a sigh, he went upstairs and sorted the laundry into two piles—uniforms and not uniforms. Back downstairs, he marched straight out to the sidewalk, trying not to pay any attention to whatever Mrs. Zhao was doing except that what she was doing was standing there with her arms crossed looking smug.

"Now what's wrong?"

"There's laundry in the basement. You're not very good

at asking for help, are you?"

"Yeah, well, you're not very good at giving it. I thought you were going to teach me to cook."

"All day you're in and out, in and out. No time to cook, I guess."

"I have time." He shifted his weight from one foot to the other. The basket was lighter without Cade's uniforms in it, but not so light that he wasn't feeling the effects of carrying it up and down the stairs twice. "Is there really laundry in the basement?"

"I'll show you. Then we'll go to the grocery store."

To get to the basement, they had to go around to the back of the house through a separate entrance, and how was Arlo supposed to have known that? He felt better about having been so oblivious. But the machines were coin-operated and there weren't any bill changers, which left him and Mrs. Zhao glowering at each other in mutual disgruntlement. She thought that if you were doing laundry, you ought to have a pocketful of quarters, and he thought that if you expected people to feed your machines with quarters, you ought to give them a way of getting said quarters. Besides, who used money anymore?

"Real laundromats take iPay."

"I'm not running a laundromat."

"Then maybe you should make the machines free."

"People would abuse them."

"How? By doing laundry they didn't really need to do?"

She shrugged. "Half loads are bad for the environment."

Arlo rolled his eyes. "Maybe we should forget the whole thing."

"You give up too easily. Typical of your generation."

She scowled at him, and he scowled back because he wasn't a quitter. A quitter would've run away from Mr. Terzini after that first incident with the stairs. Arlo had put up with a lot to make things work with his former master. He could put up with Mrs. Zhao in order to make things work with Cade. So he considered his options.

"We'll go to the store," he said. "We can get change there."

Mrs. Zhao gave him a look he could almost call approving, and together they walked back up the dark and narrow stairwell to the ground floor where Mrs. Zhao surprised him by leading him a few driveways down to an aging Honda hatchback in a dull shade of brown. He'd expected to walk to the neighborhood market, but by the time they were finished loading up their cart at the Asian market she drove them to, he understood why that wouldn't have worked. Dumpling wrappers, bok choi, Sichuan peppercorns.

"Are these really spicy?" he asked, shaking the bottle of pinkish pebbles from the passenger's seat. He didn't mind a little bite himself, but he didn't know how Cade felt about spicy food. Maybe he should've asked before he decided to cook Chinese.

"Not spicy." Mrs. Zhao commanded her car with the same ferocious determination she did everything. Whether it was a traffic light or a shrub, she fought it and won. "They'll make your mouth numb though."

"Why would I want that?" Why would he want either of them to have a numb mouth? They needed their mouths.

"Because they taste good. Are you afraid of a little numbness?"

"No." He put the bottle back into the bag full of ingredients that'd cost him more than he'd planned to spend. It would've been cheaper to stick to his original plan of taking Cade out for dinner, but Mrs. Zhao said a bottle of soy sauce was an investment he would use over and over. And this was *good* soy sauce apparently because when he'd tried to tell her Cade already had soy sauce, she'd put the bottle in the cart anyway.

When they got back to her house, she left him on the lawn while she went inside and came back out with a huge copper wok, which alarmed him all over again. He had no idea how to use a wok. This was such a terrible idea, and it

212

was all Tripp's fault. Tripp's and Mrs. Zhao's because she treated every attempt he made to back out of this plan like he was a deserter who deserved to be court martialed.

With Mrs. Zhao carrying the wok, which looked big enough to feed a family of ten, and Arlo toting their shopping bags, they climbed the stairs to Cade's apartment and he let them in. Then he ran downstairs to start the washer and got back just in time to hear a loud crack. What if the human trafficking ring had come to recapture him and was torturing Mrs. Zhao to learn his whereabouts?

He rushed into the kitchen to save her but found it empty aside from Mrs. Zhao, who was whacking the counter with a rolling pin.

"That's not how rolling pins work."

"Very funny. I'm crushing these." She gave the counter another violent whack, and this time he noticed the plastic baggy full of pink peppercorns sitting on it. "Wash your hands." She nodded toward the sink. "They're about to get dirty."

As long as they didn't get crushed. Arlo dutifully washed his hands, then followed her directions to mix the ground pork with a whole host of other ingredients, including the crushed peppercorns.

"Like making meatloaf," he observed. He'd never made meatloaf, but he remembered his mother making it when he was small enough that playing in meat had looked like fun.

Mrs. Zhao snorted at the suggestion that her dumpling filling was anything like meatloaf and directed him to wash his hands again.

"Now the hard part." She took a scoop of filling and placed it in the middle of one of the dumpling wrappers they'd bought. Thank God she wasn't trying to teach him to make dumpling dough from scratch. "Watch," she said sharply as she folded the wrapper in half and pinched the edges together until they were decoratively crinkled.

"Plunk, fold, smoosh. Got it."

213

"You try." She stepped aside to give him room.

Plunk. Fold. Smoosh. His dumpling didn't look as pretty—the edge more a mash than a crinkle—but it was functionally the same thing. Mrs. Zhao shook her head at it.

"We're just going to eat them," he said. "They don't need to win a beauty contest."

"You have to *boil* these."

"And?"

"When they're badly made, they fall apart." She made exaggerated roiling motions with her hands, like she was trying to imitate boiling water, then exploded them with a vocal whoosh. "All the filling seeps out, sinks to the bottom of the pot. You get a limp, empty dumpling instead of a plump, tasty dumpling. If you want your dumplings to survive, you have to learn to crimp. But no, he's too impatient to learn anything." She shook her head in disapproval.

Arlo sighed. "So teach me how to crimp."

"What was I doing? But then someone thought they didn't need lessons." She nudged him out of the way because the counter space was so small only one of them could stand directly in front of it at a time and did her plunk, fold, smoosh routine again. This time Arlo paid more attention to the smoosh part and saw that it was more a series of delicate pinches than a smoosh. That was why her edges were crinkled while his had been a flat mash.

He must've made a dozen dumplings before she finally pronounced one of them good enough to survive being boiled, but that didn't stop her from hovering over him as he went through the rest of them. She was obviously happiest when she was bossing him around, and he didn't mind being bossed. He'd found her intimidating when she was silently scowling at him, but now that she was giving him orders he could follow, he knew how to make her happy.

"You can freeze what you don't need right away," she

said as he surveyed the quantity of dumplings they'd made—far more than he and Cade needed for dinner tonight. "Four minutes fresh, eight minutes frozen. They'll float to the top when they're ready. You can boil water, right?"

"Now who's being funny?" He gave her a little bump with his hip.

He was feeling kind of proud. His dumplings were plump and pretty, just like they were supposed to be, and Mrs. Zhao had helped him make two sauces to serve with them. Cade was sure to be impressed. Cade acted like everything Arlo did was a big deal, even when it was just frozen lasagna or making the bed, though none of it ever convinced him Arlo was ready for a real, permanent relationship. Which meant this probably wouldn't either.

"Don't stop smiling now," Mrs. Zhao said. "Finally, he was smiling, and already it's gone."

"As if you ever smile."

"I'm old," she said with a beleaguered sigh. "What do you have to be unhappy about?"

She had no idea, and most of it he wasn't going to tell her, but he told her the main thing. "Officer Brixby wants me to move out."

"He'll say different when he sees these." She gestured at the tray of dumpling she was covering in tinfoil. "Who could resist a good dumpling? You're a good dumpling." She pinched his cheek with her strong fingers.

Aw. Arlo smiled at her, even though the gesture suggested she thought of him as a baby, just like Cade did.

"Officer Brixby thinks I need to be more grown-up. Older and, like, independent."

"Independent is good." She slid the dumplings into the refrigerator. "If you're independent, it means you're in the relationship because you want to be, not because you have to be. Maybe he thinks you only love him for his apartment."

If Arlo were going to love someone for their apartment, it would be Sebastian. But for the first time, he turned the situation around and saw it from Cade's point of view. Everyone kept saying how important it was for him not to depend on Cade—as if he couldn't just walk out the door and go back to the streets—but no one had ever said anything about how his dependence on Cade might feel to Cade. Maybe Cade thought Arlo wasn't choosing him, that Arlo had gotten stuck with him the way he had with Mr. Terzini.

That was sort of how it'd started. He'd chosen Cade's apartment over Sebastian's condo or the safehouse, but he hadn't had a lot of choices, and he hadn't even fully realized he had a right to choose. But a lot had changed since then, and he definitely chose Cade now. The apartment, he didn't care about. He liked being here, but if living somewhere else would make Cade understand that Arlo was choosing him above everyone else in the whole world, then Arlo would do that.

"Do you have anywhere else I could live?" he asked Mrs. Zhao. "Like a cheap place. Cheaper even than this." He was already calculating what he would be able to afford. Now that he was eighteen and had ID, he could get a job, but it wouldn't pay much.

"This place isn't cheap," Mrs. Zhao said like he'd insulted her. "How much could you pay?"

He named his price, and she shook her head.

"You need a roommate. Many, many roommates. But maybe..."

"Maybe?"

"Maybe you could stay at my house. I have three bedrooms—two more than I need. Would you be trouble?"

"Not even a little," Arlo promised. "I'd cook, if you taught me, and clean. I don't make any noise. I'd hardly even be home." Between working as much as he could and hopefully being allowed to date Cade, he wouldn't have time to be under her feet.

Mrs. Zhao nodded. "First, get a job," she said with a wag of her finger. "I don't do charity."

216

"I don't need charity." He could easily get a job at one of the bigger grocery stores in town. On Monday, he would go out and look. Cade was going to be so pleased. He flung his arms around Mrs. Zhao, who pinched his cheek again before disengaging.

"Hey, wait," he said as she picked up her purse to leave. "We didn't use the wok." He was relieved but also a little disappointed.

"That's for the bok choi. It needs to be fresh, so you'll make it yourself."

"But I don't know how to use a wok."

"Oh, suddenly he doesn't know everything. Watch a YouTube video. I have work to do."

"What, like alphabetize the blades of grass? Everything in the yard is perfect already."

"How do you think it gets that way?"

Arlo couldn't tell whether she was joking or not. Living with Mrs. Zhao was going to be either fun or terrifying, but either way, it wasn't going to be boring.

Chapter 24 Brixby

Thank God it was Friday. Brixby could hardly wait to pick up Arlo and bring him over to Francesca's. He was babysitting two full-grown women this weekend and intended to treat the time more like a getaway than a job.

"Hey!" The duty officer waved him down as he was about to slip out. "You were looking for overtime, right? I've got an overnight flagging gig here."

Overnight was perfect. That was where the money was. "When?"

"Tonight and tomorrow. I know it's short notice, but I got some call-outs."

The short notice explained why Brixby's name had come up on the duty roster when it was usually too far down the seniority rankings for plum assignments like this, but he had plans this weekend. Important plans.

"I really can't," he said, knowing it wouldn't endear him to the sergeant who had a spot to fill. "Another time?"

"We'll see." Which meant he could expect his name to fall even farther down the list. "Captain was asking for you, by the way. Said you should swing by before you left."

That didn't bode well either. Wondering which of his misdeeds he was about to be called out for, he took the stairs to Captain Murphy's office on the top floor.

"I got a phone call," Captain Murphy said, coming straight to the point. His expression was so stony Brixby had an inkling that pissing off the duty officer was going to be the least of his problems. "From a lawyer representing a company called DDD. You know who that is?"

"They own Hell's Bedroom."

"That's right, Brixby. They own Hell's Bedroom. And this lawyer wants to know why I had a uniform on their premises on Wednesday. So tell me, why did I have a uniform on their premises on Wednesday?"

"Just following up on something about the case."

"The case I expressly told you not to work on?"

Brixby scrambled for an excuse. The only lifeline he could come up with was the one Dobransky had extended to him. "You said I should coordinate with the FBI. Agent Dobransky's back in San Francisco. He asked if I could handle something for him locally. I thought it'd be okay, sir."

Captain Murphy looked like he knew a liar when he saw one. Slooowly, he reached for his phone. "Let's just check on that, shall we?"

Brixby swallowed. He hadn't taken a seat because Captain Murphy hadn't offered him one, so he stood at attention, not allowing himself to fidget as Captain Murphy called the FBI on speaker and got put through to Dobransky.

"Did you ask my officer to run an errand for you?"

There was a pause, during which Brixby mentally crossed his fingers. Dobransky didn't owe him anything, but he came through anyway.

"That was the, uh, interview with the security guard at Hell's Bedroom, right?"

Brixby exhaled in relief. Thank God he'd been keeping Dobransky up to date like he'd promised to.

"Is there an issue, Captain?"

"I'd appreciate a heads-up the next time you ask one of my officers to do something for you."

"Of course, of course. My apologies. The case is really heating up out here. We're all going to come out of this looking good, Captain. Nothing to worry about."

Captain Murphy disconnected the call and eyed Brixby. "Next time a Fed asks you to do something, you clear it with me first. I don't need any fucking lawyers breathing down my neck without warning."

"Yes, sir." Brixby saluted his way out of the office. He walked down the long hall and into the back stairway, relieved and freaked out all at once. In the stairwell, he put a call through to Dobransky.

"Dude, I owe you."

"Not sure how much more I can do for you," Dobransky warned. "I'm not running that sting you've got going this weekend, and I can't pretend I am."

"I get it." If they caught Mike, they'd have to book him so he could be brought to trial. Brixby couldn't just kill the man, much as he might like to. But an arrest would mean his involvement in another unauthorized operation was going to come to light.

He hung up on Dobransky and sat down on the steps, trying to figure out what to do. If he wanted to continue his career with the Boston PD, he should call Harrison and tell him he couldn't be involved in the sting this weekend. Go back to the duty officer and ask if the overtime opportunity was still available. Work his way up through the ranks and increase his earning potential. Laugh at his co-workers' jokes about hot chicks and men who didn't meet their definition of manhood. Put in his time in hopes of someday making detective, and date on the sly until he was ready to come out on some theoretical someday.

Which all sounded awful. He would love to tell Captain Murphy and the whole Boston PD to go fuck themselves, but if he didn't have a job, what did he have to offer Arlo? Officer Brixby in the hot uniform would be gone. Cade Brixby, Private Investigator, would barely earn enough to support himself. He would need to get a roommate—the paying kind, not the angelic refugee kind—and it would be the end of any ideas he had about putting Arlo through art school. Arlo deserved a future.

On the other hand, what kind of future would Arlo have if they didn't eliminate Mike and anyone else who might be a threat to him?

Brixby didn't storm back into Captain Murphy's office and offer his resignation, but he didn't stop at the desk and take the overtime assignment either. He just drove home, caught between the safe answer and the right one.

"I made dumplings!" Arlo exclaimed the moment Brixby walked in the door. Arlo's cheeks were rosy, and his eyes were so bright they shone straight into Brixby's tired soul. Arlo showed him a tray full of Chinese dumplings sitting on the kitchen counter next to a pot of boiling water. His face expressed a need for approval, so Brixby gave it to him. It was so much easier to be Arlo's Dom than to be anything else.

"You made these?"

"Mrs. Zhao helped me. But I'm going to do this part myself." He indicated the wok on the other burner where oil was starting to smoke.

"Lemme change, and I'll give you a hand."

"I've got it. Grab a beer and relax."

"Why do we have beer?" He opened the refrigerator to verify that they did, in fact, have beer. "You're underage."

"Mrs. Zhao helped me with that too. I didn't drink any, promise."

"It's fine."

It was weird. Both that Arlo had gone shopping with his landlord and that he was having sex with someone he couldn't share a drink with. He shut the refrigerator door and went to change, shucking his uniform for what might be the last time, whereupon he discovered the laundry had been done.

"You've been busy today."

"Yeah, I—ow!"

"Ow?" He rushed back to the kitchen to find Arlo shaking his hand.

"It splattered. I'm supposed to—" Arlo jiggled the wok.

"But it keeps—ow!" He jerked his hand back again. "And the dumplings have to—fuck."

Arlo sounded ready to cry, which Brixby couldn't allow, so he picked up the wok and held it away from the burner until the sizzling stopped.

"It's going to be all wilted now," Arlo said mournfully.

"Isn't bok choi always kind of wilted?"

"I have no idea."

"Well, me either, so I'll be happy with it however it comes out. How about you do the dumplings, and I'll stir this."

The kitchen was close quarters for two people trying to cook at the same time, but it was cheerful, and Arlo went back to being bright and happy, which was all Brixby really cared about. He managed to keep the bok choi from turning into charcoal while Arlo boiled dumplings and set the table. Then he popped the cap on a bottle of beer, and they sat down to eat what turned out to be very good dumplings and much less good bok choi, for which he took full responsibility.

"I was supposed to do everything," Arlo said when Brixby blamed his own lack of wok skills for the half-charred, half-wilted dish.

"But you don't have to. I mean, this is great—the dinner and the laundry. I feel really... loved." He hesitated to use the word, but Arlo beamed at it. "But it's a bonus, not a requirement. Remember what we discussed? I'd rather you concentrate on getting settled." Especially now that he was contemplating becoming completely unsettled himself. "But this is good. Really, really good. I appreciate it."

He wrapped a sticky hand around Arlo's wrist. They were both covered in dumpling sauce because they'd tried to use the chopsticks Mrs. Zhao had lent them. He raised Arlo's hand to his mouth and licked one of his fingers. Arlo tasted like red pepper and soy sauce. He giggled at the attention.

"We have to get over to Francesca's," Brixby said with

the tip of Arlo's finger still resting against his lips, "but maybe not just this minute." He waggled his eyebrows, and Arlo broke out into a grin. "Someone did a lot of work today and deserves a reward. How do you feel about a blowjob?"

"For me or for you?"

"You know, I think that's why God invented the sixty-nine." He got up from the table, which was covered in dumpling sauce just like the two of them, and tugged Arlo into his arms. He would make a decision later. For now, he just wanted Arlo.

ILONA OPENED THE DOOR DRESSED in a pair of sweatpants and a pink t-shirt featuring a giant white kitten instead of one of her usual get-ups. Kimi lurked behind her, dressed even more casually in what looked like pajamas with her hair in an artless ponytail and not a trace of makeup on her face. Ilona was wearing makeup, but it was smudged around the eyes like she might've been crying.

"What've you two been up to?" Brixby asked.

"We were just watching television," Kimi said, as if television made people cry. "Want to come into the den?" she asked Arlo.

Arlo nodded, no doubt excited by all the stuff there was to play with here. He followed Kimi down the hall, which left Brixby alone with Ilona.

"You want something to drink?" she offered.

"I'm not here as a Dom."

"I know, but you don't know where anything is."

"I'll figure it out. What were you doing before I got here?"

"Watching television, like Kimi said." Ilona drifted off in the direction the other two had gone, so he followed her. He liked the den with its masculine colors and soft edges. Even though Francesca didn't own the house, it suited her. Except for this room, which suited him.

Arlo and Kimi were in chairs next to each other, each

with a can of soda in their cup holder, watching cartoon characters prance around on the screen. Brixby snuggled into Arlo's chair with him. It was almost wide enough for them to sit side by side, but he pulled Arlo into his lap anyway. They hadn't showered after fooling around, so Arlo smelled of sex and soy sauce.

Wrapped up in enjoying Arlo's enjoyment of the television program, he lost track of Ilona, only to have her pop up at his elbow with a bottle of water.

"Why don't you get *yourself* a goddamned bottle of water?" Kimi muttered darkly.

"I didn't ask her to bring me this," Brixby said in his defense.

"I meant *her*." Kimi gestured with her chin to where Ilona had taken the only uncomfortable chair in the room— a hard-backed thing that looked like she'd carried it in from the dining room. "She's going to get a migraine."

"Is she?" He wasn't sure how he was supposed to handle that if it happened.

"She doesn't eat, she doesn't drink, she gets all emotional—"

"Whose fault is that?" Ilona asked.

Kimi didn't answer, but Brixby could guess. "Have you been annoying her?"

"She gets annoyed easy."

"And then she gets migraines."

"Well, whose fault is that?" Kimi taunted, throwing Ilona's words back at her.

"It's not anyone's fault if they're sick," Arlo said. "They're just sick."

"Yeah, but she should take care of herself. She knows what her triggers are. She just likes having Mistress take care of her."

"Well, Francesca isn't here," Brixby pointed out, "so if Ilona gets sick, you'll be the one taking care of her."

"Me?" Kimi squealed.

"Since you seem to know so much about what her

triggers are and how to prevent them, I'm putting you in charge of her migraines this weekend. What does Francesca do when Ilona gets a migraine?"

"Sits in the dark with her and pets her," Kimi said petulantly. "Holds her hair back when she barfs. Gives her a bath when she starts to feel better."

"Well, there you go. If Ilona gets a migraine this weekend, guess what you'll be doing."

Kimi's glare was so threateningly furious, Brixby wondered if she were more of a top than she realized, but she wasn't going to stare *him* down. After a few moments of trying, she rose to her feet with a weary sigh and went to the mini-fridge in the corner. She pulled out a bottle of water and brought it over to Ilona.

"You don't really want me brushing your hair, do you?"

Ilona looked as horrified at the idea as Kimi. She took the bottle and, after one genteel swallow, upended it. Kimi had been right about her needing it apparently.

"You should eat something too," Kimi said. "I'll get it for you, I guess."

She stomped out of the room, determined to be ungracious in her helpfulness, but she came back with a fruit and cheese platter that must've taken some effort to put together. She made Ilona move into one of the comfortable chairs and supervised every bite she took, which amused Brixby no end. He'd found a way to make them get along, apparently, and if Kimi was a little dictatorial in her ministrations, Ilona didn't seem to mind.

Arlo turned his face up with a smirk, and Brixby held a finger to his lips. No point breaking the spell he'd managed to cast. By the time the platter was half empty, Ilona and Kimi were both eating off it as Kimi explained the television program to Ilona, who knew as little about it as Brixby. Ilona was looking decidedly better than when they'd arrived—no longer so pinched and sad. He eavesdropped on them while Arlo watched the television with his mouth parted just a little and his eyes fixed on the bright screen.

"So I guess you two are together now," Kimi observed.

Brixby was about to tell her that their relationship was none of her business, but Arlo jumped on the question. "We signed a contract."

"That wasn't a contract," Brixby reminded him. And they hadn't signed anything—just made a list of bullet points.

"It's *like* a contract," Arlo told Kimi. "It says what I want and what Cade wants. And after he catches Mike, we can sign a real one."

That wasn't exactly what Brixby had said, but Arlo sounded so happy about it, and Ilona and Kimi looked so happy for him, he decided not to clarify. He kept saying their relationship couldn't be permanent, but he'd accepted that he wanted it to be. More importantly, Arlo wanted it to be, and Arlo tended to get what he wanted.

Chapter 25 Arlo

Ilona had made up separate bedrooms for him and Cade, but Arlo didn't need a separate room. Besides, the room Kimi showed him to while Cade was making a patrol of the perimeter, or doing some kind of cop/Dom thing before they could go to sleep, had been decorated for a child—a *small* child—with Pooh and Piglet dancing on the walls and a single bed with a white picket headboard and a comforter covered in bees.

"Just take me wherever Cade is sleeping," he told Kimi.

She smirked like she'd known there was no way he was going to sleep in a Winnie-the-Pooh room and led him farther down the hall to a room guarded by heavy double doors with matching brass doorknobs. The doors looked like a portal to something important. Kimi opened them with a push that made them swing inward to reveal the room beyond.

"Holy shit." He took a few steps into the room, which was about as big as his parents' whole house. The carpet was so thick his feet sank into it, and he swore he could feel how soft it was even through his socks. The walls were a creamy beige. *Everything* was a creamy beige, like a picture from the French Renaissance come to life except softer—gold muted down to cream. A massive four poster bed occupied the far wall, all draped in netting like Cleopatra slept there. Or like they were expecting mosquitos.

"It's Mistress's room." Kimi stood in the doorway with

her hands behind her back, surveying the room like a kid who'd been told not to touch anything.

"She sleeps here alone?" That bed slept four, easy.

"With Ilona."

"On the floor?" He wouldn't even mind sleeping on the floor with a carpet this soft.

"Why would they sleep on the floor?"

"Never mind." He didn't want to talk about what Terzini had done to him. He'd thought Ilona had things so strict, but even she got to sleep in the bed, next to her mistress who cherished her instead of treating her like a dog. Not even a dog. Lots of people let their dogs sleep on their beds.

"Where's Ilona going to sleep tonight then?" Definitely not in the bed with him and Cade.

Kimi cackled. "I'll show you."

Arlo dropped his ratty backpack on the downy rug and followed Kimi back down the hallway. "In the Winnie-the-Pooh room?"

"Worse." Kimi flicked on the lights in the room next to Winnie-the-Pooh and stood back so Arlo could peer inside. "Barbies."

The room was so pink it hurt Arlo's teeth, but Ilona might like it.

"She's kind of the princess type," he observed. He got the sense Ilona enjoyed being all dressed up, whereas Kimi would probably rather look the way she did now, like she'd just rolled out of bed on a Saturday morning.

"She really does get migraines," Kimi said. "I feel bad for her."

"You do?" Ilona had snuck up on them.

"Of course I do." Kimi had her back to the doorjamb, leaning against it like she was lounging, but Arlo could feel the tension emanating off her. "No one likes to be in pain."

"Except people who do," Ilona joked.

"I only like a little pain," Arlo said, trying to keep things light. "I like spankings."

"Spankings mean I've been bad," Ilona said with a

frown.

"I'm always going to be bad," Kimi said with a shrug. The three of them were clustered in the doorway to the Barbie room. It was a little awkward. "I might as well enjoy it."

"You don't have to be bad," Ilona said. "You could be good."

"Like you?"

"Mistress *likes* subs who behave themselves. It's fine for people to be bratty if that's their deal, but that's not what Mistress wants. You're making her stressed."

"You're both making her stressed," Cade said. Great. Now all four of them were lurking in the doorway of a Barbie-themed bedroom.

"How am *I* making her stressed?" Ilona asked.

"By fighting all the time. You told Francesca she could bring Kimi home to help her get back on her feet, but you've been making it difficult. And you," Cade said, turning to Kimi, "could be more grateful. Because Ilona did allow it. You wouldn't be here if she didn't have sympathy for your situation, but how are you repaying her? By trying to co-opt her mistress? By turning her home into a battlefield?"

Arlo had a crush on Cade—he *loved* Cade—but that only explained some of the raw lust sweeping through him right now. Cade was so strong and fierce and sure of himself, his eyes steely and his mouth a hard-set line. Arlo wanted to jump him. He licked his lips and tried to communicate through a puppy-eyed softness how eager he was to stop hanging out with Ilona and Kimi and move to a bed, but dominant Cade was also relentless Cade, and his attention was fixed on the women.

"There's a reason Francesca left the two of you behind this weekend," he told them. "You're exhausting her. Is that how a good sub behaves?"

"No, sir," Ilona said. "I'll do better, I promise."

"Don't tell *me*. Tell Francesca." He turned his eyes on Kimi. "Francesca really does like obedience, which means she might not be the right mistress for you. I know you didn't choose her, but that's exactly the problem. Random chance doesn't make the best matches."

Kimi turned her face away from Cade, which meant she was facing Arlo now. He could see she wanted to argue, but if she argued, she would only prove Cade right.

"There aren't that many lesbian dominants," she said finally.

"You're not wrong about that," Ilona agreed.

"Maybe someday you'll be one," Cade suggested. His kind patience was as much of a turn-on for Arlo as the steely determination had been. Arlo really needed to get him alone.

"Are you a switch?" Ilona asked Kimi.

"No." Kimi looked trapped, nervous. She tried to push away from the doorjamb, but they were all too crowded together in the narrow space of the hallway for her to have anywhere to go.

"Maybe you could be," Arlo told her. She was definitely bossy. Plus, she didn't seem all that into submitting, now that he thought about it. She was into *Francesca*, but that was more like a territorial dispute. Whereas Arlo wanted to crawl on the ground for Cade, wanted to merge into him and be part of him and live in the circle of his arms.

"I don't even know why we're talking about this." Kimi managed to force her way between Cade and Ilona so she could escape down the hall. Ilona watched her go with a thoughtful expression.

"Is this where we're sleeping?" Cade asked with a quick glance into the pink-washed room. Arlo thought he saw him shudder.

"I'm sleeping here," Ilona said, and Arlo thought she might've shuddered too, so maybe she wasn't as princess-y as he'd imagined. "You're sleeping in the master."

"Isn't that your room? We'd be fine here."

Oh, *please* no. Arlo wanted to do dirty things with Cade, which required a bed big enough for dirty things and a décor that didn't make him feel like he would be corrupting little girls if he did them. Fortunately, Ilona insisted that "Mistress said," and Cade didn't try to argue with that.

"I'll show you where we're sleeping." Arlo tugged him down to the other end of the hall where the double doors stood open to reveal the giant bedroom. "I bet we have a hot tub." He dashed into the bathroom and yep. Hot tub! This weekend was going to be excellent.

Cade shut the double doors. They clicked into place against each other with a solid thunk, formidably sturdy, as though no one could ever intrude. Arlo sank to his knees and bowed his head, not because that was how Terzini had taught him to kneel but because he felt the need to be small in the presence of his Dom.

Cade's fingers carded through his hair. "In the mood to play, are you?"

"To serve you, Officer Brixby." He leaned against Cade's thigh, thinking about how jealous he'd been of Kimi because the traffickers had matched her with someone who was keeping her. But now he saw that Francesca was just who Kimi had ended up with. Like him and Terzini. Francesca was nicer and more ethical than Terzini. She didn't hit Kimi or make her spend her days in a cage. But their kinks didn't line up.

"Is Francesca really going to send Kimi away once those guys get caught?"

"Not send her away, but help her get set up somewhere on her own."

"But what if she'd rather stay with Francesca?"

"This isn't really about Kimi, isn't it?" Cade sighed like the world was too heavy for him to bear, like he wasn't feeling either dominant or frisky. "Let's talk somewhere more comfortable. Go run a tub for us."

Arlo went as ordered, but his enthusiasm for it had dwindled. They were going to have that conversation again, the one that inevitably ended with Cade saying he had to move out. At least he was prepared for it this time.

Cade came into the bathroom naked. He was so well made, with such strong, lean muscle everywhere. Arlo would rather be servicing him than talking about how to leave him.

"Francesca must have some bubble bath around here somewhere. Ah, here we go. Attar of Rose. Sounds perfect." Cade upended the bottle, and a frothy roil of fragrant bubbles went up. He slid his long body into the water, which had risen high enough that his dick bobbled in the foam. He tipped his head back like he was relaxing, but his shoulders were too tense for that to be true.

Arlo got naked and climbed into the tub to straddle his lap, desperate to be close to him because he seemed so far away. Cade put his thumbs on the points of Arlo's hips.

"You're still not eating, are you?" He traced up over his ribs. "You eat when I'm watching, but these bones tell me it's not enough."

"If you want me to put on weight, I will. Mr. Terzini liked me to be skinny, but if you'd rather—" He stopped when Cade shook his head sternly.

"This is exactly what I mean when I say you can't be so dependent on me, Arlo. You need to eat for you, not for me. And I need to know that if I told you to starve yourself, you'd tell me to fuck off. Because otherwise I have too much power over you. Do you understand what I'm saying?"

Arlo did, or at least was beginning to. He understood that Terzini had been his captor, not his Dom, that Mike had been his kidnapper, not his friend, and that he hadn't been a street-smart kid going after his dreams. He'd been an inexperienced neophyte who'd fallen prey to a human trafficking ring because he hadn't known any better.

But he knew better now. Lots better. He understood what kind of sub Tripp was and what kind of sub Harrison was, what kind of sub Ilona was and—most importantly— what kind of sub he was. He was a boy who didn't want to be called boy in search of a Daddy he didn't want to call Daddy. He wanted to be loved and coddled, but he didn't need to be dressed up or spoiled. He wanted to be teased and spanked, but not whipped or burned. He wanted attention, but also freedom.

In short, he wanted Cade. And if the only way he could keep him was to leave him, then he would. But when it came to what he needed to survive—to not just survive, but thrive—a place to live was the least of it.

Chapter 26 Brixby

"I'm going to the club tomorrow night. I'm going to be part of the sting."

Arlo's words sent a sharp spike of fear through Brixby's chest, almost as if Arlo were already in a dangerous situation Brixby could see but not prevent rather than straddling his lap in a tub still filling with water.

"We discussed that," Brixby reminded him.

"No, we didn't. You just said no. But if it's a choice between obeying you or taking care of myself, I get to tell you to fuck off. You just said so."

Brixby groaned. "Arlo. This isn't about power exchange. Going to the club would be dangerous. You're a civilian."

"So are Tripp and Francesca and Sebastian and—"

"I can't stand the thought of you getting hurt." He leaned forward to rub his cheek against Arlo's. "Haven't you been through enough already?"

"That's why I have to do it. I won't be safe until Mike is caught and the ring is dismantled, which means the investigation is more my business than anyone's. They hurt me, and I'm allowed to be mad about it."

Brixby was glad Arlo had finally developed a full realization of how angry he had a right to be, but his timing was terrible. Couldn't he just obey his Dom until the perpetrators were safely behind bars?

"You know I'm the best bait," Arlo insisted.

"And you know how I feel about using you as bait."

"Also, I have the best chance of spotting Mike if he's there."

That was a fair point, but the answer was still no. "I thought we were going to enjoy the hot tub. Where's the button to make the jets go?"

"Don't change the subject."

"I don't want to talk about the club. I'm not even sure *I'm* going to the club." He turned off the faucet and cranked the timer to its highest setting, then sank into the churning water and tried to let it relax away his fear of Arlo being back at the scene of the crime. Which had just been added to the fear of losing his job.

"Why wouldn't you be going to the club?" Arlo asked with a frown.

"I have to make a decision." He'd been trying to keep his problems to himself, but sometimes Doms needed comfort too. "I don't know how to make it."

"A decision about me?"

"Not everything is about you, angel." Though it sort of was. Take care of Arlo or catch the guy who'd hurt him? How was he supposed to choose? "If I go to the club tomorrow, there's a good chance I'll get fired. I'm struggling to support you as it is. If I get fired, I'll be struggling to support myself."

He smiled at Arlo weakly, unmanned by the admission he'd just made. He hadn't wanted Arlo to know exactly how poorly he compared to Sebastian, but now it was out there.

"I got a new ATM card today," Arlo said after a moment.

"That's good. I'm glad you're getting everything sorted out."

"I have money in my account from when I worked before. It's not a lot, but I paid for all the stuff I used to make dinner tonight. The money you left this morning is still on the coffee table. I don't know if you noticed."

"I didn't, but thank you. It was sweet of you to buy me dinner." Twenty dollars wasn't going to save him, but he definitely appreciated the thought.

"I guess I didn't mention it before, but I ordered a new phone from my parents' plan. It's coming on Monday."

That was good news. He hadn't wanted to nag Arlo about how fast he was going through data, but he'd noticed.

"And I'm going to get a job," Arlo continued. "I have a lot of experience working in grocery stores. Now that I'm eighteen, I can be a checker. They make more money than baggers."

"God, Arlo. I don't want you working in a grocery store."

"Why not?"

"You don't see Ilona working at a grocery store."

"No, 'cause she's a graphic artist, like Cash."

She was? All this time, he'd been imagining Francesca could afford to keep Ilona as a pet. The fancy outfits, the elaborate lifestyle, everything he couldn't do for Arlo.

"But you deserve to be spoiled."

"I never asked to be. It's not on my list. Is that why I can't live with you? Because you think I need something fancy? I don't care if we live in a cardboard box. I just want to be with you." Arlo sat still for a moment, his face scrunched up in concentration. "I have another place to stay," he said after a moment.

"You do?" That was a surprise, and not a welcome one, despite how he'd been harping on it. "Where?"

"Mrs. Zhao said I could rent her spare bedroom. But if I stay with you, I can help pay rent on your place instead, and then if you lost your job, it wouldn't be such a problem. I'm sorry I made you feel like you had to take care of me financially. Mr. Terzini never would've let me have anything he hadn't given me himself, so I guess I thought..." Arlo trailed off, then shook his head resolutely. "I never wanted his money. I wanted him to love me. The way you do."

Brixby hadn't told Arlo he loved him, but somehow Arlo knew it anyway.

"And besides," Arlo said, perking up a little, "you don't have to worry about losing your job because you don't have to go to the club tomorrow. Not if I'm the bait."

"You're absolutely not going to that club without me."

"But we have to find Mike."

"We will. Promise." Sometimes doing the right thing had unfortunate consequences, but protecting people like Arlo was why Brixby had become a cop in the first place. Better to be a protector and not a cop than a cop and not a protector. "I shouldn't have said I might not be going to the club tomorrow. Of course I'm going."

"And I get to come too, right?"

Brixby sighed. If Tripp was allowed to be part of their SWAT team, why couldn't Arlo be? Only because Brixby loved him.

"I'll talk to Harrison about it," was all he would promise. "Now let me enjoy my soak. What do you think Ilona does for Francesca when she's in the bath?"

"Probably washes her and shit."

"Then you should get to it."

"You're already covered in bubbles," Arlo pointed out. "How much more washed can you get?"

"These aren't scrubbing bubbles. The scrubbing is your job."

"Okay." Arlo started a motion that could've been called scrubbing if it had involved a washcloth and more than one particular part of Brixby's anatomy.

"Starting up here." He moved Arlo's hand up to his neck. Twenty minutes or so of Arlo rubbing him all over should have him both relaxed enough and revved up enough to take Arlo to bed and fuck him so thoroughly he'd be too tired to go to Hell's Bedroom tomorrow. "And use one of those thingies." He gestured at the fluffy ball hanging from a plastic hook. Was it rude to use someone else's shower pouf? Oh well. He would owe Francesca a new one.

The netting on the pouf scraped over his skin with exactly the right amount of roughness as Arlo warmed to his task, sloshing water and bubbles everywhere as he crawled over and around Brixby to get to every part of him— first those parts that were above water like his neck and shoulders, then submerging the pouf to run it across his belly. He raised one of Brixby's arms up out of the water so he could clean it from fingertip to armpit, then repeated the motion on the other side.

His face grew reflective, even admiring, as his hands moved Brixby's limbs with gentle reverence. Brixby let his eyes flutter shut, giving himself up to physical sensation. The bubble bath made the water almost oily—slick and nourishing—and the jets burbled with the background hiss of white noise, sealing out the outside world. One of the jets was hitting him right between the shoulder blades, and all the while, Arlo's little hands ran over him.

"Ouch." Brixby reached down to still the motion of netting over his ball sack. What had been stimulating on the rest of his skin was a bit much there. Arlo grinned like he'd known he was going too far. "Careful with that if you want it to work," he warned, but his cock was working just fine. Full steam ahead. "Maybe use your hands in that area."

"Can I get you off?" Arlo asked as his hands went to work. "I want to see if I can make you shoot so hard you break the water."

"I was thinking I'd fuck you," Brixby said lazily.

"Ooh, good idea. Can't we do both?"

"I don't think so." Not considering what they'd gotten up to earlier. "You pick, angel." He hauled Arlo against him, making water slosh over the side of the tub.

"Fuck," Arlo chose quickly.

"Time to get you cleaned up then." He hooked his hands under Arlo's knees and yanked, upending him so Arlo almost went completely under.

"Hey." He kicked out, trying to rearrange himself.

"Be good."

"Yes, Officer Brixby." Arlo made the switch so quickly, so completely. It amazed Brixby every time—that snap from half-grown man to perfectly obedient, perfectly beautiful, perfectly submissive Arlo.

With fondness threatening to overwhelm him, he got Arlo situated more comfortably, then applied the pouf to his ass. Yep, he definitely owed Francesca a new one. He scraped the netting between Arlo's thighs and over his balls, exactly the way he'd complained about being done to him, enjoying Arlo's squeals that said it hurt but he loved it. Arlo separated his legs to let him in, making only the smallest whimper of protest when Brixby worked the pouf right up against his pucker. He had his lower lip sucked between his teeth and his eyes squeezed shut, but his cock rose like a pontoon trying to breach the surface.

The water was so slick Brixby didn't need lube to worm a finger inside him, cleaning him in theory but really just teasing him, stroking over his prostate to get him nice and hungry until he was squirming so much he made waves. Time to bring this to bed.

Brixby pulled the plug, then turned on the shower so they could rinse off. Bubbles were a cute look on Arlo, but they were bound to taste nasty. Then he herded Arlo into the bedroom where he surveyed the giant bed with annoyance. It was covered in about twenty pillows plus extra tasseled tapestry things. He wished they'd planned ahead because their dicks were pointing at each other as they stripped the bed like a married couple on an old-fashioned sitcom.

Brixby got into the bed on one side and Arlo got into it on the other and they lay on their backs next to each other, sandwiched between dusky pink sheets, until they both started laughing.

"Do you really think I want to live like this?" Arlo asked. He rolled onto his side and propped his head up on his palm. "I'm afraid to get lube on these sheets." He ran his hand over them. They were really, really smooth.

"Fuck these sheets then." Brixby swept the top sheet out of his way so he could see the glory of Arlo's body instead of a sea of rose. He rolled onto Arlo, smashing him down into the bottom sheet, which was just going to have to get sticky. Arlo arched up to meet him. Their groins ground into each other, their dicks already primed. The skin of Arlo's erection was silkier than the sheets.

"This is what I want," Arlo gasped. "Only this, only you. I love you."

Brixby wanted to say it back, but he didn't feel like he had the right. Arlo was healing, growing. He'd taken huge steps in the right direction tonight, but he was still an eighteen-year-old who'd been held captive by a poser of a Dom. Brixby had to hold firm, insist on a period of separation and some time for Arlo to learn more about himself and D/s relationships before Brixby gobbled him up like a greedy stalker.

He couldn't keep Arlo, but he could fuck him. Refusing to let Arlo up at all, wanting the feel of their bodies mashed together and the dominance of holding him down, he worked two lube-slick fingers into Arlo's ass until Arlo was loose and ready.

Then he scrunched Arlo in half until Arlo's knees were up by his ears. Arlo seemed made to fold, as if he'd been formed out of wishes and fantasy. He mewled at being forced into such a compromising position, but Brixby slapped the backs of his thighs in a stinging rebuke that changed the protest into a groan, then lined his cock up with Arlo's hole and pressed in.

God, it felt so good. Every time. Brixby dipped his forehead down to let it rest against Arlo's as he regained his composure, but Arlo wouldn't stay still long enough to let the sensations settle. He was squirming and bucking, straining closer and seeking out Brixby's lips with his own. Their tongues played together as Brixby started shallow thrusts, rocking gently in and out, the moment unexpectedly sweet. He'd meant to fuck Arlo into the mattress as an antidote to Arlo's declaration of love, but love crept in anyway.

It was Arlo who broke the kiss, tilting his head back with a gasp. "Officer Brixby?"

"What, angel?"

"Aren't you going to fuck me?"

"What do you think I'm doing?"

Arlo whimpered, and Brixby took pity on him. He put his hands under Arlo's hips and increased the speed and force of his thrusts, ramping up the intensity until Arlo was hollering out his pleasure with one hand on his cock and the other clenched in his hair like he needed a touch of pain to hold himself together.

Brixby caught the inside of Arlo's thigh with his teeth, biting down next to the faded remains of the scars Terzini had left, making his own mark to claim Arlo as his own.

Arlo screamed and came. He spurted straight up to hit Brixby on the chin, and Brixby laughed and tried to reach the errant drops with his tongue even as his own climax swamped him. His eyes squeezed shut, blanking out the sight of Arlo's hazy blue eyes blinking up at him with satisfaction.

Chapter 27 Brixby

The next morning, Brixby left Arlo with Ilona and Kimi so he could run over to Cash's and discuss the change in plans with Harrison. Harrison didn't have any objection to Arlo being part of their sting. The only one who'd ever had any objection to it was him, and he'd capitulated now.

"I'll let Knight know," Harrison said. "So he won't be confused if Arlo ends up in his office. Anything else you want to tell me?" They were in the living room where Cash was giving them privacy by rattling pots and pans in the kitchen and Mr. Moo was giving them privacy by not giving two fucks about their existence.

"Not that I can think of," Brixby answered.

Arlo would be allowed to roam Hell's Bedroom seemingly on his own, but Brixby would be following at a distance. Cash would be there too, keeping an eye out for anyone taking too much notice of him, and Harrison would be outside waiting to nab anyone who might follow Arlo out. The plan made Brixby nervous, but it was clear enough. Harrison was acting like Brixby had something to confess.

"I hear you're staying at Francesca's this weekend."

"She didn't want to leave the girls alone."

"And I hear," Harrison said portentously, as if he were about to say something way dramatic. "That there's only... one... bed."

"Oh."

"Yeah, oh. Apparently the nature of your relationship with Arlo has changed. How come I'm not hearing about it from you?"

"Come on, you've seen us together."

"I have. And I've also heard you swear up and down it wasn't like that. You were just taking care of the poor damaged sub, remember? So when did taking care of transition to fucking?"

"Um, a week or so ago?" He was trying not to sound guilty, but it was hard not to sound guilty when you felt guilty. "I shouldn't have, I know."

"Why not?" Harrison leaned back with a chuckle. "He's sweet and cute and he worships you. Seems like a good match."

"Because he's undergone physical and psychological trauma." He thought about Arlo's legs—the scars Terzini had left there and the bite mark he'd left next to them. It'd felt right at the time, but waking up this morning in a tangle of rose sheets, he'd been startled by the sight of those red indentations. "He should be given time to heal. I shouldn't be bothering him."

"*Are* you bothering him? Because if you are, I'll definitely have to beat you up." Harrison had maybe eighty percent of Brixby's body weight, but Brixby wouldn't want to tangle with him. He had a feeling Harrison fought dirty. "It seems like he's into you."

"He's into me. That's not the problem."

"Then I'm failing to see what the problem is. He could use a positive authority figure. Isn't that how this whole Daddy Dom thing works?"

"Who says I'm a Daddy Dom?" Brixby asked, his voice breaking in an embarrassing way.

"Oh, come on. I know what a Daddy Dom is. Cash has been explaining things to me." Harrison gave Brixby an evaluating look that made Brixby wish Cash hadn't been explaining things to him.

"Even if I am," Brixby admitted, "that's a dynamic best

explored when the sub is in a position where he's emotionally strong enough that he doesn't need anyone propping him up."

"So, wait. Let me see if I've got this straight. Arlo can only lean on you if he doesn't actually need to?"

"Um." Put like that, it didn't sound right. "Of course he can lean on me. I want him to. I just..." God, complicated. "Seriously, Harrison, don't you think it's a bad idea for him to jump straight from one D/s relationship into another?"

"Was he having a D/s relationship with Terzini?"

"No, that was a hostage situation."

"So show him better. Arlo knew what he wanted. He didn't get it. How is that a reason to keep him from getting it now? Brixby." Harrison put a hand on his knee. "I trust you with him. So does Cash. Trust yourself."

Wow. That was what it came down to, wasn't it? He'd been thinking he wasn't enough for Arlo but also that he was too much for him. He hadn't considered that he might be exactly right. They'd negotiated what was—if Brixby could only admit it to himself—a pretty good contract, and Arlo had demonstrated every time they played how thoroughly he was on board with its terms, that he hadn't just agreed to them because he was afraid of displeasing his Dom. Their play was honest. Their love was honest.

"You don't think Arlo should get his own apartment?"

"I mean, if you don't want him there."

"No, I do." He did. Whether he had a studio in an attic or a grand bedroom with a two-person hot tub, he wanted to share it with Arlo. And if Arlo got a job and paid rent, that would definitely help with his impending financial crisis.

"What does Arlo want?" Harrison asked.

"He says he wants to stay."

"Then he should get to decide that, don't you think?"

Fuck. Of course. Brixby had been so insistent on what he thought would be good for Arlo, he hadn't been giving any credence to Arlo's stated preferences.

"Are you trying to tell Brixby how to top?" Cash yelled from the kitchen. So maybe all that pot banging wasn't giving them as much cover as Brixby had imagined.

"Just standard relationship advice," Harrison called back. "Seriously," he said to Brixby, "I'm happy for you. You told me once it was okay to let Cash love me. I'm telling you the same thing. Let Arlo love you."

"He already does." And it was time to tell Arlo the feeling was mutual. But first they had a sting to get through.

BRIXBY SURVEYED ARLO, WHO WAS STANDING in the Hell's Bedroom changing area wearing nothing except Harrison's booty shorts. He traced his thumbs over the bony points of Arlo's collarbones. Arlo had eaten lunch today, serving himself out of Francesca's giant refrigerator that was stocked with literally everything. Brixby had watched him, pretending not to and wondering if he would ever trust Arlo to take care of himself or if he would always feel compelled to make sure he was doing it.

"I'm proud of you for being here, but I don't want you to take any unnecessary chances."

"Yes, Officer Brixby."

"That's my angel." He framed the naked column of Arlo's throat. Someday soon he would get Arlo a real collar, but for now, he unfastened the medallion from around his own neck. "Would you like to wear this?"

"Your necklace?"

"My collar."

Arlo's big, blue eyes grew damp as Brixby hung it on him, and he wrapped his hand around the medallion as if it were crusted with diamonds. Brixby just wished it still had a GPS tracker attached to it. He was going to have to give Arlo a little space in there, and he didn't want to.

As he led Arlo toward the double doors that opened into the play area, a cold autumn wind blew through the lobby.

He threw a glance over his shoulder and saw a patron in a wheelchair entering as a man held the door for her. Brixby had known that door wasn't ADA compliant, and he felt a flash of annoyance about it until his focus shifted from the door to the man holding it.

He was one of the valets, probably. Dressed in dark clothes similar to the Hell's Bedroom security guards but without a Hell's Bedroom logo on the pocket. He had white skin and short, brown hair, was a little shorter than average and neither thin nor fat. Hopelessly generic, in other words.

If it weren't for how exactly he matched the portrait Arlo had drawn of him.

"Is that Mike?" He nudged Arlo to get him to look in that direction even as he used his body to block the valet's view of Arlo.

Arlo peered around him. "I think so," he whispered.

The patron wheeled herself over to the reception desk, and Mike let the door swing shut behind him as he left the building. He was about to get in the van idling at the curb and drive away. Brixby needed to go after him, but what was he supposed to do with Arlo?

"Go inside. Find Cash and stay with him." He pushed Arlo toward the playroom, then grabbed his phone and wallet out of his locker and dashed for the front door. "Call Mr. Knight," he barked at the woman behind the reception desk. "Tell him Officer Brixby needs him in the lobby. Now!" he yelled when she just stared at him. He made it out front in time to see the van's taillights turn the corner.

Harrison jogged up to him from across the street. "What's up?"

"That was Mike. Hey," he yelled at Patrick, who was a few doorways down. "That guy who took the van, is he on his way to the lot?"

"Mike? Yeah, sure. Where else would he be going?"

Mike. The guy's name was literally Mike.

"Let's go get him," Harrison said. "Looks like we found our man."

Chapter 28 Arlo

The doors swung shut behind Arlo, a solid layer between him and Mike, the person who'd once offered him what he'd thought was his dream. Arlo's heart gave an erratic thump, but Mike couldn't hurt him now, not with Cade here. Cade would take care of it. He reached for the medallion Cade had fastened around his neck, clasping the metal disc in his hand as his heartrate slowed.

A collar. He'd been too overwhelmed to ask Cade what it meant, but he hoped it meant Cade was going to keep him. Doms didn't put collars on people they were going to kick to the curb, right? With this medallion fastened around his neck, he had to believe he was loved.

Keeping one hand on it, he moved into the play space. He'd only been inside once, seemingly ages ago. He'd been so foolishly confident then, ready to dive all the way in. None of the acts on display had seemed too far out there, and he hadn't stopped to ask himself whether he wanted to participate in them or not.

Now, as he meandered from scene to scene looking for Cash, he viewed them with a more critical eye. Paddling was a maybe. Cade would be gentle with it, not give him more than he could handle, and he liked the illicit naughtiness of it. Paddlings were like spankings for extra bad boys—less love, more pain. Whippings were a no though. He'd gotten more whippings than he would ever need from Terzini. Whippings were all pain, no love.

Then there was a woman being tickled, which he hadn't even realized counted as BDSM. She was laughing and screaming all at the same time. It looked like fun and also like torture, and he could imagine squirming like that for Cade, eating up Cade's attention even as he begged for it to stop.

Next to the tickling, a guy was having a rod inserted in his urethra. Arlo had no idea how he felt about that. Confused, mostly. Cash must like it though because he was one of the people watching, and his lips were slightly parted like he was about to lick them.

Arlo sidled up to him. "What does that feel like?"

Cash swung around with a grin. "Hey, Arlo. Is sounding something that interests you?"

"Not sure." He would need to know more about it before he decided.

"It doesn't hurt. At least, so I've heard."

"From Harrison?"

"I tell no tales." Cash put a finger to his lips. "But if you want me to give Brixby some tips, I happen to be a certified sounding master."

"Is that actually a thing?"

"No, but I do know what I'm doing. Speaking of Brixby, where is he? I wasn't expecting him to let you that far out of his sight."

"He and Harrison are chasing after Mike."

"You found him already? So it wasn't that guy, huh?" Cash pointed to a man in a suit who had his back to them, watching the woman being tickled.

"I don't know who that is." All Arlo could see was a suit jacket and a head of medium brown hair.

"Name's Popinjay. He's the Dom who signed in Jessica, and his car was here both nights in question."

The name was familiar from some of the discussions in Cash's living room, but Arlo had no idea whether he'd ever seen the man before. From the back, he could be almost anyone, even Terzini. Except that Terzini was dead, he

248

reminded himself, not standing right over there listening to a woman scream-laugh as a guy attacked her feet with an ostrich feather.

"Maybe I should take a peek." He pulled on Cash's shirt sleeve, and they circled around together to a spot from which Arlo could see Popinjay's face.

"Anything register?"

"He might've been here the last time I was here."

"He was," Cash reminded him. "We know that. Did you talk to him?"

Arlo shook his head. He didn't think so. He'd only been in the club for about fifteen minutes before he got thrown out, and he hadn't talked to anyone except Uncle Bob. Speaking of Uncle Bob, he was watching the scene on the other side where a woman was whipping a man. Arlo waved to him.

"He doesn't seem to be paying any attention to you," Cash said.

"Huh?"

Uncle Bob had definitely waved back.

"Popinjay." Cash directed Arlo's attention back to the guy in the suit. "Maybe you should stay out of his line of vision, though. Just in case he's part of this whole thing."

Arlo seriously doubted he'd ever talked to the man, but he was happy to see Uncle Bob. Uncle Bob had been so nice to him—listening to him ramble about his dreams and signing him into Hell's Bedroom so he could try to fulfill them.

"Let's go out to the lobby," Cash said, interrupting Arlo's thoughts. "I want to let Harrison know Popinjay's here."

"I should stay in here. Mike is out there."

"Right, but—" Cash gestured to Popinjay again.

"I don't think he's got anything to do with it. I'm going to talk to Uncle Bob."

"Yeah, okay. Good idea. Stick with Bob." Cash clapped him on the back, then strode briskly for the doors that led out to the lobby.

Arlo wrapped his arms around himself as Uncle Bob crossed over to him. With Cash gone, he felt a little cold and vulnerable. Not that Popinjay was likely to jump him in the middle of a busy floor with security guards at every juncture. There was one right there, staring at him—a Black guy with dreads who looked kind of familiar.

"Hey!" Uncle Bob wrapped him up in a hug. His bare chest was comfortable—furry and very warm. "It's so good to see you. Where have you been? You look amazing. And you're eighteen now, right? Who signed you in?"

"That's a lot of questions," Arlo said with a grin.

Uncle Bob had always been so interested in him. It'd been like medicine to his seventeen-year-old soul.

"Let's go find somewhere we can talk." Uncle Bob wrapped an arm around his shoulders and used it to lead him over to the edge of the floor where the bar was. "I'm going to grab a drink. You want something? I'll put it on my account."

Arlo asked for a Diet Coke, then changed his mind and asked for a real Coke. He waited at the edge of the bar space while Uncle Bob went to fetch it. His body was on high alert, though he wasn't sure why. Popinjay hadn't moved, and the Black security guard was in the same stance Arlo had last seen him in—keeping an eye on him but not moving toward him. There was no threat from either of those quarters.

"Here you go." Uncle Bob handed him a tall glass full of Coke and ice, then tapped his own glass against it. "To reunions. So who did you say you're here with?"

"My Dom," Arlo said proudly. He sipped from his glass, then realized he was actually pretty thirsty and took a bigger gulp. "It's kind of a secret though. Did you know I got kidnapped?"

"Kidnapped?" There was a funny edge to Uncle Bob's voice—an artificial surprise, like he was on a game show pretending to be excited. "Did your new Dom rescue you? He's a police officer, isn't he?"

Arlo nodded. Uncle Bob was so clever, always knowing everything. Not like Arlo who was naïve and sort of dizzy. He took another swallow of soda, searching for sharpness in the cool, caffeinated liquid.

"So where is he?" Bob asked. "Your Dom," he clarified when Arlo only looked at him.

His Dom. Where was his Dom? He knew the answer to that, didn't he? "Mike."

"Mike," Bob repeated, as if he knew what Arlo was talking about, even though Arlo wasn't sure himself. "Finish that up for me, boy."

Arlo didn't like boy. He'd told Cade no, and Cade had promised. But this wasn't Cade. It wasn't Terzini either. It was Uncle Bob. Uncle Bob, who was tipping the glass up to his mouth and making him drink from it. Uncle Bob, who was setting the glass down on one of the little round tables and leading him toward the hallway where the private rooms were. Uncle Bob, who—

Arlo yanked his arm away as what remained of his consciousness made the connection at last. Bob had set him up. He'd sent Mike after him and told him exactly what to say because Bob knew all about him and what he wanted. And now Bob was trying to kidnap him again, take him somewhere Cade wouldn't be able to find him.

"I'm not—" he tried, but the words came out all wrong, his tongue as thick and heavy as his legs.

"Not feeling well, I know." Bob wrapped an arm around him, hooking it under his arms to keep him upright. "I'm going to bring you somewhere you can lie down."

Bob wasn't particularly big, but he was bigger than Arlo, and Arlo's body wasn't obeying him. He'd been drugged, he realized, feeling like he should've realized it before. But there was so much to figure out, so much that was coming to him, and it was all a jumble.

"Don't wanna," he mumbled, but no one took any notice.

Bob was just like Terzini, thinking he could do whatever

251

he wanted with Arlo's body, and Arlo was allowing it again, impotent and helpless, about to be hurt by someone older and more experienced who should be watching out for him instead of taking advantage of him. It made him angry, but he couldn't turn the anger into motion or work it out of his tongue-tied mouth.

"Here we go," Bob said, stopping in front of a closed door. "You're going to have a nice rest in here until I figure out what to do with you." Bob's voice was jolly, pitched low in a friendly intimacy. He was a fucking evil, horrible person who Arlo badly wanted to punch, but he could barely stay on his feet when Bob leaned him up against the wall to get the door open.

If Arlo went in there, Cade would never find him. Bob would deliver him back to Terzini, back to the cage. He raised a heavy hand to the medallion around his neck. Cade's collar. The talisman that was supposed to keep him safe.

With the last bit of strength left in his body, he gave the chain a hard yank, then let the necklace slip quietly to the floor, leaving it there as a silent plea to the man who'd claimed him.

Chapter 29 Brixby

"You should read him his rights," Harrison said. So far they'd only told Mike that Security needed to talk to him and left him to fidget in Knight's office while they consulted out in the hallway about the best way to handle him.

"Yeah, let's get that taken care of." If Sebastian found out he hadn't done everything exactly by the book, he would never hear the end of it.

"Oh, come on," Mike said after Brixby mirandized him. "No one drives twenty-five on that street. I'd be run over."

"This isn't a traffic stop," Brixby told him.

"Look, if that van was used to rob a bank or something, you gotta understand I was just parking it. I never seen it ten minutes ago."

"It's not about the van either." He was making Mike guess, waiting to see what he might come up with.

"Um, I don't know anything about anything else." Mike's expression was starting to shift from *hey, we're all buds here, right?* to *fuck, this might be bad.* "This club is kind of freaky, but I just park the cars. I'm not even employed by them. I don't report to you," he told Knight in a more aggressive tone than he'd been using with Brixby. "If one of your guys fucked up, that's not on me."

"I feel like you might know more about what goes on here than you're letting on," Harrison said.

"Yeah, well, I don't." Mike rubbed the wooden arms of

his chair, then planted both hands firmly and started to rise to his feet.

Brixby laid his hand on Mike's shoulder hard enough to suggest he sit down.

"Are you charging me with something?" Mike asked as he settled back into his seat. "Because otherwise I don't gotta stay here."

"I guess you don't," Harrison agreed with a shrug. "But there's a lot about to go down, in a very big way. And you're a very small cog. It's always the little guys who get hit the hardest, isn't it, Brixby?"

"Unless they cooperate," Brixby said. "Just my experience. When the cards start to fall, it's the guy at the bottom they fall on."

"I don't know what you're talking about," Mike said. But he did, and he knew that they knew that he did. He was going to crack, Brixby could see it. Right now he was calculating what kind of charges they could pin on him, trying to think his way out of them.

Knight's phone buzzed. "That's the front desk," he said. "I gotta grab it."

Brixby gave him permission with a wave. Didn't hurt to let Mike stew a while longer. Truth was, they didn't have much on him—just Arlo's identification of him as the guy who'd bought him a bus ticket and maybe stole his backpack.

"Yeah, send him back," Knight said into the receiver. He lifted his eyes to Harrison. "Cash is looking for you."

Harrison stepped out into the hallway to wait for Cash, and Brixby followed him out there. Sometimes it was helpful to let a perp sit with his thoughts for a bit.

"Where's Arlo?" Brixby asked when Cash arrived breathless and alone. "He was supposed to be with you."

"He's all right. I left him with Bob Jones. I wanted to let you know Popinjay is here. You were thinking there might someone on the inside helping Mike out, right?"

"Don't you think it could be Jones just as well as

Popinjay?"

Cash frowned like no, he hadn't thought that at all, but maybe they'd been looking at this backward the whole time. They'd been focusing on Doms because the scheme benefited Doms, but who served Doms? Subs. And money was the same shade of green regardless of your sexual preferences. Jones had every sub's ear and a house that looked like its owner had fallen on hard times.

"Shit." He didn't waste time talking about it. He didn't stop to put his phone back in his locker either, just pushed through the doors that led to the playroom. Cash was on his heels, so Brixby sent him to make a clockwise circuit while he swept the floor counterclockwise, moving as fast as he could past one scene after another while scanning every face, following every pair of booty shorts, and keeping his eyes peeled for a bright flash of blond curls. By the time he ran into Cash halfway around the circle, an acidic weight burned in the center of his chest.

"I saw Popinjay," Cash said. "Right where I left him. He didn't have Arlo."

"Any sign of Bob Jones?"

Cash shook his head solemnly. "You don't really think...?"

Brixby didn't have time to make Cash feel better about having left Arlo alone right now. He started moving again, continuing around the circle even though Cash had already swept this half. Maybe he would see something Cash hadn't. He went through the bar area, praying he would spot Arlo having a friendly chat with his friend Uncle Bob, but there was no sign of him at any of the tables crowded with people in fetish gear who were being watched over by a security guard. A security guard he recognized.

"Denzel, right? Officer Brixby, Boston PD. We talked about this kid the other day. You remember him?" He flashed Arlo's picture on his phone.

"Phones aren't allowed—"

"I don't give a fuck what's allowed. Have you seen this

255

kid?" He pushed the phone right into Denzel's face.

"Yeah, he was here," Denzel said with a rueful shake of his head. "Knew I'd seen him somewhere, but I couldn't place it. He was in the bar with an older guy wearing purple shorts and a chest harness. They had a drink, then headed that way." He indicated the hallway down which the private rooms were located.

Brixby sprinted down the hall and opened the first door he came to. The room was empty, the lights off. The next door was locked, so he banged on it with his fist.

"Hey." Denzel grabbed him by the arm. "You can't bust in on people."

"Call Knight and ask him. I'll break down every one of these doors if I have to."

Something in his face must've said he would do it because Denzel released him to pull a walky-talky out of his pocket. Brixby waited impatiently, sighting down the hallway to count how many rooms needed to be searched. On the floor outside one of the doors, something gold sparkled. His medallion.

"Arlo?" He tried the door and found it locked.

"You gotta wait for Mr. Knight to come."

Brixby shook his head. Anything could be happening in there. He reared back and aimed a kick at the door plate. The door trembled but didn't crack. Denzel put a hand on his arm, trying to hold him back, but Brixby brushed it off.

"If you're not going to help, then get the fuck out of my way." He raised his leg to deliver another kick. God, what he wouldn't give for a battering ram right now. But before he could follow through, Denzel hip-checked him off-balance.

"I'm trying to give you the key, for fuck's sake."

Brixby's hands shook as he opened the door. Inside the small room, Arlo lay on his side on a cot, his curly head cradled on a pillow and his eyes closed like the most handsome Sleeping Beauty ever. His wrists had been bound with a coil of green rope, and at the foot of the bed, Jones stood with another hank of rope. Brixby flung Jones into Denzel's waiting arms as he moved to the head of the cot.

"Angel?"

Arlo didn't answer, but his whisper-soft breath washed over Brixby's hand. Brixby brushed the matted strands of hair off Arlo's face, then trailed his fingers down to Arlo's neck where a pulse beat with reassuring regularity.

Chapter 30 Brixby

They were back in a hospital. Brixby lay on the bed with Arlo on top of him and a tangle of cords and tubes trailing off to the side. Arlo had opened his eyes once, his heartrate spiking and his lips moving like he had something important to say, but Brixby had told him he was safe and could sleep as long as he needed to. He'd been resting quietly since then, motionless other than the gentle rise and fall of his breath.

When the door opened, Brixby prepared himself for another lecture. Every time a nurse came in, they tsked at him. Made him lay Arlo down with the covers smoothed over him. Then as soon as they went away, Brixby picked him up again. But the face peeping around the door at him this time belonged to Harrison rather than to an annoyed nurse.

Brixby motioned him in.

"How's he doing?" Harrison asked.

"Doctor says he'll be fine once the drug works its way through his system. A hangover maybe, but no lasting harm."

"Good news. He's been through a lot."

"Yeah." He nudged his nose into Arlo's hair. Arlo's eyelashes fluttered open, then shut again. "How are things at the club?"

"Chaos personified. The place is swarming with uniforms, and everyone's riled. Uncle Bob was an institution."

"That's how he did it. Who better to pick out the weak members of the herd? You know he's the one who got Arlo tossed that night, right? Signed him in, reported him, and had Mike waiting outside to pick him up. Fucking bastard. Sebastian had better put him away."

"I'm sure he'll do his best. I called to let him know what went down, but his phone is off. He and Tripp must be having a good time in New York. I haven't heard from Francesca either. You want me and Cash to run over to her place tonight?"

"If you wouldn't mind." He was going to be here until they discharged Arlo, and then he'd be taking Arlo home.

"Anything else you need?"

"A job?"

"You got it. Might be a little slow at first. We gotta get you licensed, take on some new clients."

"I'll manage. Arlo's going to get a job too."

That hurt to say, but he'd been telling Arlo he had to be an adult, and Arlo was going to be one. Which meant Brixby wasn't wholly responsible for his welfare. It also meant that sometimes Arlo might be the one taking care of *him*—a tough pill for a Daddy Dom to swallow, but a vital part of any real partnership. If Ilona could contribute to the household expenses, then so could Arlo. They would figure out how to send him to art school in time.

"You're sure you want to leave the force?" Harrison asked. "I can't see Captain Murphy forcing you out over this, not with the press it's going to get. You rescued a drugged teenager from a kinky cabal."

"And got caught at a BDSM club dressed in fetish-ware." There'd been at least one reporter taking photos.

"So say you were undercover."

Brixby shook his head. "I'm done being undercover. This is who I am, and Arlo is who I want."

"Then I've got you." Harrison crossed over to him. "Welcome aboard, partner."

Brixby freed up a hand to shake, and Arlo gave a sleepy

protest.

"It's okay," Brixby whispered to him as Harrison tiptoed out. "I'm right here. You just sleep, angel."

"Not sleepy," Arlo's very sleepy voice murmured against his chest.

Brixby huffed out an amused breath. Arlo might be small and light and submissive, but he was tough.

"Did you get him?" Arlo's words were a little clearer now, but his eyes were still shut.

"Jones? Yeah, we got him. Mike too."

Arlo lifted a hand to his throat.

"Are you thirsty?" There was a pitcher of water on the bedside table, but Arlo shook his head. His curls tumbled around his face as he hitched himself up a bit.

"My collar. I left it outside the door so you'd know where I was."

"I know. That's how I found you. Very clever of you."

"Where is it?"

Brixby fished it out of his pocket. "It needs a new chain."

"I'm sorry."

"Don't be. It did its job, which was to keep you safe. Here." He looped the chain around Arlo's throat and tied it in a knot. The remaining chain sat closer to Arlo's neck, more like a real collar, and the medallion rested in the dip at the base of his throat. Brixby could kiss that medallion. "I'll get you something nicer."

Arlo's hand closed around it. "I like this one."

"That knot's going to make it difficult to take off."

"I don't want to take it off. It's a collar. It means you're keeping me, right?"

"Now's probably not the time to talk about it. You've been drugged and traumatized, and—"

"Don't you dare say I have to start all over again. I fought for myself, just like you wanted me to. I'm not helpless. I'm not a baby. And I know what I want."

Brixby had to agree Arlo had earned the right to make

his own decisions. "You're sure I'm what you want though? You wouldn't rather be with someone better positioned to take care of you?"

"Like who?"

"Like—"

"Like nobody, that's who. You don't have to support me. Just love me."

God help him, he did. This bundle of innocence was everything he'd ever dreamed of. A little too soon and a little too young, but both those things would change over time. And Brixby intended to make sure they had a lot of time.

"Then I guess you're stuck with me."

Arlo flung his arms around him with an excited squeal.

"There's not going to be any more Officer Brixby though," Brixby warned.

Arlo pulled away, his expression switching from ecstatic to worried in a flash. "I can't be your sub? Only your boyfriend?"

"No, no. You can be my sub. I just meant I'm leaving the force."

Arlo waved that off. "I don't care if you're a real cop. You'll always be Officer Brixby to me. But, um, can you still wear the uniform sometimes?"

"Sure." As long as he didn't wear it out of the house.

"And it's forever, right?"

"Arlo, I need you to understand that you'll always be free to—"

"*Right?*" Arlo insisted. "You're keeping me this time. Forever and ever."

Brixby gave up trying to be properly ethical about it. "Forever and ever," he promised his boyfriend, his sub, his angel. "I love you, Arlo, and yes, I'm going to keep you."

~~The End~~

Need more? The series concludes in Upsy-Daisy Dom, starring Sebastian and Tripp.

Book 3 of Hell's Bedroom
Upsy-Daisy Dom

TANYA CHRIS

It's really rude to wish you'd been kidnapped. Especially when your best friend actually was. But Tripp wishes *something* would happen to him. He likes his sex kinky, and he likes his kink on the fun side of risky. Which means he's got his eye on Sebastian Gage, the incredibly handsome, incredibly rich, incredibly dangerous Dom.

Sebastian makes subs cry, and he's not sorry about it. He *is* sorry his bent toward emotional sadism means none of his playmates ever stick around, but he's not going to let any of his newfound friends know that. All they know is he's a cruel Dom and a brilliant attorney, and now's the time to concentrate on the brilliant attorney part instead of getting sidetracked by a gangly young sub with a smart mouth and a penchant for danger.

Because Sebastian will do anything to make sure the perp who's been targeting vulnerable subs gets everything the law can throw at him, maybe even sacrifice Tripp, the only sub who can take everything Sebastian has to offer.

Book 1 of Hell's Bedroom
Kitchen Sink Dom

Harrison's new case isn't going the way he'd hoped. Wearing a collar, pretending he's submissive, searching for a Dom who can get him into Hell's Bedroom—his first time working undercover is really stretching his boundaries. He's always wondered if BDSM might be for him, but how can he be honest about what he wants sexually when he can't be honest about anything else?

When Cash meets the handsome man brimming with energy, he feels like he's struck gold. Cash isn't the most dominant top, but he's got a wide repertoire of skills, and he'd be happy to practice every single one of them on Harry, the sub who's so new to the scene he doesn't even know his own kinks. But the closer he gets to Harry, the more obvious it becomes that Harry isn't who he claims to be.

As Harrison flirts with both BDSM and Cash, one missing person turns into two. Someone at Hell's Bedroom is abducting vulnerable subs, and it's going to take more than just Harrison to bring them home. It's going to take a whole kinky village.

Aftercare

ONE MAN TO SAVE HIS BROTHER, ONE MAN TO HEAL HIS HEART

AFTERCARE

AN M/M BDSM ROMANCE BY

TANYA CHRIS

Aayan Denir knows Garrett Hillier was once a high-powered defense attorney, and—thanks to a leaked photograph—he knows Garrett is sexually submissive, which makes him ideally qualified to defend Aayan's brother from the charge of murdering his sub. Aayan would do anything to protect Syed, even if he doesn't understand how Syed could hurt someone he loves. He could never hurt Garrett. He only wants to take care of him—love him, serve him, cherish him. And maybe torture him. Just a little.

Garrett probably shouldn't be dating his client's brother. Right? And what's the use in a confirmed sub dating a guy who doesn't want to be a Dom anyway? The important thing is to get Syed cleared of the discriminatory murder charge he's facing. Aayan is a distraction. But for the first time in the three lonely years since Garrett's husband died, he's feeling hope, ambition, and desire. Can he give up the pain he craves to find the love he needs?

As Syed's trial date looms, Aayan and Garrett explore what a BDSM relationship means for them, and what they mean to each other.

Deep Under

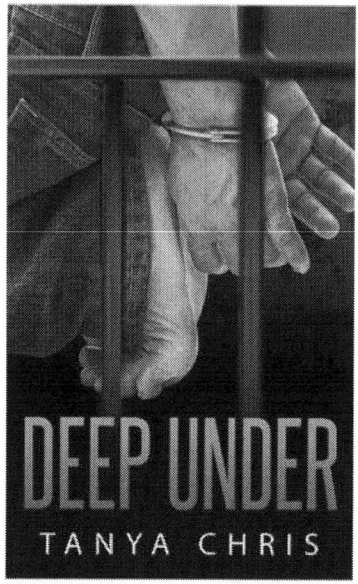

DEEP UNDER

TANYA CHRIS

It was a routine traffic stop until the submissive in Jack recognized the Dominant in Maddox. Now Maddox and Jack are walking a dangerous line: on opposite sides of the law by day, on the same side of the bed at night.

Can Maddox trust a man with Jack's past, and does Jack even want him to? One thing's for sure: Jack needs to be punished, and Maddox is just the man to do it.

Manufactured by Amazon.ca
Bolton, ON